Fairy Tales and

Fantastic Stories

Terry Jones

Fairy Tales and Fantastic Stories

Illustrated by Michael Foreman

PAVILION

This edition published in Great Britain in 1997 by
PAVILION BOOKS LIMITED
26 Upper Ground, London SE1 9PD

Text copyright © Terry Jones 1981, 1992
Illustrations copyright © Michael Foreman 1981, 1992

Fairy Tales first published in hardback in 1981
Fantastic Stories first published in hardback 1992

Designed by Bet Ayer

A CIP catalogue record for this book is available
from the British Library.

ISBN 1 85793 996 4

Set in Revival
Printed in Italy by Conti Tipocolor

2 4 6 8 10 9 7 5 3 1

This book can be ordered direct from the publisher. Please contact
the Marketing Department. But try your bookshop first.

601918485

CONTENTS

FANTASTIC STORIES

Fairy Tales

THE CORN DOLLY

 FARMER WAS CUTTING HIS CORN, when he thought he could hear someone crying far away. Well, he kept on cutting the corn, and the crying got louder and louder until he had only one more shock of corn to cut, and it seemed as if the crying were coming right from it. So he peered into the last bit of corn and sure enough, there was a little creature made of corn stalks, sitting sobbing its heart out.

'What's the matter with you?' asked the farmer.

The little creature looked up and said: 'You don't care,' and went on crying.

The farmer was a kindly man, so he said: 'Tell me what your trouble is, and perhaps there is something I can do.'

'You farmers don't care what happens to us corn dollies,' said the creature.

Now the farmer had never seen a corn dolly before, so he said: 'What makes you think that?'

The corn dolly looked up and said: 'We live in the standing corn, we keep it safe and do no harm to anyone, and yet every year you farmers come with your sharp scythes and cut down the corn and leave us poor corn dollies homeless.'

The farmer replied: 'We have to cut the corn to make the flour to make the bread we eat. And even if we didn't cut it, the corn would wither away in the autumn and you corn dollies would still be homeless.'

But the corn dolly burst into tears again and said: 'Just because we're small and made of straw, you think you can treat us anyhow, and leave us with nowhere to live in the cold winter.'

The farmer said: 'I'll find somewhere for you to live.' And he picked up the corn dolly and took it to the barn and said: 'Look! You can live here and be snug and warm all through the winter.'

But the corn dolly said: 'You live in a fine house made of stone, but just because us corn dollies are small and made of straw, you don't think we're good enough to live in a proper house.'

The farmer said: 'Not at all,' and he picked up the corn dolly and carried it into his house and sat it on the window-sill in the kitchen.

'There,' he said, 'you can live there.'

But the corn dolly scowled and said: 'Just because we're small and made of straw, you think we're not good enough to sit with you and your wife.'

The farmer said: 'Not at all,' and he picked up the corn dolly and carried it to the fireside, and he pulled up a chair and sat the corn dolly down between himself and his wife. But still the corn dolly was not happy.

'What's the matter now?' asked the farmer.

'Just because we're small and made of straw,' said the corn dolly, 'you've sat me on a hard chair, while you and your wife sit in soft chairs.'

'Not at all,' said the farmer, and he gave the corn dolly a soft chair. But still the corn dolly was not happy.

'Is there still something the matter?' asked the farmer.

'Yes,' said the corn dolly. 'Just because I'm small and only made of straw, you've sat me over here, while you and wife sit next to the fire and keep nice and warm.'

The farmer said: 'Not at all. You can sit wherever you like,' and he picked the corn dolly up and put it next to the fire. And just then a spark flew out of the fire and landed on the corn dolly. And, because it was only made of straw, it burst into flames, and, because it was only very small, it was all gone before the farmer or his wife could do anything to save it.

THE SILLY KING

KING HERBERT XII HAD RULED WISELY and well for many years. But eventually he grew very old and, although his subjects continued to love him dearly, they all *had* to admit that as he had grown older he had started to do *very* silly things. One day, for example, King Herbert went out of his palace and walked down the street with a dog tied to each leg. Another time, he took off all his clothes and sat in the fountain in the principal square, singing selections of popular songs and shouting 'Radishes!' at the top of his voice.

Nobody, however, liked to mention how silly their king had become. Even when he hung from the spire of the great cathedral, dressed as a parsnip and throwing Turkish dictionaries at the crowd below, no-one had the heart to complain. In private they would shake their heads and say: 'Poor old Herbert – whatever will he do next?' But in public everyone pretended that the King was as grave and as wise as he had always been.

Now it so happened that King Herbert had a daughter whom, in a moment of slightly more silliness than usual, he had named Princess Fishy – although everyone called her Bonito. Rather conveniently, the Princess had fallen in love with the son of their incredibly rich and powerful neighbour, King Rupert, and one day it was announced that King Rupert intended to pay a state visit to King Herbert to arrange the marriage.

'Oh dear!' said the Prime Minister. 'Whatever shall we do? Last time King Herbert had a visitor, he poured custard over his head and locked himself in the broom cupboard.'

'If only there was someone who could make him act sensibly,' said the Lord Chancellor, 'just while King Rupert's here at any rate.'

So they put up a notice offering a thousand gold pieces to anyone who could help. And from the length and breadth of the land came doctors offering their services, but it was all no use. One eminent doctor had a lotion which he said King Herbert must rub on his head before going to bed, but King Herbert drank it all on the first night, and was very ill. So a second eminent doctor produced a powder to cure the illness caused by the first doctor, but King Herbert put a match to it, whereupon it exploded and blew his eyebrows off. So a third doctor produced a cream to replace missing eyebrows, but King Herbert put it on his teeth and they all turned bright green overnight.

Not one of the doctors could make King Herbert less silly, and he just got ill from their lotions and potions and creams and powders.

Eventually the day of the state visit arrived, and King Herbert was still swinging from the chandeliers in the throne room and hitting people with a haddock.

Everyone was very agitated. The Prime Minister had chewed his nails right down to nothing, and the Lord Chancellor had gnawed through his chain of office, but no-one had any idea of what to do. Just then the Princess Fishy stood up and said: 'Since no-one else can help, let me try.'

'Don't talk nonsense, Bonito!' said the Prime Minister. 'Fifty of the most eminent doctors in the land have failed to cure the King, what could *you* possibly do?'

'I may not be able to cure the King,' said the Princess, 'but if I could show you how to turn an egg into solid gold, then would you do as I said?'

And the Lord Chancellor said: 'Princess, if you could indeed show us how to turn an egg into solid gold, then we should certainly do as you told us.'

'For shame!' said the Princess. 'Then you should do as I say now.

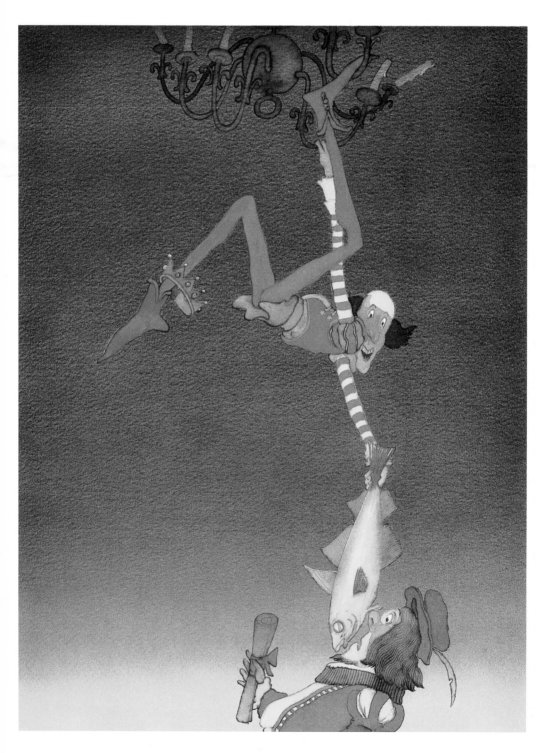

I can no more turn an egg into solid gold than you can, but even if I could it wouldn't prove that I could help my father.'

Well, the Lord Chancellor and the Prime Minister looked at each other and, because they had no ideas themselves, and because they had no other offers of help, they agreed to do what the Princess told them.

Shortly afterwards, King Rupert arrived. There were fanfares of trumpets; drums rolled; the people cheered, and they looked for King Rupert's son, but they couldn't see him. King Rupert was dressed in gold and rode a white horse, and on his head he bore the richest crown anyone had ever seen. The Lord Chancellor and the Prime Minister met him at the gates of the town and rode with him down the main street.

Suddenly, just as they were about to enter the palace, an old woman rushed out of the crowd and threw herself in front of King Rupert's horse.

'Oh, King Rupert!' she cried. 'Dreadful news! An army of fifty thousand soldiers is marching through your country!'

King Rupert said: 'Surely that cannot be!' But just then a messenger in King Rupert's own livery rode up on a horse and cried: 'It's true, your Majesty! It's more like a million of them – I've never seen so many!'

King Rupert went deadly pale and fell off his horse in a faint.

They carried him into the throne room, where King Herbert was standing on his head, balancing a box of kippers with his feet. Eventually, King Rupert regained consciousness, and found his son and the Princess looking down at him.

'I am afraid we are homeless now, my dear,' said King Rupert to the Princess. 'An army of fifty million soldiers has overrun our country. Do you think your father will let us stay here to live?'

'Of course he will,' said the Princess. 'Only you mustn't mind if he's a bit silly now and again.'

'Of course not,' said King Rupert, 'we're all a bit silly now and again.'

'That's true,' said the Prince. 'For example, the old lady who stopped you outside the palace was none other than the Princess here, but you didn't recognize her.'

'Indeed I did not,' said King Rupert.

'And the messenger was none other than your own son,' said the Princess, 'and yet you didn't even recognize him.'

15

'Indeed I did not,' said King Rupert.

'Moreover,' said the Princess, 'you didn't even stop to consider how you could defeat that army of a million soldiers.'

'I have no need to consider it,' said King Rupert. 'How could I possibly deal with an army of such a size?'

'Well, for a start you could pour a kettle of boiling water over them,' said the Princess, 'for they're only an army of soldier ants.'

Whereupon King Rupert laughed out loud at his own silliness, and agreed that the Princess should marry the Prince without delay, and he didn't even mind when King Herbert poured lemonade down his trousers and put ice-cream all over his crown.

THE WONDERFUL CAKE-HORSE

 MAN ONCE MADE A CAKE shaped like a horse. That night a shooting star flew over the house and a spark happened to fall on the cake-horse. Well, the cake-horse lay there for a few moments. Then it gave a snort. Then it whinnied, scrambled to its legs, and shook its mane of white icing, and stood there in the moonlight, gazing round at the world.

The man, who was asleep in bed, heard the noise and looked out of the window, and saw his cake-horse running around the garden, bucking and snorting, just as if it had been a real wild horse.

'Hey! Cake-horse!' cried the man. 'What are you doing?'

'Aren't I a fine horse!' cried the cake-horse. 'You can ride me if you like.'

But the man said: 'You've got no horse-shoes and you've got no saddle, and you're only made of cake!'

The cake-horse snorted and bucked and kicked the air, and galloped across the garden, and leapt clean over the gate, and disappeared into the night.

The next morning, the cake-horse arrived in the nearby town, and went to the blacksmith and said: 'Blacksmith, make me some good horse-shoes, for my feet are only made of cake.'

But the blacksmith said: 'How will you pay me?'

And the cake-horse answered: 'If you make me some horse-shoes, I'll be your friend.'

But the blacksmith shook his head: 'I don't need friends like that!' he said.

So the cake-horse galloped to the saddler, and said: 'Saddler! Make me a saddle of the best leather – one that will go with my icing-sugar mane!'

But the saddler said: 'If I make you a saddle, how will you pay me?'

'I'll be your friend,' said the cake-horse.

'I don't need friends like that!' said the saddler and shook his head.

The cake-horse snorted and bucked and kicked its legs in the air and said: 'Why doesn't anyone want to be my friend? I'll go and join the wild horses!' And he galloped out of the town and off to the moors where the wild horses roamed.

But when he saw the other wild horses, they were all so big and wild that he was afraid they would trample him to crumbs without even noticing he was there.

Just then he came upon a mouse who was groaning to himself under a stone.

'What's the matter with you?' asked the cake-horse.

'Oh,' said the mouse, 'I ran away from my home in the town, and came up here where there is nothing to eat, and now I'm dying of hunger and too weak to get back.'

The cake-horse felt very sorry for the mouse, so it said: 'Here you are! You can nibble a bit of me, if you like, for I'm made of cake.'

'That's most kind of you,' said the mouse, and he ate a little of the cake-horse's tail, and a little of his icing-sugar mane. 'Now I feel much better.'

Then the cake-horse said: 'If only I had a saddle and some horse-shoes, I could carry you back to the town.'

'I'll make you them,' said the mouse, and he made four little horse-shoes out of acorn-cups, and a saddle out of beetle-shells, and he got up on the cake-horse's back and rode him back to town.

And there they remained the best of friends for the rest of their lives.

THE FLY-BY-NIGHT

A LITTLE GIRL WAS LYING in bed one night when she heard a tapping on her window. She was rather frightened, but she went to the window and opened it, telling herself that it was probably just the wind. But when she looked out, do you know what she saw? It was a little creature as black as soot, with bright yellow eyes, and it was sitting on a cat that appeared to be flying.

'Hello,' said the creature, 'would you like to come flying?'

'Yes, *please!*' said the little girl, and she climbed out of the window on to the cat and off they flew.

'Hang on tight!' cried the creature.

'Where are we going?' asked the little girl.

'I don't know!' called the creature.

'Who are you?' asked the little girl.

'I haven't got a name,' said the creature, 'I'm just a fly-by-night!' And up they went into the air, over the hills and away.

The little girl looked around her at the bright moon, and the stars that seemed to wink at her and chuckle to themselves. Then she looked down at the black world below her, and she was suddenly frightened again, and said: 'How will we find our way back?'

'Oh! Don't worry about *that!*' cried the fly-by-night. 'What does it matter?' And he leant on the cat's whiskers and down they swooped towards the dark earth.

'But I must be able to get home!' cried the little girl. 'My mother and father will wonder where I am!'

'Oh! Poop-de-doo!' cried the fly-by-night, and he pulled back on the cat's whiskers and up they soared – up and up into the stars again, and all the stars were humming in rhythm:

> Boodle-dum-dee
> Boodle-dum-da,
> Isn't it great,
> Being a star!

And all the stars had hands, and they started clapping together in unison. Then suddenly the Moon opened his mouth and sang in a loud booming voice:

> I'm just the Moon,
> But that's fine by me
> As long as I hear that
> Boodle-dum-dee!

And the cat opened its mouth wide and sang: 'Wheeeeeeee!' and they looped-the-loop and turned circles to the rhythm of the stars.

But the little girl started to cry and said: 'Oh please, I want to go home!'

'Oh no, you don't!' cried the fly-by-night, and took the cat straight up as fast as they could go, and the stars seemed to flash past them like silver darts.

'Please!' cried the little girl. 'Take me back!'

'Spoilsport!' yelled the fly-by-night and he stopped the cat dead, then tipped it over, and down they swooped so fast that they left their stomachs behind them at the top, and landed on a silent hill.

'Here you are!' said the fly-by-night.

'But this isn't my home,' said the little girl, looking around at the dark, lonely countryside.

'Oh! It'll be around somewhere, I expect,' said the fly-by-night.

'But we've come miles and miles from my home!' cried the little girl. But it was too late. The fly-by-night had pulled back on the cat's whiskers and away he soared up into the night sky, and the last the little girl saw of him was a black shape silhouetted against the moon.

The little girl shivered and looked around her, wondering if there were any wild animals about.

'Which way should I go?' she wondered.

'Try the path through the wood,' said a stone at her feet. So she set off along the path that led through the dark wood.

As soon as she got amongst the trees, the leaves blotted out the light of the moon, branches clutched at her hair, and roots tried to trip up her feet, and she thought she heard the trees snigger, quietly; and they seemed to say to each other: 'That'll teach her to go off with a fly-by-night!'

Suddenly she felt a cold hand gripping her neck, but it was just a cobweb strung with dew. And she heard the spider busy itself with repairs, muttering: 'Tut-tut-tut-tut. She went off with a fly-by-night! Tut-tut-tut-tut.'

As the little girl peered into the wood, she thought she could see eyes watching her and winking to each other and little voices you couldn't really hear whispered under the broad leaves: 'What a silly girl – to go off with a fly-by-night! She should have known better! Tut-tut-tut-tut.'

Eventually she felt so miserable and so foolish that she just sat down and cried by a still pond.

'Now then, what's the matter?' said a kindly voice.

The little girl looked up, and then all around her, but she couldn't see anyone. 'Who's that?' she asked.

'Look in the pond,' said the voice, and she looked down and saw the reflection of the moon, smiling up at her out of the pond.

'Don't take on so,' said the moon.

'But I've been so silly,' said the little girl, 'and now I'm quite, quite lost and I don't know how I'll *ever* get home.'

'You'll get home all right,' said the moon's reflection. 'Hop on a lily-pad and follow me.'

So the little girl stepped cautiously on to a lily-pad, and the moon's reflection started to move slowly across the pond, and then down a stream, and the little girl paddled the lily-pad after it.

Slowly and silently they slipped through the night forest, and then out into the open fields they followed the stream, until they came to a hill she recognized, and suddenly there was her own house. She ran as fast as she could and climbed in through the window of her own room, and snuggled into her own dear bed.

And the moon smiled in at her through the window, and she fell asleep thinking how silly she'd been to go off with the fly-by-night. But, you know, somewhere, deep down inside her, she half-hoped she'd hear another tap on her window one day, and find another fly-by-night offering her a ride on its flying cat. But she never did.

THREE RAINDROPS

A RAINDROP WAS FALLING out of a cloud, and it said to the raindrop next to it: 'I'm the biggest and best raindrop in the whole sky!'

'You are indeed a fine raindrop,' said the second, 'but you are not nearly so beautifully shaped as I am. And in my opinion it's shape that counts, and *I* am therefore the best raindrop in the whole sky.'

The first raindrop replied: 'Let us settle this matter once and for all.' So they asked a third raindrop to decide between them.

But the third raindrop said: 'What nonsense you're both talking! *You* may be a big raindrop, and *you* are certainly well-shaped, but, as everybody knows, it's purity that really counts, and I am purer than either of you. I am therefore the best raindrop in the whole sky!'

Well, before either of the other raindrops could reply, they all three hit the ground and became part of a very muddy puddle.

The Butterfly Who Sang

A BUTTERFLY WAS ONCE SITTING ON A LEAF looking extremely sad.

'What's wrong?' asked a friendly frog.

'Oh,' said the butterfly, 'nobody really appreciates me,' and she parted her beautiful red and blue wings and shut them again.

'What d'you mean?' asked the frog. 'I've seen you flying about and thought to myself: that is one hell of a beautiful butterfly! All my friends think you look great, too! You're a real stunner!'

'Oh *that*,' replied the butterfly, and she opened her wings again. 'Who cares about *looks*? It's my singing that nobody appreciates.'

'I've never heard your singing; but if it's anywhere near as good as your looks, you've got it made!' said the frog.

'That's the trouble,' replied the butterfly, 'people say they can't hear my singing. I suppose it's so refined and so high that their ears aren't sensitive enough to pick it up.'

'But I bet it's great all the same!' said the frog.

'It is,' said the butterfly. 'Would you like me to sing for you?'

'Well . . . I don't suppose my ears are sensitive enough to pick it up, but I'll give it a try!' said the frog.

So the butterfly spread her wings, and opened her mouth. The frog gazed in wonder at the butterfly's beautiful wings, for he'd never been so close to them before.

The butterfly sang on and on, and still the frog gazed at her wings, absolutely captivated, even though he could hear nothing whatsoever of her singing.

Eventually, however, the butterfly stopped, and closed up her wings.

'Beautiful!' said the frog, thinking about the wings.

'Thank you,' said the butterfly, thrilled that at last she had found an appreciative listener.

After that, the frog came every day to listen to the butterfly sing, though all the time he was really feasting his eyes on her beautiful wings. And every day, the butterfly tried harder and harder to impress the frog with her singing, even though he could not hear a single note of it.

But one day a moth, who was jealous of all the attention the butterfly was getting, took the butterfly on one side and said:
'Butterfly, your singing is quite superb.'

'Thank you,' said the butterfly.

'With just a little more practice,' said the cunning moth, 'you
could be as famous a singer as the nightingale.'

'Do you think so?' asked the butterfly, flattered beyond words.

'I certainly do,' replied the moth. 'Indeed, perhaps you already
do sing better than the nightingale, only it's difficult to concentrate
on your music because your gaudy wings are so distracting.'

'Is that right?' said the butterfly.

'I'm afraid so,' said the moth. 'You notice the nightingale is
wiser, and wears only dull brown feathers so as not to distract from
her singing.'

'You're right!' cried the butterfly. 'I was a fool not to have realized that before!' And straight away she found some earth and
rubbed it into her wings until they were all grey and half the
colours had rubbed off.

The next day, the frog arrived for the concert as usual, but when
the butterfly opened her wings he cried out: 'Oh! Butterfly! What
have you done to your beautiful wings?' And the butterfly
explained what she had done.

'I think you will find', she said, 'that now you will be able to
concentrate more on my music.'

Well, the poor frog tried, but it was no good, for of course he
couldn't hear anything at all. So he soon became bored, and
hopped off into the pond. And after that the butterfly never *could*
find anyone to listen to her singing.

JACK ONE-STEP

 BOY NAMED JACK WAS ON HIS WAY to school, when he heard a tapping noise coming from an old log. He bent down and put his ear to the log. Sure enough, it sounded as if there was something inside it. And then he heard a tiny voice calling out: 'Help! Please help!'

'Who's that?' asked Jack.

'Please,' said the voice, 'my name is Fairy One-Step, and I was sleeping in this old hollow log when it rolled over and trapped me inside.'

'If you're a fairy,' said Jack, 'why don't you just do some magic and escape?'

There was a slight pause, and then Jack heard a little sigh and the voice said: 'I wish I could, but I'm only a very small fairy and I can only do one spell.'

So Jack turned the log over and, sure enough, a little creature the size of his big toe hopped out and gave him a bow.

'Thank you,' said the fairy. 'I would like to do something for you in return.'

'Well,' said Jack, 'since you *are* a fairy, how about granting me three wishes?'

The fairy hung his head and replied: 'I'm afraid I haven't the magic to do that – I'm only a very small fairy, you see, and I only have one spell.'

'What is that?' asked Jack.

'I can grant you one step that will take you wherever you want to go,' said the fairy.

'Would I be able to take one step from here to that tree over there?' asked Jack.

'Oh – farther than that!' said the fairy.

'Would I be able to take one step all the way home?' asked Jack.

'Farther, if you wanted,' said the fairy.

'You mean I could take one step and get as far as London?' gasped Jack.

'You could take your one step right across the ocean, if you wanted – or even to the moon. Would you like that?'

'Yes, *please*!' said Jack.

So Fairy One-Step did the spell and Jack felt a sort of tingle go down his legs.

Then the fairy said: 'Now *do* think carefully where you want to go.'

'I will,' said Jack. Then he thought for a bit, and asked: 'If I have only one step, how do I get back again?'

Fairy One-Step went a little red and hung his head again and replied: 'That's the snag. If *only* I wasn't such a small fairy.' And with that he flew off, and Jack went on his way to school.

All that day he hardly listened to what his teacher said, he was so busy thinking of where he would like to step to.

'I'd like to go to Africa,' he thought, 'but how would I get back? I'd like to go to the North Pole, but I'd be stuck there. . . .' And try as he might, he *couldn't* think of anywhere that he wouldn't want to get back from.

That night, he couldn't sleep for thinking but, the next morning, he leapt out of bed and said: 'I know where I'll go!'

He went out of the house and said aloud: 'I'll take my step to where the King of the Fairies lives.' As soon as he'd said it, he felt a tingle down his legs, and he took a step and found himself rising into the air. Up and up he went, above the trees, higher and higher, and, when he looked back, his home was like a doll's house on the earth below, and he could see his mother waving frantically up at him. Jack waved back, but he felt his step taking him on and on, over hills and valleys and forests, and soon he found himself over the ocean, going so fast that the wind whistled past his ears. On and on he went, until in the distance he could see a land with high mountains that sparkled as if they were made of cut-glass. And he found himself coming down from the clouds . . . and down . . . until he landed in a green valley at the foot of the cut-glass mountains. And there on a hill up above him was a white castle with towers and turrets that reached up into the sky. From it he could hear strange music, and he knew that this must be the castle where the King of the Fairies lived.

There was a path leading up the hill to the castle, so he set off along it. Well, he hadn't gone more than a couple of steps when a cloud of smoke appeared in front of him. When it cleared away, he found himself staring straight into the eyes of a huge dragon that was breathing fire out of its nostrils.

'Where do you think you're going?' asked the dragon.

'To see the King of the Fairies,' replied Jack.

'Huh!' replied the dragon, and breathed a long jet of flame that set fire to a tree. 'Go back where you came from.'

'I can't,' replied Jack. 'I came by one magic step and I haven't got another.'

'In that case,' said the dragon, 'I shall have to burn you up.'

But Jack was too quick for him. He sprang behind the dragon's back, and the dragon span round so fast that it set fire to its own tail, and Jack left it trying to put out the flames by rolling in the grass.

Jack ran as hard as he could, right up to the door of the castle, and rang the great bell. Immediately the door flew open and an ogre with hair all over his face looked out and said: 'You'd better go back where you came from or I'll cut you up into pieces and feed them to my dog.'

'Please,' said Jack, 'I can't go back. I came by one magic step and I haven't got another. I've come to see the King of the Fairies.'

'The King of the Fairies is too busy,' said the ogre, and pulled out his sword that was six times as long as Jack himself. And the ogre held it over his head and was just about to bring it down, when Jack jumped up and pushed the ogre's beard up his nose. And the ogre gave a terrible sneeze and brought down his sword and cut off his own leg.

Jack dashed inside, and shut the door. The castle was very dark, but in the distance Jack could still hear the fairy music that he had heard before. So he crept through corridors and down passageways, expecting at any moment to meet another monster. He found himself walking past deep black holes in the wall, from which he could

hear horrible grunts and the chink of chains, and he could smell brimstone and the stench of scaly animals. Sometimes he would come to deep chasms in the floor of the castle, and find himself looking down thousands of feet into seething waters below, and the only way across was a narrow bridge of brick no wider than his shoe. But he kept on towards the fairy music, and at length he saw a light at the end of the passage.

When he reached the door, he found himself standing in the great hall of the Fairy King. There were lights everywhere, and the walls were mirrors so that a thousand reflections greeted his gaze and he could not tell how large the hall really was. The fairies were all in the middle of a dance, but they stopped as soon as they saw him. The music ceased, and at the end of the hall sat the King of the Fairies himself. He was huge and had great bulging eyes and a fierce beard and a ring in his ear.

'Who is this?' he cried. 'Who dares to interrupt our celebration?'

Jack felt very frightened, for he could feel the power of magic hovering in the air, and all those fairy eyes, wide and cold, staring at him.

'Please,' said Jack, 'I've come to complain.'

'Complain!' roared the King of the Fairies, turning first blue and then green with rage. 'No-one dares to complain to the King of the Fairies!'

'Well,' said Jack, as bravely as he could, trying to ignore all those glittering fairy eyes, 'I think it's most unfair to leave Fairy One-Step with only one spell – and that not a very good one.'

'Fairy One-Step's only a very small fairy!' bellowed the King of the Fairies, and he stood up and he towered above all the other

fairies. Then he held his hands in the air, and everything went deathly silent.

Jack felt even more frightened, but he stood there bravely and said: 'You ought to be ashamed of yourself. Just because you're the biggest of the fairies, that's no reason to treat the small ones badly.'

Well, the King of the Fairies went first green then purple then black with anger. But just then a little voice at Jack's elbow said: 'He's right!' and Jack looked down and found Fairy One-Step standing by him.

Then another voice at the other end of the hall said: 'That's true! Why should small fairies be worse off than big fairies?'

And suddenly another fairy said: 'Why?' and soon all the fairies were shouting out: 'Yes! *Why?*'

The King of the Fairies drew himself up, and looked fearfully angry and roared: 'Because I'm more powerful than *any* of you!' and he raised his hands to cast a spell.

But the fairies called out: 'But you're not more powerful than *all* of us!' and do you know what happened then? In a flash, all the other fairies disappeared and, before he could stop himself, the King of the Fairies had cast his spell right at his own reflection in one of the mirrors. The King of the Fairies shook and trembled, and first his beard fell off, then he shrank to half his size and fell on all fours and turned into a wild boar and went charging about the hall of mirrors.

Then the other fairies reappeared, and threw him out of the castle. And they made Fairy One-Step their King, and granted Jack one more magic step to take him home.

And that's just where he went.

THE GLASS CUPBOARD

HERE WAS ONCE A CUPBOARD that was made entirely of glass so you could see right into it and right through it. Now, although this cupboard always appeared to be empty, you could always take out whatever you wanted. If you wanted a cool drink, for example, you just opened the cupboard and took one out. Or if you wanted a new pair of shoes, you could always take a pair out of the glass cupboard. Even if you wanted a bag of gold, you just opened up the glass cupboard and took out a bag of gold. The only thing you had to remember was that, whenever you took something *out* of the glass cupboard, you had to put something else back *in*, although nobody quite knew why.

Naturally such a valuable thing as the glass cupboard belonged to a rich and powerful King.

One day, the King had to go on a long journey, and while he was gone some thieves broke into the palace and stole the glass cupboard.

'Now we can have anything we want,' they said.

One of the robbers said: 'I want a large bag of gold,' and he opened the glass cupboard and took out a large bag of gold.

Then the second robber said: 'I want two large bags of gold,' and he opened the glass cupboard and took out two large bags of gold.

34

Then the chief of the robbers said: 'I want three of the biggest bags of gold you've ever seen!' and he opened the glass cupboard and took out three of the biggest bags of gold you've ever seen.

'Hooray!' they said. 'Now we can take out as much gold as we like!'

Well, those three robbers stayed up the whole night, taking bag after bag of gold out of the glass cupboard. But not one of them put anything back in.

In the morning, the chief of the robbers said: 'Soon we shall be the richest three men in the world. But let us go to sleep now, and we can take out more gold tonight.'

So they lay down to sleep. But the first robber could not sleep. He kept thinking: 'If I went to the glass cupboard just *once* more, I'd be even richer than I am now.' So he got up, and went to the cupboard, and took out yet another bag of gold, and then went back to bed.

And the second robber could not sleep either. He kept thinking: 'If I went to the glass cupboard and took out two more bags of gold, I'd be even richer than the others.' So he got up, and went to the cupboard, and took out two more bags of gold, and then went back to bed.

Meanwhile the chief of the robbers could not sleep either. He kept thinking: 'If I went to the glass cupboard and took out three more bags of gold, I'd be the richest of all.' So he got up, and went to the cupboard, and took out three more bags of gold, and then went back to bed.

And then the first robber said to himself: 'What am I doing, lying here sleeping, when I could be getting richer?' So he got up, and started taking more and more bags of gold out of the cupboard.

The second robber heard him and thought: 'What am I doing, lying here sleeping, when he's getting richer than me?' So he got up and joined his companion.

And then the chief of the robbers got up too. 'I can't lie here sleeping,' he said, 'while the other two are both getting richer than me.' So he got up and soon all three were hard at it, taking more and more bags of gold out of the cupboard.

And all that day and all that night not one of them dared to stop for fear that one of his companions would get richer than him. And they carried on all the next day and all the next night. They didn't stop to rest, and they didn't stop to eat, and they didn't even stop to drink. They kept taking out those bags of gold faster and faster and more and more until, at length, they grew faint with lack of sleep and food and drink, but still they did not dare to stop.

All that week and all the next week, and all that month and all that winter, they kept at it, until the chief of the robbers could bear it no longer, and he picked up a hammer and smashed the glass cupboard into a million pieces, and they all three gave a great cry and fell down dead on top of the huge mountain of gold they had taken out of the glass cupboard.

Sometime later the King returned home, and his servants threw themselves on their knees before him, and said: 'Forgive us, Your Majesty, but three wicked robbers have stolen the glass cupboard!'

The King ordered his servants to search the length and breadth of the land. When they found what was left of the glass cupboard, and the three robbers lying dead, they filled sixty great carts with all the gold and took it back to the King. And when the King heard that the glass cupboard was smashed into a million pieces and that the three thieves were dead, he shook his head and said: 'If those thieves had always put something back into the cupboard for every bag of gold they had taken out, they would be alive to this day.' And he ordered his servants to collect all the pieces of the glass cupboard and to melt them down and make them into a globe with all the countries of the world upon it, to remind himself, and others, that the earth is as fragile as that glass cupboard.

KATY-MAKE-SURE

HERE WAS ONCE A LITTLE GIRL called Katy, who found an old shoe inside a hollow tree. It was a funny little shoe with a pointed toe and it was no more than an inch long.

'I wonder who it can belong to?' she thought, and she slipped it into the pocket of her dress, and went on her way. She hadn't gone very far before she heard a sound like this:

> tippity-tap
> tippity-tap
> tippity-tap

She looked round a large oak tree and saw a little goblin hopping around on one foot. 'Excuse me,' she said, 'but is this your shoe?'

Well, the goblin danced for joy.

'At last!' he cried. 'Without my shoes I can't go back to Goblin City.'

So Katy gave the goblin his shoe, and he put it on, and danced around the tree, singing:

> Short or long to Goblin City?
> The straight way's short,
> But the long way's pretty!

Then he stopped, and said to Katy: 'If you come with me to Goblin City, the King of the Goblins will give you a reward.'

'Well, I *could* come,' said Katy, 'but how would we get there?'

The goblin just hopped up and down on one leg and chanted:

> Short or long to Goblin City?
> The straight way's short,
> But the long way's pretty!

'But how do I know if it's worth going the pretty way, or if it'll take too long?' asked Katy.

The goblin jumped in the air, twirled round three times before he landed on one toe, and said:

> Short or long to Goblin City?
> The straight way's short,
> But the long way's pretty!

'How can I be sure it's not better to go the short way?' asked Katy.

The goblin jumped in the air, landed on his head, and span round and round like a top until he disappeared into the ground, and then reappeared just behind Katy and cried:

> Short or long to Goblin City?
> The straight way's short,
> But the long way's pretty!

'How can I be sure I'll like it, whichever way we go?' asked Katy.

The goblin did a somersault, and landed on one finger. Then he snapped his finger so hard that he rose into the air, up and up, and then came tumbling down and landed in a dandelion puff-ball, and cried:

> Goblin City's far and near!
> If you want to make sure,
> You'd better stay here!

With that, a puff of wind caught the dandelion and scattered it to the four corners of the world, and the goblin was gone too.

And poor Katy never went to Goblin City either way.

THE WOODEN CITY

HERE WAS ONCE A POOR KING. He had a threadbare robe and patches on his throne. The reason he was poor was that he gave away all his money to whom ever needed it, for he cared for his people as if each of them was his own child.

One day, however, a wizard came to the city while the King was away. The Wizard summoned all the people into the main square, and said to them: 'Make me your king, and you shall have all the gold and silver you ever wanted!'

Now the townsfolk talked amongst themselves and said: 'Our King is poor, for he has given all his money away, and while it is certainly true that there are no beggars in this kingdom, it is also true that none of us are very rich nor can expect to be as long as our present King reigns.' So at length they agreed that the Wizard should become their king.

'And will you obey my laws – whatever I decree?' cried the Wizard.

'If we can have all the gold and silver we ever wanted,' they replied, 'you may make what laws you wish.'

Whereupon the Wizard climbed to the top of the tallest tower in the city. He took a live dove, and tore out its feathers, and dropped them one by one out of the tower, chanting:

Gold and silver shall be yours
And blocks of wood shall serve my laws.

Now that poor dove had as many feathers on its back as there were people in that city and, by the time the Wizard had finished, everyone in the city had been turned to wood.

When the King arrived back, he found the gates of the city shut and no-one to open them. So he sent his servant to find out what was the matter. The servant returned, saying he could not find the gatekeeper, but only a wooden mannequin dressed in the gatekeeper's uniform, standing in his place.

At length, however, the gates were opened, and the King went into the city. But instead of cheering crowds, he found only wooden people, each standing where they had been when the Wizard cast his spell. There was a wooden shoemaker sitting working at a pair of new shoes. Outside the inn was a wooden innkeeper, pouring some beer from a jug into the cup of a wooden old man. Wooden women were hanging blankets out of the windows, or walking wooden children down the street. And at the fish shop, a wooden fishmonger stood by a slab of rotten fish. And when the King entered his palace, he even found his own wife and children turned to wood. Filled with despair, he sat down on the floor and wept.

Whereupon the Wizard appeared, and said to the King: 'Will you become my slave if I bring your people back to life?'

And the King answered: 'Nothing would be too much to ask. I would become your slave.'

So the Wizard set to work. He ordered a quantity of the finest wood, and took the most delicate tools, with golden screws and silver pins, and he made a little wooden heart that beat and pumped for everyone in that city. Then he placed one heart inside each of the wooden citizens, and set it working.

One by one, each citizen opened its wooden eyes, and looked stiffly around, while its wooden heart beat: tunca-tunca-tunca. Then each wooden citizen moved a wooden leg and a wooden arm, and then one by one they started to go about their business as before, except stiffly and awkwardly, for they were still made of wood.

Then the Wizard appeared before the King and said: 'Now you are my slave!'

'But', cried the King, 'my people are still made of wood, you have not *truly* brought them back to life.'

'Enough life to work for me!' cried the wicked old Wizard. And he ordered the wooden army to throw the King out of the city and bolt the gates.

The King wandered through the world, begging for his food, and seeking someone who could bring his subjects back to life. But he could find no-one. In despair, he took work as a shepherd, minding sheep on a hill that overlooked the city, and there he would often stop travellers as they passed to and fro and ask them how it was in the great city.

'It's fine,' they would reply, 'the citizens make wonderful clocks and magnificent clothes woven out of precious metals, and they sell these things cheaper than anywhere else on earth!'

One night, however, the King determined to see how things were for himself. So he crept down to the walls, and climbed in through a secret window, and went to the main square. There an extraordinary sight met his eyes. Although it was the dead of night, every one of those wooden citizens was working as if it had been broad daylight. None of them spoke a word, however, and the only sound was the tunca-tunca-tunca of their wooden hearts beating in their wooden chests.

The King ran from one to the other saying: 'Don't you remember me? I am your King.' But they all just stared at him blankly and then hurried on their way.

At length the King saw his own daughter coming down the street carrying a load of firewood for the Wizard's fire. He caught hold of her and lifted her up and said: 'Daughter! Don't you remember me? Don't you remember you're a Princess?'

But his daughter looked at him and said: 'I remember nothing, but I have gold and silver in my purse.'

So the King leapt on to a box in the main square and cried out: 'You are all under the Wizard's spell! Help me seize him and cast him out!'

But they all turned with blank faces and replied: 'We have all the gold and silver we ever wanted. Why should we do anything?'

Just then, the Wizard himself appeared on the steps of the palace, arrayed in a magnificent robe of gold and silver, and carrying a flaming torch.

'Ah ha!' he cried. 'So you thought you'd undo my work, did you? Very well . . . .' And he raised his hands to cast a spell upon the

King. But before he could utter a single word, the King seized the bundle of firewood that his daughter was carrying and hurled it at the Wizard. At once the flame from the Wizard's torch caught the wood, and the blazing pieces fell down around him in a circle of fire that swallowed him up. And as the fire raged, the spell began to lift.

The King's daughter and all the others shivered, and the tunca-tunca-tunca of their wooden hearts changed to real heartbeats, and they each turned back into flesh and blood. And when they looked where the Wizard had been, there in his place they found a molten heap of twisted gold and silver. This, the King had raised up on a pedestal in the main square, and underneath he had written the words:

'Whoever needs gold or silver may take from here.'

But, do you know, not one of those townsfolk ever took a single scrap of it as long as they lived.

I wonder if it's still there?

The Ship of Bones

N the days when sailing ships crossed the oceans, blown by the winds, there was one ship that all sailors dreaded to see. It was called the Ship of Bones. Its sails were deathly white and its figurehead was a skull and all along its length were carved the names of drowned sailors, and they say that the hull was made from their bones.

This is the story of the only man who went aboard the Ship of Bones and lived to tell the tale. His name was Stoker, Bill Stoker, and he sailed on the ship *Mayfly*, that left Portsmouth on 1 June 1784. . . .

They hadn't been gone more than a week when they were caught in a storm . . . in a terrible storm. The waves towered up six times as high as the mainmast, and the little ship was tossed about the ocean like a bit of cork in the foam. One moment it was rising up the head of a mighty wave and the next minute it was dashed down into the trough, and the waters blotted out the sun and it all went still, until another wave crashed down on her bows.

Well, the storm raged on for four days and four nights, and on the fourth night the sailors had given themselves up as good as dead. Their sails were in shreds, the rudder was broken, and half

the crew were lying sick in their hammocks or being tossed across the cabin by the force of the sea.

Old Bill Stoker was lying in his bunk, thinking this would be his last night on this earth, when he heard a cry from up on deck, and this sailor comes running down to the cabin as white as a sheet.

'It's the Ship of Bones!' he cries. 'We've had it now for sure, mates!'

Now old Bill Stoker was not one to take things lying down. 'I don't believe in no Ship of Bones,' he says, and leaps out of his bunk and climbs up on deck.

It was a dreadful night. The rain lashed across his face, and the wind was blowing up the sea like so many mountains. Bill Stoker peers into the storm, and – sure enough – across the tops of the raging waters he can just make out the whitest ship you ever saw. Its sails were almost glowing white in the darkness.

'Well!' shouts Bill Stoker. 'If that's the Ship of Bones, I'll eat my hat!'

Just then, a mighty wave smashes across the deck and, before he knows what's hit him, Bill Stoker finds himself lifted high up in the air on top of the wave. He looks down and there – a hundred feet below – is his own ship. Then suddenly, he's thrown through the air by the force of the wave, and he lands slap in the middle of another, and he goes right under. Well, just as he's beginning to gasp for breath, he finds himself shooting out and up into the air again on another monstrous wave. And this time he looks down, and just catches sight of the white ship below him, when he finds himself hurtling downwards again. Then everything goes deathly quiet and still.

Well, he opens his eyes and looks around. Sure enough he's lying right there on the deck of the Ship of Bones. He can see the black night and the storm raging all about. But the ship itself is quite still – scarcely moving, like, as if it were becalmed. And there's not a sound.

Bill Stoker puts his hand out and feels the deck. It's smooth like ivory and, even though the rain and the waves are lashing the ship, the deck itself is quite, quite dry. Well, Bill looks around and sees that he's all alone, except for an old sailor who's winding in the anchor. So he gets to his feet and calls out: 'Ahoy there!' But the old sailor doesn't turn round – he just keeps on a-winding in that anchor. So Bill Stoker walks across the deck and says: 'Ahoy there, matey! What's to do?'

The old sailor turns round, and do you know? He hasn't got a face – leastwise, not what you'd *call* a face – more of a skull . . . . And his hands are skeleton hands. And his jaws open and a cracked voice says: 'Welcome to the Ship of Bones, Bill!' And he puts out a boney hand to take hold of Bill Stoker. But old Bill Stoker – he backs away. Then he turns on his heels and runs as hard as he can, and ducks below decks. But he can hear the skeleton coming after him, so he shuts the hatch and skids down those steps as fast as he can.

Inside the ship there's a curious smell, like you get around tombstones. Bill Stoker grabs the rail as he goes down, and he notices that everything's made out of bones – white and yellow, old and new. But he can still hear the skeleton footsteps coming after him, so he goes right on down into the hold.

It's so dark, he can't see for a bit . . . then suddenly he hears a shout: 'Why! Here's Bill Stoker! Hello there, Bill! Welcome to the Ship of Bones!'

Bill's eyes are used to the dark by now, and he can just see some shapes rising up off their beds and coming towards him. Well! He doesn't stop to see who they are: he doubles back on himself and runs back up the steps. And there's the skeleton sailor, standing at the top, grinning down at him.

Well, old Bill Stoker wasn't a man to be scared easily, so he runs up the steps, gets out his cutlass and strikes at the creature. But the skeleton sailor hops out of the way, and grabs Bill's shirt as he runs past. But it's an old shirt, and it rips apart before the thing can get its boney fingers over Bill's throat. In a trice, Bill's up on deck again, sprinting across to the bridge house.

Once inside, he locks the door . . . but he can hear the boney steps coming nearer and nearer. Then he sees that horrible grinning skull's face, leering in at the window.

Bill wasn't a man to give up, like, so he thinks to himself: 'They're just a lot of old bones – all of them – they must be scared of *something*.' Then he gets an idea.'I know what'll see old bones off!' he cries, and he drops down on all fours and starts barking like a dog. Well, the skull's face sort of frowns. Old Bill flings the door open and leaps out – barking like mad. And do you know? That horrible creature just turns and runs. Whereupon old Bill takes his chance, and leaps over the side. Immediately he feels the waves picking him up and flinging him across the water again. . . .

Well, I don't know what happened next, and I don't think old Bill knew, but he finally found himself back on his own boat, with his shipmates all standing around him and pointing. And Bill looked out into the night and he saw that Ship of Bones going off as fast as it could – to wherever it came from.

Not long after that, the storm died down, and they came out into calmer waters, and old Bill Stoker told his story to his ship-mates, and they all listened with bated breath. But do you know? Not one of them believed it. But that didn't worry old Bill Stoker. And that evening he sat right down and – can you guess what he did? He *ate his hat*!

Simple Peter's Mirror

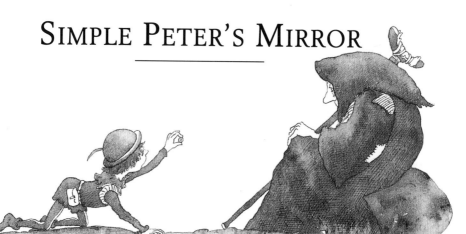

SIMPLE PETER WAS WALKING TO WORK in the fields one morning when he met an old woman sitting beside the road.

'Good morning, old woman,' he said, 'why do you look so sad?'

'I have lost my ring,' said the old woman, 'and it is the only one like it in the whole world.'

'I will help you find it,' said Simple Peter, and he got down on his hands and knees to look for the old woman's ring.

Well, he hunted for a long time, until at last he found the ring under a leaf.

'Thank you,' said the old woman. 'That ring is more precious than you realize,' and she slipped it on to her finger. Then she took a mirror out of her apron and gave it to Peter, saying: 'Take this as a reward.'

Now Simple Peter had never seen a mirror before and so, when he looked down and saw the reflection of the sky in his hands, he said: 'Have you given me the sky?'

'No,' said the old woman, and explained what it was.

'What do I want with a mirror?' asked Peter.

'That is no ordinary mirror,' replied the old woman. 'It is a magic mirror. Anyone who looks into it will see themselves not as they are, but as other people see them. And that's a great gift, you know, to see ourselves as others see us.'

Simple Peter held the mirror up to his face and peered into it. First he turned one way, then he turned the other. He held the mirror sideways and longways and upside down, and finally he shook his head and said: 'Well, it may be a magic mirror, but it's no good to me, I can't see myself in it at all.'

The old woman smiled and said: 'The mirror will never lie to you. It will show you a true reflection of yourself as other people see you.' And with that she touched her ring, and the oak tree that was standing behind her bent down and picked her up in its branches, and carried her away.

Well, Simple Peter stood there gaping for a long while, and then he looked in the mirror again, and still he could not see himself, even when he put his nose right up against it.

Just then a farmer came riding past on his way to market. 'Excuse me,' said Simple Peter, 'but have you seen my reflection? I can't find it in this mirror.'

'Oh,' said the farmer, 'I saw it half an hour ago, running down the road.'

'Thank you,' said Peter, 'I'll see if I can catch it,' and he ran off down the road.

The farmer laughed and said to himself: 'That Simple Peter is a proper goose!' and he went on his way.

Simple Peter ran on and on until he came to the blacksmith.

'Where are you running so fast, Peter?' called the blacksmith.

'I'm trying to catch my reflection,' replied Peter. 'John the farmer said it ran this way. Did you see it?'

The blacksmith, who was a kindly man, shook his head and said: 'John the farmer has been telling you stories. Your reflection can't run away from you. Look in the mirror, and you'll see it there all right.'

So Peter looked in the magic mirror, and do you know what he saw? He saw a goose, with a yellow beak and black eyes, staring straight back at him.

'There, do you see your reflection?' asked the blacksmith.

'I only see a goose,' said Peter, 'but *I'm* not a goose. I'll show you all! I'll seek my fortune, and then you'll see me as I really am!'

So Peter set off to seek his fortune.

Before long, he came to a wild place in the mountains, where he met a woodcutter and his family with all their belongings on their backs.

'Where are you going?' he asked them.

'We're leaving this country,' said the woodcutter, 'because there is a dragon here. It is fifty times as big as a man and could eat you up in one mouthful. Now it has carried off the King's daughter and is going to eat her for supper tonight.' And with that they hurried on their way.

Peter went on, and the mountains grew steeper and the way became harder. All at once he heard a sound like a grindstone. He looked round a rock and there he saw the dragon. Sure enough, it was fifty times as big as himself and it was spinning a stone round in its front claws to sharpen its teeth.

'Oh ho! Are you the dragon?' asked Peter. The dragon stopped sharpening its teeth and glared with great fierce eyes at Peter.

'I am!' said the dragon.

'Then I shall have to kill you,' said Peter.

'*Indeed?*' said the dragon, and the spines on its back started to bristle, and tongues of flame began to leap out of its nostrils. 'And how are *you* going to kill *me?*'

And Peter said: 'Oh, *I'm* not, but behind this rock I have the most terrible creature, that is fifty times as big as you, and could eat *you* up in one mouthful!'

'Impossible!' roared the dragon, and leapt behind the rock. Now Peter, who was not *so* simple after all, had hidden the magic mirror there, and so when the dragon came leaping round the rock it ran slap bang into it, and there, for the first time, it saw itself as it appeared to others – fifty times as big and able to eat itself up in one mouthful! And then and there that dragon turned on its tail and ran off over the mountains as fast as it could, and was never seen again.

Then Peter went into the dragon's cave, and found the King's daughter, and carried her back to the palace. And the King gave him jewels and fine clothes and all the people cheered him to the skies. And when Peter looked in the magic mirror now, do you know what he saw? He saw himself as a brave, fierce lion, which was how everyone else saw him. But he said to himself: 'I'm not a lion! I'm Peter.'

Just then the Princess came by and Peter showed her the mirror and asked her what she saw there.

'I see the most beautiful girl in the world,' said the Princess. 'But *I'm* not the most beautiful girl in the world.'

'But that's how you appear to me,' said Peter, and he told the Princess the whole story about how he had come by the mirror, and how he had tricked the dragon.

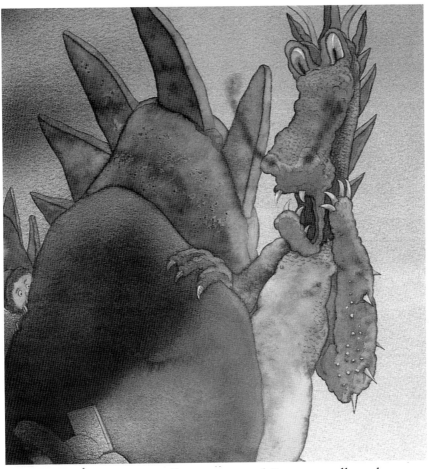

'So you see, I'm not really a goose, and I'm not really as brave as a lion. I'm just Simple Peter.'

When the Princess heard his story, she began to like him for his straightforwardness and honesty. Pretty soon she grew to love him, and the King agreed that they should be married, even though Peter was just a poor ploughman's son.

'But, my dear!' said the Queen. 'People will make fun of us because he is not a real prince.'

'Fiddlesticks!' replied the King. 'We'll make him into the finest prince you ever did see!' But the old Queen was right. . . .

On the day of the wedding, Peter was dressed up in the finest clothes, trimmed with gold and fur. But when he looked in the magic mirror, do you know what he saw? Instead of a rich and magnificent prince, he saw himself in his own rags – Simple Peter. But it didn't worry him. He smiled and said to himself: 'At last! Everyone sees me as I really am!'

BRAVE MOLLY

LITTLE GIRL WAS ONCE CAUGHT IN A THUNDERSTORM. The day grew dark, and the wind started to blow, and suddenly a fork of lightning streaked across the sky and a great clap of thunder rolled all around her. Poor Molly trembled with fright, and she wished she were back at home with her mother. Then it started to rain. Such a cloudburst it was! The heavens just opened up and down came the rain in great big drops the size of your fist.

In the distance, Molly could see a little hut, so she ran up to it and, finding the door open, she slipped into the gloomy inside. No sooner had she shut the door than a deep growling voice said: 'Grrrr! Who are you?'

Molly looked around her, but the inside of the hut was quite dark, and she couldn't see anyone.

'P-p-p-please . . . my name's M-M-M-Molly,' she said. 'Who are you?'

'Grrrr! I'm a Terrible Monster – that's who!' said the voice.

Just then a bolt of lightning lit up the inside of the hut for a fraction of a second and, in that moment, Molly saw a huge black shape crouching against the far end of the hut. 'Ohhhhh!' she cried.

'What's the matter?' growled the Terrible Monster. 'Frightened, are you?'

'Indeed I am,' said Molly. 'You're as black as coal, as big as a house and covered in hair.'

'And I've got a terrible roar,' said the Monster. 'AAAAAAAA-RRRRRRRGH!'

Poor Molly fell over backwards in her fright. And the thunder crashed over their heads, and another flash of lightning lit up the Monster, and Molly could see that he had great black claws and glowing eyes and huge yellow teeth.

'Pretty frightening, huh?' bellowed the Monster.

'Oh y-y-y-yes!' cried Molly.

'*And* I'm as strong as two hundred oxen!' he cried and, as the lightning flashed, Molly saw the Monster rear up on his legs and throw the roof of the hut high into the air.

'Oh . . . please don't!' cried Molly, as the rain started to pour down on her and the thunder crashed.

'*And* I eat little girls for my supper!' roared the Monster. And he bent down and put one glowing eye right up against poor Molly, and said: 'How about *that*?'

'Well,' Molly thought to herself, 'it's no use being frightened. If he's going to eat me – he's going to eat me.' So she picked up her satchel and hit that Monster right on the nose. And do you know what happened? Well, the Monster didn't pick her up in his huge claws, and he didn't gobble her up with his great yellow teeth. Do you know what he did? First he turned green, then he turned black and then he turned bright pink, and a bunch of flowers grew out of the top of his head.

'Why! You're not a frightening monster at all!' cried Molly.

'Aren't I?' said the Monster.

'No!' said Molly, and a beautiful ribbon tied in a bow suddenly appeared right round the Monster's middle. And Molly took hold of the ribbon and pulled it and the Monster opened up and inside was a little rabbit who looked very frightened and said: 'Oh please! Don't put me in a pie!'.

And Brave Molly said: 'I won't put you in a pie this time, but don't go around trying to frighten little children in future.'

'No . . . I promise,' said the rabbit, and scuttled off out of the hut.

And just then the sky cleared and the sun came out, and Brave Molly set off home again, and she didn't meet another monster all the rest of the way.

THE SEA TIGER

HERE WAS ONCE A TIGER who told the most enormous lies. No matter how hard he tried, he just couldn't tell the truth.

Once the monkey asked the tiger where he was going. The tiger replied that he was on his way to the moon, where he kept a store of tiger-cheese which made his eyes brighter than the sun so that he could see in the dark. But in fact he was going behind a bush for a snooze.

Another time, the snake asked the tiger round for lunch, but the tiger said that he couldn't come because a man had heard him singing in the jungle, and had asked him to go to the big city that very afternoon to sing in the opera.

'Oh!' said the snake. 'Before you go, won't you sing something for me?'

'Ah no,' said the tiger. 'If I sing before I've had my breakfast, my tail swells up and turns into a sausage, and I get followed around by sausage-flies all day.'

One day, all the animals in the jungle held a meeting, and decided they'd cure the tiger of telling such enormous lies. So they sent the monkey off to find the wizard who lived in the snow-capped mountains. The monkey climbed for seven days and seven nights, and he got higher and higher until at last he reached the cave in the snow where the wizard lived.

At the entrance to the cave he called out: 'Old wizard, are you there?'

And a voice called out: 'Come in, monkey, I've been expecting you.'

So the monkey went into the cave. He found the wizard busy preparing spells, and he told him that the animals of the jungle wanted to cure the tiger of telling such enormous lies.

'Very well,' said the wizard. 'Take this potion, and pour it into the tiger's ears when he is asleep.'

'But what will it do, wizard?' asked the monkey.

The wizard smiled and said: 'Rest assured, once you've given him this potion, everything the tiger says will be true all right.'

So the monkey took the potion and went back to the jungle where he told the other animals what they had to do.

That day, while the tiger was having his usual nap behind the bush, all the other animals gathered round in a circle and the monkey crept up very cautiously to the tiger and carefully poured a little of the potion first into one of the tiger's ears and then into the other. Then he ran back to the other animals, and they all called out: 'Tiger! Tiger! Wake up, tiger!'

After a while, the tiger opened one eye, and then the other. He was a bit surprised to find all the other animals of the jungle standing around him in a circle.

'Have you been asleep?' asked the lion.

'Oh no,' said the tiger, 'I was just lying here, planning my next expedition to the bottom of the ocean.'

When they heard this, all the other animals shook their heads and said: 'The wizard's potion hasn't worked. Tiger's still telling as whopping lies as ever!'

But just then the tiger found himself leaping to his feet and bounding across the jungle. 'But it's true!' he cried to his own surprise.

'What are you doing, tiger?' they asked.

'I'm going to fly there!' he called and, sure enough, he spread out his legs and soared up high above the trees and across the top of the jungle.

Now if there's one thing tigers don't like, it's heights, and so the tiger yelled out: 'Help! I *am* flying! Get me down!'

But he found himself flying on and on until the jungle was far behind him and he flew over the snow-capped mountains where the wizard lived. The wizard looked up at the tiger flying overhead and smiled to himself and said: 'Ha-ha, old tiger, you'll always tell the truth now. For anything you say will become true – even if it wasn't before!'

And the tiger flew on and on, and he got colder and colder and, if there's one thing tigers hate worse than heights, it's being cold.

At length he found himself flying out over the sea, and then suddenly he dropped like a stone, until he came down splash in the middle of the ocean. Now if there's one thing that tigers hate more than heights and cold, it's getting wet.

'Urrrrgh!' said the tiger, but down and down he sank, right to the bottom of the ocean, and all the fish came up to him and stared, so he chased them off with his tail.

Then he looked up and he could see the bottom of the waves high above him, and he swam up and up, and just as he was running out of breath he reached the surface. Then he struggled and splashed and tried to swim for the shore.

Just then a fishing-boat came by, and all the fishermen gasped in amazement to see a tiger swimming in the middle of the ocean. Then one of them laughed and pointed at the tiger and said: 'Look! A sea tiger!'

And they all laughed and pointed at the tiger, and, if there's one thing tigers hate worse than heights and cold and getting wet, it's being laughed at.

The poor tiger paddled away as fast as he could, but it was a long way to the shore, and eventually the fishermen threw one of their nets over him and hauled him on to the boat.

'Oh ho!' they laughed. 'Now we can make a fortune by getting this sea tiger to perform tricks in the circus!'

Now this made the tiger really angry because, if there's one thing tigers hate more than heights and cold and getting wet and being laughed at, it's performing tricks in the circus. So as soon as they landed he tore up the net, and leapt out of the boat, and ran home to the forest as fast as his legs would carry him.

And he never told any lies, *ever* again.

THE WIND GHOSTS

HEN THE WIND IS HOWLING ROUND THE HOUSE and tearing at the clouds, our ears are filled with noise. Chimney pots rattle, doors bang, windows shake. But in between the blasts, when the wind is still for a moment, you can sometimes hear, very faintly, the pitter-patter footsteps of the ghosts who follow the wind. Here is the story of one such ghost.

Once there were two friends who set off to seek their fortunes. On the first day, they came to a wide river, and did not know how to get across. So they walked along the river bank until they came to a little tumbledown hut, where an old woman was sitting making a necklace of bones.

'How do we get across this river, old woman?' they asked.

The old woman kept on threading the bones on the string as if they were beads, and said: 'There are two ways to cross the river. One is free, and one will cost you.'

'How can that be?' asked the two friends.

'Well,' said the old woman, 'one way is to swim across. That's free. The other way is to take the boat that leaves from here at midnight, but that will cost you, for once you step on board you must give the boatmen whatever he asks for.'

'I don't want to get wet,' said the first friend, whose name was Jonathan. 'I'll take the boat.'

'Who knows what the boatman might ask for!' said David. 'I'll swim.'

So the two friends agreed to meet the next day on the other side. Then David tied all his belongings in his shirt, and put them on his head, and swam across. It was a wide river, and the current took him a long way downstream, but eventually he got to the other side. There he lit a fire and waited until his friend Jonathan arrived.

'Well?' asked David. 'What did the boatman ask for?'

'Oh . . . he wanted the moon,' said Jonathan.

'So what did you give him?' asked David.

'Oh . . . I just got out my cup and dipped it in the river and handed it to him so that, when he looked into it, there was the moon, shining up at him.'

Well, the two friends went on their way, and on the second day they came to a deep chasm. There they found a little old man, sitting outside a cave.

'How do we get across this chasm?' they asked.

'There are two ways,' said the little old man. 'One way will take a minute, the other way will take a month.'

'How can that be?' they asked.

'Well, one way is to walk all round the edge of the chasm, and that will take you a month,' said the little old man. 'The other way is to ask the eagle that lives on this mountain to give you a ride on his back. But if he does, you must answer any question he asks you as you fly over, otherwise he will drop you into the chasm.'

'I'm not going to risk that!' said David. 'I'll walk round the edge, even if it takes a month.'

'I can answer any question,' said Jonathan. 'I'll fly on the eagle's back.'

So the two friends agreed to meet in a month's time. David walked and walked for a whole month, and eventually he reached the spot on the other side of the chasm where they had agreed to meet, and there – sure enough – was his friend Jonathan waiting for him.

'What was the eagle's question?' asked David.

'Oh . . . he wanted to know where he could always find the summer sun in midwinter,' replied Jonathan.

'What did you tell him?' asked David.

'Oh . . . I told him to find one blade of grass, for you must know that all plants store the summer sun in their leaves.'

So the two friends went on their way until they came to the shore of a sea. There they found an old sailor, so they asked him how they could cross the sea.

'There are two ways,' said the old sailor. 'One way is dangerous, the other way is safe.'

'How can that be?' they asked.

'One way is to sail across on a boat. That will be full of danger, for the sea is deep and there are storms and high waves and sea-monsters. The other way is to go to the wizard of the sea, and ask him to get you across by his magic. That is quite safe, but with this warning: you will have to do whatever the wizard of the sea wants first, or else you will never get across at all.'

'I will sail across,' said David, 'for I would rather face the dangers of the sea than put myself in the wizard's hands.'

'I can do whatever the wizard asks me to,' said Jonathan. 'I'll go by magic.'

So Jonathan went to the wizard and swore to do whatever the wizard asked of him.

'There's only one thing you need do for me,' said the wizard, 'and that's not so difficult for someone who can give the moon away and who knows where to find the summer sun in midwinter.'

'What is it I must do?' asked Jonathan.

'You must catch the wind,' said the wizard. And just then a breeze blew across the shore, and Jonathan set off after it.

Meanwhile David had built himself a boat. He spread his sail, and the wind blew him across the ocean. Sometimes the wind blew up a storm, and sometimes it blew him the wrong way, and he fought with the rain and the cold and the sea-monsters, but at length he got to the other side. There he built a windmill, and the wind turned the sails of the mill, and he became a miller. He never grew rich, but he was never poor, and – for all I know – he was happy enough.

Jonathan, however, never *was* able to catch the wind, and to this day he chases after it, and in between the blasts of a storm you may hear the pitter-patter of his footsteps. He cannot stop and he cannot catch it, for he is now a wind ghost. And yet – for all I know – he *too* is happy enough . . . in his way.

THE BIG NOSES

 HERE WAS ONCE AN ISLAND in the middle of the ocean, where everybody's nose was far too big. The chief of the island got in a boat, and sailed to the place where the wisest of all men lived.

'Now, what is the problem?' asked the wisest of all men.

'Well,' said the chief of the island, 'all my people are unhappy because their noses are too big. We can't get our sweaters over our heads because our noses are so big. We can't enjoy a drink without hitting our noses on the other side of the cup. We can't kiss each other, because our noses get in the way. But worst of all, we don't even like each other, because of our ugly great noses. Can you help us by making our noses smaller?'

'Well,' said the wisest of all men, 'I cannot make your noses smaller. Only the magician who lives by the burning lake could do that – and even he could not do it for *all* your people. But come back in three days' time, and perhaps I shall be able to help you.'

So the chief of the island stayed in that land for two days and two nights. And while he was there, he went to the magician who lived by the burning lake and the magician cast a spell over his nose and made it very small indeed. And on the third day, the chief went back to the wisest of all men, and said: 'Well, have you thought of an answer?'

The wisest of all men looked at the island chief in amazement. Finally he said: 'Is that really *you*?'

And the chief said: 'Yes, of course it is.'

And the wisest of all men said: 'But what has happened to your nose?' So the chief of the island told him how he had been to the magician. And the wisest of all men shook his grey head, and said: 'You seek one solution for yourself and another for your people, and that's not good.'

'Well, it's too late now,' replied the chief, 'so what is your solution for my people?'

'First,' said the wisest of all men, 'you must go to the volcano that lies on the other side of this land, and take the ashes from its mouth, and rub them into your hair and hands and all over your body. Then put on these robes, and return to your people and tell them that you are Chan Tanda.'

The chief looked amazed, and said: 'But *you* are Chan Tanda, the wisest of all men. Why should I pretend to be you?'

'You must,' said Chan Tanda, 'and, believe me, you will thank me for it.'

So the chief took the clothes and Chan Tanda told him what he was to say to his people, and then he went to the volcano, and climbed to the very top, where the smoke and flames came billowing out of the ground. And he rubbed the ashes into his hair and hands and all over his body until he was a dusty grey colour, just like Chan Tanda himself. And he put on the clothes and sailed back to his people.

When he arrived, they all said: 'Where is our chief?'

And he replied, as he had been instructed: 'Your chief says he will not come back to this island until his people have become more reasonable.'

'What does he mean?' they all cried. 'We may have big noses, but we're not fools! Tell him to come back!'

'He says he won't come back until you've changed some of your foolish ways,' said the chief of the island.

'What foolish ways?' they said. 'What does he mean?'

'For a start, he says you must stop sitting out in the rain playing ludo.'

'But we like sitting out in the rain playing ludo!' they cried.

'Secondly, you must stop using egg-cups for your tea.'

'But we like drinking tea out of egg-cups!' they cried.

'And thirdly, you must bend your heads to one side when you kiss.'

'But we've always kept them upright!' they cried.

'Otherwise your chief will never return,' said the chief of the island.

Well, they held a meeting, and decided to do what was asked so that their leader would return. And before long they discovered that when they didn't sit out in the rain playing ludo, their sweaters didn't shrink, and they were able to put them on over their heads without their noses getting in the way. And when they gave up drinking tea out of egg-cups, they found that their noses no longer hit the other side. And when they bent their heads to one side, they could kiss just fine. Before long, they even started to like each other, and soon they were all living happily enough, and realized that there never had been anything wrong with their noses in the first place.

But the chief of the island had to return to the wisest of all men, and get him to persuade the magician who lived by the burning lake to change *his* nose back to its proper size again, before he dared to go home to his own people.

A Fish of the World

A HERRING ONCE DECIDED TO SWIM right round the world. 'I'm tired of the North Sea,' he said. 'I want to find out what else there is in the world.' So he swam off south into the deep Atlantic. He swam and he swam far far away from the seas he knew, through the warm waters of the equator and on down into the South Atlantic. And all the time he saw many strange and wonderful fish that he had never seen before. Once he was nearly eaten by a shark, and once he was nearly electrocuted by an electric eel, and once he was nearly stung by a sting-ray. But he swam on and on, round the tip of Africa and into the Indian Ocean. And he passed by devilfish and sailfish and sawfish and swordfish and bluefish and blackfish and mudfish and sunfish, and he was amazed by the different shapes and sizes and colours.

On he swam, into the Java Sea, and he saw fish that leapt out of the water and fish that lived on the bottom of the sea and fish that could walk on their fins. And on he swam, through the Coral Sea, where the shells of millions and millions of tiny creatures had turned to rock and stood as big as mountains. But still he swam on, into the wide Pacific. He swam over the deepest parts of the ocean, where the water is so deep that it is inky black at the bottom, and the fish carry lanterns over their heads, and some have lights on their tails. And through the Pacific he swam, and then he

turned north and headed up to the cold Siberian Sea, where huge white icebergs sailed past him like mighty ships. And still he swam on and on and into the frozen Arctic Ocean, where the sea is forever covered in ice. And on he went, past Greenland and Iceland, and finally he swam home into his own North Sea.

All his friends and relations gathered round and made a great fuss of him. They had a big feast and offered him the very best food they could find. But the herring just yawned and said: 'I've swum round the entire world. I have seen everything there is to see, and I have eaten more exotic and wonderful dishes than you could possibly imagine.' And he refused to eat anything.

Then his friends and relations begged him to come home and live with them, but he refused. 'I've been everywhere there is, and that old rock is too dull and small for me.' And he went off and lived on his own.

And when the breeding season came, he refused to join in the spawning, saying: 'I've swum around the entire world, and now I know how many fish there are in the world, I can't be interested in herrings anymore.'

Eventually, one of the oldest of the herrings swam up to him, and said: 'Listen. If you don't spawn with us, some herrings' eggs will go unfertilized and will not turn into healthy young herring. If you don't live with your family, you'll make them sad. And if you don't eat, you'll die.'

But the herring said: 'I don't mind. I've been everywhere there is to go, I've seen everything there is to see, and now I know everything there is to know.'

The old fish shook his head. 'No-one has ever seen everything there is to see,' he said, 'nor known everything there is to know.'

'Look,' said the herring, 'I've swum through the North Sea, the Atlantic Ocean, the Indian Ocean, the Java Sea, the Coral Sea, the great Pacific Ocean, the Siberian Sea and the frozen Arctic. Tell me, what else is there for me to see or know?'

'I don't know,' said the old herring, 'but there may be something.'

Well, just then, a fishing-boat came by, and all the herrings were caught in a net and taken to market that very day. And a man bought the herring, and ate it for his supper.

And he never knew that it had swum right round the world, and had seen everything there was to see, and knew everything there was to know.

TIM O'LEARY

UNDREDS OF YEARS AGO a goblin sat on the bank of a river, dipping his toes in the water. Towards the end of the day, a farmer came walking home from his fields. When he saw the little goblin he rubbed his eyes and looked again.

'What sort of thing are you?' he asked.

'I'm Tim O'Leary,' said the goblin.

'How can that be?' said the farmer. 'Tim O'Leary's my best friend, and he don't look a bit like you.'

'Ah!' sighed the goblin. 'I found a cave that was full of witch's treasure, and I would have carried it all off, but I cut my feet on some magic rocks, and turned into a goblin as you can see.'

'But what are you doing with your feet in the river?' asked the farmer.

'I'm trying to wash the magic off my feet,' replied the goblin, 'but it's no good.'

'Oh deary me, Tim,' said the farmer, 'whatever can we do?'

'The only way to turn me back into Tim O'Leary is to steal the witch's treasure and throw every single bit of it into the deepest ocean.'

'I'll do that!' cried the farmer.

'But mind you don't cut your feet on the magic rocks!' said the goblin.

72

'I won't,' said the farmer, 'I have on my toughest boots.' And he set off to find the cave.

It was almost night when he found it, so he lit a torch and ventured in. First he came to a long tunnel, where the floor and the walls and the ceiling were all of sharp rocks. So he walked very slowly and very carefully along the tunnel, and he managed to get to the other end of it without cutting himself.

There he found three great doors. One was made of wood. One was made of iron. And one was made of stone. Just as he was wondering which one to try, he heard a croak behind him. He turned round and found a frog sitting on a rock.

'You want to know what lies behind the doors?' asked the frog.

'Yes,' said the farmer.

'Very well, I'll tell you, if you promise to give me a jewel from the witch's treasure.'

'I can't do that,' replied the farmer, 'I have to throw every single bit of the witch's treasure into the ocean, so that the goblin can turn back into Tim O'Leary.'

'Huh!' said the frog. 'Don't believe that goblin. He's no more Tim O'Leary than I am. He just wants to get his hands on the witch's treasure.'

'Well, why doesn't he come and get it himself?' asked the farmer.

'He's a water-goblin,' said the frog. 'Very powerful, you know, but he must keep touching water. That's why he sits with his toes in the river.'

Well, the farmer didn't know who to believe, but he said to himself: 'I set out to save Tim O'Leary, and that's what I'll do.'

'Come,' said the frog, 'you can give me a jewel from the witch's treasure and then keep the rest for yourself.'

'No,' replied the farmer, 'I must save Tim O'Leary.'

'You fool!' screamed the frog, shaking with anger. Then he grew larger and larger, and turned brown and then black and suddenly there was a little old elf.

'You fool!' he screamed. 'You'll never get the witch's treasure now! It lies behind one of the doors, but behind another lies a monster that will tear you to pieces, and behind the third lies a hole that will suck you in. Now you won't know which is which and I shan't tell you!' And he disappeared in a puff of smoke that smelt curiously of nettle beer.

Well, the farmer was very frightened, but he was determined to help Tim O'Leary. So he covered himself from head to foot in mud and got a long pole that stretched the length of the three great doors. Then he opened the first door that was made of wood. Immediately there was a whooshing noise and he saw a terrible black hole, and he felt himself being sucked towards it. And suddenly stones and rocks from the cave were flying past him, and all disappearing into that terrible black hole. But the farmer clung tight to his pole, and because it was wider than the doorway it couldn't go through. So the farmer struggled and strained and eventually he managed to shut the door with a great bang, and the sucking wind died down and the cave grew still again.

'Phew!' said the farmer. 'Now which of the next two doors has the treasure, and which has the monster that will tear me to pieces?'

Finally he decided to try the iron door. He opened it very, very cautiously, expecting a terrible monster to leap out at him at any moment. But all was quiet. He looked in and found himself gazing

into a high hall, lit by candles, and in the centre of the hall was a great iron chest, with a golden lock.

The farmer looked around the hall and there on the wall hung a great golden key. So he took the key and eagerly opened up the treasure chest. Whereupon there was a terrible roar and out jumped a hideous monster with great claws and bulging eyes. And it stretched out its claws to seize the farmer, but, because he was all covered in mud, he slipped through them, and ran as hard as he could for the door. He got there in the nick of time and slammed it shut just as the monster sprang again, so that it crashed against the great door and the iron rang and the monster roared.

Then the farmer opened the last of the three doors, that was made of stone. And there lay the witch's treasure. The poor man had never seen so many precious stones and so much gold and silver.

'It would be a crime', he said to himself, 'to throw all that into the ocean but, if that's the only way to save Tim O'Leary, that's what I must do.'

So he put it all into a great sack and carried it down to the river and put it into a boat and set off for the sea.

Well, he hadn't gone very far before he heard singing coming from the back of the boat, and there he found the goblin sitting trailing a toe in the water. In this way, they sailed out into the wide open ocean, until the goblin suddenly said: 'Here we are!'

And the farmer picked up the sack of treasure, and he took one last look at it and said: 'I shall never see such wealth again. But if this is the only way to turn you back into Tim O'Leary, away it goes!' And he emptied all the precious jewels and silver and gold into the sea.

'Ah ha!' cried the goblin. 'Thank you very much! I was never Tim O'Leary and he was never me!' And with that he jumped into the waves and disappeared with the treasure.

Well, the farmer went home, and he found Tim O'Leary sitting on a wall.

'Oh,' said the farmer, 'because of you, I've lost the richest treasure I've ever seen,' and he told him the whole story. And Tim O'Leary put his arm round the farmer and said: 'Leave the treasure to the goblins. You've proved yourself a true friend to me and a true friend I'll be to you, and that's worth more than all the gold and silver and precious jewels in the world.'

THE WITCH AND
THE RAINBOW CAT

SMALL GIRL WAS WALKING along the banks of a river on a hot summer's day when, quite by chance, she came across a little house. It had a front door and windows and a chimney and a little garden that ran down to the river, but it was very, very small. The girl could touch the roof if she reached up, and she had to bend her head to look in at the windows.

'I wonder if anyone's at home?' she said to herself. So she knocked on the door and waited, but there was no answer. So she tried the door and it opened easily.

'Hello?' she called. 'Is there anyone at home?' But there was no answer. Now the little girl knew that she shouldn't go into a strange house without being invited, but it was all so curious and so small that she just *had* to look inside. So she bent her head, and stepped into the house.

Everything in the house was perfect, but half the size of normal things. She didn't have to stand on tip-toe to look on to the tables. She didn't have to stand on a chair to reach the kitchen sink or look out of the windows, and the door handles were all just the right height. There was a sitting-room with a fireplace and a mirror over the mantelpiece, and she could see into the mirror perfectly well, just like her mother could at home, without having to climb on anything. But she noticed one very curious thing: the reflection of herself that she saw in the mirror was quite grown-up.

At first she thought it was a trick of the light, and she looked around the room at the other things, but when she turned back to the mirror, sure enough – instead of a little girl, there was a fully grown-up woman looking back at her. She blinked and stared again. It was definitely *her* reflection: the dress it was wearing was exactly the same as the dress she was wearing, and when she touched her nose the reflection touched *its* nose, and when she touched her ear, the reflection touched *its* ear . . . and suddenly she realized she was looking at herself as a grown-up woman.

How long she stood there, staring into that mirror, I don't know, but suddenly she heard the latch on the front door open, and she heard some footsteps coming slowly into the house . . . tip . . . tap . . . tip . . . tap . . . and all at once she remembered that she shouldn't be there, so she quickly hid herself behind a little cupboard, feeling very frightened.

She heard the footsteps go into the kitchen . . . tip . . . tap . . . tip . . . tap . . . and then go out of the kitchen and slowly start to come towards the sitting-room . . . tip . . . tap . . . tip . . . tap. Nearer and nearer they came and the little girl's heart beat faster and faster, until suddenly the footsteps stopped and turned and went upstairs. The little girl took her chance and ran for the front door, but it was locked. She ran to the back door, but that too was locked, and there was no key. She tried the windows but they were all tight shut, and she couldn't open any of them. And so she ran back and hid behind the cupboard in the sitting-room.

Well, she crouched there for quite a long time, wondering what on earth she was going to do, when she heard the footsteps coming downstairs again . . . tip . . . tap . . . tip . . . tap. This time they turned towards the sitting-room and kept on coming, closer and closer, until they walked right in. The little girl peered out from behind the cupboard, and do you know what she saw? She saw a little old witch in a green hat and a green cloak, and on her shoulder was a cat that was all the colours of the rainbow.

The little girl didn't know what to do, so she just kept quiet. And the little old witch stopped and looked about her, and said: 'Who's been looking in my mirror? I can see a child there!'

The poor girl trembled with fright and kept just as quiet as she could, but she heard the little old witch coming towards the cupboard, and suddenly there she was, looking down at her with piercing green eyes.

'Who are you?' asked the old witch. 'What are you doing in my house?'

'Please,' said the little girl, 'my name is Rose and I didn't mean any harm.'

'*Didn't* mean any harm?' screamed the old witch. 'Didn't mean any *harm*! You've looked in my mirror!'

'Please,' said Rose, 'shouldn't I have?'

'Of course you shouldn't have!' screamed the witch. 'Now I'll have to keep you here for ever!'

'Oh please, let me go home,' cried Rose, 'and I'll never come and bother you again.'

'No! You've looked in my mirror!' cried the witch. 'You can't go back now! You'll stay here and be my servant!'

Well, poor Rose wept and pleaded with the little green witch, but there was nothing she could do. The witch took her up to the attic at the top of the little house and locked her in. The attic had no windows and was bare and dark and full of cobwebs. Poor Rose sat down on the dusty floor and cried, for she didn't know what she was going to do.

Suddenly she felt something soft brushing up against her, and she nearly jumped out of her skin. But when she looked down she found it was just the rainbow-coloured cat, rubbing itself up against her legs.

'Hello,' said the rainbow cat. 'You can ask me three questions.'

Rose was so astonished to hear the cat talk that, without stopping to think, she exclaimed: 'But how is it you can talk?'

The rainbow cat yawned and replied: 'I would have thought that was obvious – the witch put a spell on me. Two questions left. If I were you, I'd think more carefully about the next.'

Rose thought carefully about the next question, and then asked: 'Why doesn't the witch like me looking in her mirror?'

'A better question,' replied the cat, stretching itself. 'She doesn't like you looking in the mirror because she is the Witch of the Future, and in that mirror she sees the things that are to come. She is the only person that can know those things, and once you know them she'll never let you go. One question left.'

Rose thought very carefully about what was the best question to ask the rainbow cat next, but try as she might she could not decide. She thought: 'If I ask him how to escape from here, that

wouldn't stop the old witch catching me again. If I ask him how I can get home, that wouldn't stop the old witch from finding me there. . . .'

At length the rainbow cat asked: 'Well? Have you thought of your last question?'

'Not yet,' replied Rose.

'Very well,' said the cat, 'I'll wait.'

Just then the door flew open and in burst the witch. She thrust a bundle of old clothes towards Rose and said: 'Here is a servant's uniform. You must put it on, or I'll turn you into a mad dog.'

Poor Rose trembled with fright, but she took off her own clothes and put the uniform on. It was grey and drab, and it made her feel miserable.

'Now,' said the witch, 'you must start to work for me.' And she made poor Rose scrub the floors from morning till evening, all that day and all the next day. And when Rose begged to be allowed to do some other work, the Witch of the Future shook her head and said: 'No! You must keep your eyes on the floor so that you don't go looking in my mirror again.'

Poor Rose had to scrub the witch's floors day in, day out, and at night she was so exhausted that she would go to bed without once raising her eyes from the floor. Day after day, week after week, the witch kept her at it, until poor Rose's back was bent and her hands were sore, and she never raised her eyes from the floor ever. And she worked so hard that she forgot about everything else until, one day, when the witch was out in the forest collecting toads, Rose suddenly felt the rainbow cat rubbing itself up against her leg.

'Rainbow cat! I'd forgotten about you!' she cried.

'Well,' said the cat, 'have you thought of your last question yet?'

Rose stopped her scrubbing for a moment, and then said: 'I'll ask you my last question tomorrow.'

'Very well,' said the cat, 'I'll wait.'

All that night, although she was exhausted from her scrubbing, Rose couldn't sleep. She was too busy trying to work out the best question to ask the rainbow cat, but she still couldn't decide.

The next morning she could hardly get up to scrub the floors, and she kept yawning and feeling faint.

'Now then!' screamed the Witch of the Future. 'What are you

80

doing? Get on with your scrubbing, girl, or I'll turn you into a cabbage and make you into cabbage soup!'

Then the witch went out to the forest to catch some bats. Rose was scrubbing the doorstep, watching the witch go, when she noticed a small bird in the garden, with its leg caught in one of the witch's traps. Although Rose knew that the witch would be very angry, she couldn't bear to see the bird in such pain, and so she put down her scrubbing brush and went and released it, and then went back to her scrubbing.

The next moment, she felt something rub against her leg and there was the rainbow cat again.

'Well,' said the rainbow cat, 'have you thought of your last question?'

'Not quite,' said Rose.

'I can't wait any longer,' replied the rainbow cat.

Just then, the bird flew down and landed on Rose's shoulder, and said: 'I can tell you what to ask.' And it whispered in Rose's ear, and then flew off again.

'Well,' said the rainbow cat, 'what is your question?'

Rose looked at the cat and took a deep breath and then said as the bird had told her: 'Tell me, rainbow cat, why can't I choose my own future?'

At these words, the rainbow cat looked up and smiled, and his colours all started changing and glowing and spinning round and round. 'But you can!' he cried. 'The Witch of the Future has no power without her mirror – break that and you are free.'

Just then, Rose looked up and saw the witch coming out of the wood towards her. Without another word, Rose turned and ran back into the little house, and took the mirror off the wall and hurled it to the ground so that it smashed into smithereens. Everything went still. Then there was a dreadful scream, and there glaring at her in the doorway stood the Witch of the Future, only she looked a thousand years older. Rose summoned up all her courage but, before she could speak, the witch stumbled and fell to the floor. At that moment Rose heard a creak, and saw the wall of the house start to crumble. So she ran, and she didn't stop running until she reached the gate at the bottom of the garden. There she turned, in time to see the little house collapse in a cloud of dust, and an ordinary black cat walked out and rubbed up against her legs.

'Is that you, rainbow cat?' asked Rose. But the cat didn't reply. It simply strolled off into the wood. And Rose changed back into her own clothes, and ran home as fast as she possibly could.

THE MONSTER TREE

HERE WAS ONCE A TREE THAT GREW in a wood not far from here. It was a very special tree. Its leaves were red and its trunk was green and on it grew apples that were bright blue. And nobody ever ate the bright blue apples that hung from the tree, because they knew that if they did they would meet a monster before the day was out.

One day a boy was walking with his mother in the wood, and they passed the Monster Tree. 'Oh, can I have one of those bright blue apples?' said the boy.

'No,' said his mother, 'you know you mustn't, because anyone who eats one will meet a monster before the day is out.'

The little boy didn't say anything, but he thought to himself: 'Piffle!' and he resolved there and then that he would try one of those bright blue apples for himself.

So that night, when his mother and father were safely tucked up in bed, he took his satchel and stole out of the house and down the garden and through the village. The moon made everything blue and silver, and the houses looked dark and sinister, and he began to feel a little bit frightened at being all on his own.

Soon he came to the end of the village, and he looked along the lonely path that led to the wood where the Monster Tree grew, and he felt even more frightened. 'But I don't believe in monsters,' he said to himself, and he set off along the path.

Before long he came to the edge of a wood. The trees stretched up high above him, and the wood was dark and full of strange noises, and he didn't like it at all. But he said to himself: 'I'm not scared of monsters.' Then he summoned up all his courage, and stepped into the dark wood.

Well, he hadn't gone very far before he heard a hideous noise, and he saw a horrible pair of yellow eyes peering out at him from the darkness, and a terrible voice said: 'You'll make a tasty meal for the monsters in the wood.'

He was so frightened that his knees knocked together, but he kept on walking. And he hadn't gone much farther when there was an awful screech, and something flew out of a tree and pulled his hair and screamed: 'The monsters are hungry tonight! The monsters are hungry tonight!'

Now he was so scared that his teeth started chattering, but he kept on walking towards the Monster Tree.

And just as he was passing an old hollow oak, a terrible creature leapt out in front of him, with great long nails and burning eyes and fire coming out of its ears and it screamed: 'They'll break your bones! They'll drink your blood! Go back at once!'

And the boy was so frightened that his hair stood on end, and he nearly turned right round and ran home to his bed. But he didn't. And the creature gave a terrible shriek and rushed at him. The boy jumped up and grabbed a branch, and then leapt over the creature's head, and ran as fast as he could until he reached the Monster Tree. He pulled off as many of the bright blue apples as he could carry in his satchel, and ran home as fast as his legs could take him. And when he got home, he jumped into bed, hid under the blankets and ate one of the bright blue apples from the Monster Tree all alone in the dark, and then he fell asleep.

In his dreams that night he met more monsters than you could ever imagine in a whole year. And when he woke up the next morning, he told his mother all about the Monster Tree and his terrible journey in the night. His mother was very cross, and she took his satchel and opened it up to throw those apples from the Monster Tree on the fire. But when she looked into the satchel she couldn't see any bright blue apples – they were just ordinary apples. And that morning, the villagers went into the wood to cut that Monster Tree down, but do you know what? They couldn't find it. And to this day it has never been seen again.

THE SNUFF-BOX

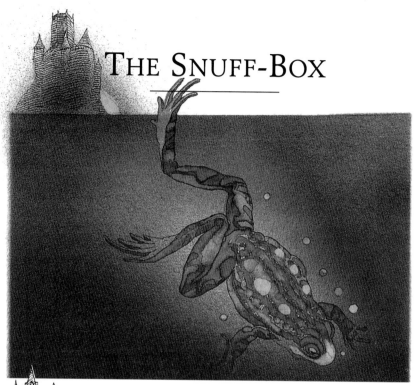

HERE WAS ONCE A DARK CASTLE that stood on the edge of a black and bottomless lake. People said that once the castle had been full of light and laughter, but now it stood empty because no-one dared live in it, for they said that something horrible lay in the black lake.

One day, however, a wicked witch came to the dark castle, and gazed down into the dark, deep waters of the bottomless lake. She picked up a toad that was sitting on the bank, and put a spell on it.

'Now then toad,' she said, 'I want you to swim down to the bottom of the lake, and bring me what you find there.'

So the toad disappeared under the water, and was gone for a whole day. At length, however, its head bobbed up to the surface again, and it said: 'Witch! I swam down, and I swam down, deeper and deeper, where there is no sound, and there is no light, but I could not find any bottom to the lake.'

'There must be a bottom, toad!' cried the witch. 'Try again!'

This time the toad disappeared into the dark, deep waters, and was gone for two whole days. When it came up to the surface again it said: 'Witch! I swam down and I swam down, deeper and deeper, where there is no sound and no light, and at last I did indeed reach the bottom, but I could not see anything, and I could not stay there, for it is as black and cold as the grave.'

The witch cried: 'You lazy toad! Here is a lantern – go down and look again!'

So the toad took the lantern, and disappeared into the dismal waters once more. This time it was gone for three whole days. And twilight fell on the fourth, and still the old witch sat waiting by the black lake. At last the toad reappeared, and said: 'Witch! I swam down, and I swam down, deeper and deeper, where there is no sound and there is no light, and at last I reached the bottom where it is as black and cold as the grave, and no bird has ever sung. I searched that foul floor by the dim light of this lantern and at last I found this. . . .' And it opened its hand, and there lay a small snuff-box.

'Give it to me at once!' cried the witch.

But the toad held on to it, and said: 'What is my reward?'

'Give me the snuff-box,' replied the witch, 'and I will turn you into a prince!'

'Very well,' said the toad, and it gave the witch the snuff-box.

The moment it did so, the witch burst into a cackle of evil laughter. 'Impertinent creature!' she cried. 'You think I'd turn you into a prince, do you? Very well! I will!' And with that she waved her hands, and the toad did indeed turn into a prince, but into the ugliest, hunch-backed prince you ever could imagine, with one leg shorter than the other and warts on his face.

'Ah-ha!' cried the witch. 'Enjoy your reward!' And she vanished into the dark castle, clutching the snuff-box.

Now the wicked witch knew that in the snuff-box, many, many years ago, a demon had been imprisoned, who had once brought terror on all the people of that land. So she held it tight, and whispered: 'Demon in the box, are you there?'

And a tiny voice said: 'Oh! Yes. Please open the box. I've been in here *so* long. . . .'

But the witch held on to it all the tighter, and said: 'If I release you, you must promise to be my slave and do as I command you for one whole year and a day, so that I become rich and rule all this land. Then you will be free to go where you will.'

'Indeed I shall!' cried the small voice. So the witch opened the snuff-box, and immediately there was a terrifying roar, and a blast of scalding air threw the witch back against the wall, and smoke poured into the room, as out leapt the demon with a terrible cry: 'At last!'

'Don't forget you are my slave for one whole year and a day!' cried the witch.

'I am nobody's slave!' cried the demon, and he touched the witch on the nape of the neck, and she turned into a millstone, and he cast her into the cold, black lake.

Meanwhile, the toad-prince had clambered in at the window of the dark castle, and he had seen all that had happened between the witch and demon of the snuff-box. And he said to himself: 'I fetched this demon up from the bottom of the bottomless lake. I must send him back there.' So he jumped down into the great hall.

'Who dares to enter my castle?' roared the demon.

'Demon!' said the toad-prince. 'Are you going to rob the people of this land?'

'Indeed I am!' roared the demon.

'Are you going to kill their dogs and steal their children?' asked the toad-prince.

'Indeed I am!' cried the demon.

'And will you make them poor and live in terror of you?'

'Indeed I shall!' bellowed the demon.

'Then let me help you!' said the toad-prince. 'For, as you see, I am ugly and unwanted, and I should like to do all the harm I can.'

'Very good!' cried the demon.

'But first,' said the toad-prince, 'I must know how powerful you really are.'

'I can easily show you,' said the demon, and he waved his hand, and a ball of fire appeared in mid-air. It circled round them once, and then flew out of the window.

'Hmmm,' said the toad-prince. 'Can't you do anything else?'

'Come with me,' said the demon, and he took the toad-prince on to the roof of the castle. 'Watch this,' he said, and spread his wings, and flew up into the air so high that he tore a hole in the sky, and a strange light shone down upon the earth. Then the demon plucked up a pine tree, threaded a trailing vine through its roots, and sewed the sky up again.

'Well,' said the toad-prince, 'that's not bad, but it's still not what I would call *really* powerful.'

'And what would *that* be?' roared the demon who was, perhaps justly, rather piqued.

The toad-prince bent down, and picked up a speck of dust, and said: 'Now if a creature as big and powerful as you could get inside that grain of dust – *that's* what I'd call *really* powerful!'

'Child's play!' exclaimed the demon, and made himself smaller and smaller, until he was no bigger than a speck of dust. Whereupon, before he could change back again, the prince picked him up and put him back in the snuff-box, and fastened the lid tight. Then he threw the snuff-box back into the black lake.

After that, the toad-prince lived in the castle, and ruled the land about with kindness and justice. And, although he was hunch-backed, the people of that land loved him, and laughter and light returned to the dark castle once again.

THE MAN WHO OWNED THE EARTH

A POOR MAN ONCE WENT to a wizard and said: 'Make me the richest man in the world.'

So the wizard gave him a ball of clay and three potions, and said: 'You must use these very carefully, for they are very strong magic. The first is very powerful, for if you were to pour it all on to the ball of magic clay, all the gold in the world would be yours. The second is even more powerful, for if you were to pour all *that* on the ball of clay, all the silver in the world would be yours. But the third is the most powerful of all, for if you poured *that* on to the clay, all the wood in the world would be yours.'

The man was very pleased, and said: 'If I had all the gold there is, I wouldn't need wood or silver! I would own the earth!'

'Indeed you would,' replied the wizard. 'But that must never be. One drop of each potion will make you rich beyond your wildest dreams. The rest you must bring back to me or you will end your days as poor as you are now.'

Well, the man went home, and immediately he opened the first potion and let a drop fall on to the ball of magic clay, and a soldier looked in at the window, and then emptied a huge sackful of gold into the room. It was more wealth than the poor man had ever imagined was possible, but even so – before he put the stopper

88

back on the potion – he couldn't resist letting just one more drop fall on to the ball of magic clay. The clay quivered in his hand, and then – suddenly – everything in the house turned to gold: the tables, the chairs, the bed, the wardrobe, the cups and plates and knives and forks, the old iron grate, the bucket by the door, even the door itself – all turned to gold.

Then the man was overcome with greed. 'All the gold in the world can be mine!' he cried, and he poured all the remaining potion on to the ball of magic clay.

Immediately the air was filled with the whirring of thousands of wings, and the sky became black with every conceivable shape and size of bird, all flying towards his house. And each bird carried in its beak a little bag of gold. One by one, they flew over the house, and one by one they dropped their bag of gold, until a huge mountain was formed. Then the birds flew off, and the sky became light again, and the noise of the wings subsided.

The man looked out of his window at the golden mountain outside, and could hardly believe his eyes. 'Now I am, without doubt, the richest man in the world!' he said. Then he built himself a palace and lived like a prince.

It was not long, however, before he heard a banging on his doors, and he went and found a hundred ragged men there. 'Who are you?' he cried.

'Once we were all kings,' they replied, 'but, since you have taken all the gold there is in the world, we have lost our kingdoms, and now we go around on foot, begging for our food.'

'I am sorry to hear that,' said the man, and he gave them each one gold piece, and then turned them out to beg their way again.

Then the man thought to himself: 'What if all those kings should try to steal my gold? I had better get some silver, for then I could pay a hundred soldiers to guard my gold.'

So he took the second potion the wizard had given him, and let a drop fall on to the ball of magic clay and, sure enough, the floors of his palace all turned to silver. Then he let another drop fall, and a silver ball the size of six houses rolled down the road and came to rest in the palace gardens. Then he was overcome with greed to see what all the silver in the world looked like, and he took the potion and poured it *all* on to the ball of clay. And there was a terrible sound like thunder, and the sky grew black and it started to rain silver pieces. They fell on to roofs and chimney pots and then into the gutters, and formed little streams of silver. And all the

streams joined into one great river that flowed down into his palace gardens, and there formed a huge lake of silver.

And he took some of the silver, and hired a hundred soldiers to guard his gold.

But, before long, he heard a banging on his doors, and he went and found a thousand ragged men there. 'Who are *you?*' he cried.

'Once we were all rich merchants,' said the men, 'but, since you have taken all the silver in the world, we have nothing to buy and sell with, and we are ruined as you see.'

'I am sorry for you,' said the man, 'but there is nothing I can do for so many.' And he turned them out of the palace to beg their way in the world.

Then the man said to himself: 'I need to build a chest to hold all that silver and gold. It will be so large that I shall need a lot of wood – I shall need that third potion after all.'

So he took the third potion and poured it all on to the ball of magic clay, and suddenly there was the rushing sound of a million leaves rustling in the wind, and he looked up and there was a forest in the sky coming up from the west. And from the south came another, and from the north and the east as well. And they blotted out the whole sky, and their roots hung down over the earth.

At this all the people looked up and cried: 'What has happened to the day?' And when they found they had no wood to build their homes, no wood to burn on their fires, and no wood for chairs or tables or to make their tools, they all rose up together. And together they beat down the doors of the palace, and took back everything, and the richest man in the world was as poor as he had been before.

WHY BIRDS SING
IN THE MORNING

 LONG, LONG TIME AGO, before you or I were ever thought of, and before there was any distinction between day and night, the King and Queen of the Light had a baby daughter. She was the most beautiful of all creatures. When she first opened her eyes, they were so bright that they filled the world with light. Everywhere she went, creatures were glad to see her. Plants grew at her touch, and animals would come out of their holes just to sit and watch her go by.

In a cave not far away there lived the Witch of the Dark. She too had an only child – a son. He was a sickly boy, he was always pale and sometimes he grew very thin and had to be nursed back to strength.

One day, however, the old Witch of the Dark brought her son to court and proposed a marriage between him and the Princess. When the King of the Light refused, the old Witch flew into a rage, and that very night she and her son broke into the King's palace and stole the beautiful Princess. They took her and locked her up in a dark cave on the other side of the mountains, and there she stayed for a long time. She cried and cried, but it was no good. The Witch would not let the Princess out until she agreed to marry her son.

Meanwhile the animals went to the King and said: 'Where is your daughter? When she is away from us all the world is dark. The plants do not grow and many of us have nothing to eat.'

The King of the Light told the animals what had happened, and the animals all agreed that they would help him look for his daughter.

So the lions and tigers went into the jungle and searched there. The rabbits and moles looked under the earth, and the fish and the turtles searched the seas, but none of them could find any trace of her. Meanwhile the birds were looking in the air and treetops, and the eagle flew off into the mountains. It flew up and up, until it was flying over their very summits. Still it flew on, over the other side and down into a region where it had never been before.

At length, the eagle grew tired and was forced to rest amongst some rocks. He hadn't been there long, however, before he heard a beautiful voice singing a sad song. Immediately he recognized it was the Princess, and he called out to her. But the eagle had only a raucous screech for a voice, and the Princess thought it was the old Witch returning. So she stopped her singing and would not make another sound. The eagle sat there, wondering what to do, when all at once he saw a black speck in the sky. It was the Witch's son, coming to visit the Princess on his mother's broomstick.

The eagle hid, and watched as the Witch's son rolled aside the great stone at the entrance of the cave. Immediately a great brightness flooded out from the cave, as the beautiful Princess came out, and filled everywhere with light. But she had tears in her eyes, and a rainbow shone all around her.

'Ah!' cried the Witch's son. 'I'm tired of waiting!' And he took hold of the beautiful girl, and threw her on the ground. Whereupon the eagle swooped down on them, snapping his beak fiercely at the Witch's son, and lifted the Princess up on his back. The Witch's son grabbed his mother's broomstick, and started hitting out at the eagle. By accident, however, he struck the Princess a blow on the side of her head, so hard that the broomstick broke in two. But the Princess held tight to the eagle, and they soared up into the sky.

The eagle carried the Princess back across the mountains, and wherever they flew they lit up the world that had been lying dark for so long. And the Witch's son got on the broomstick and followed after them. But because the broomstick was broken, he could never quite catch up with them. At length, however, the

eagle had to rest again. He let the Princess down off his back and told her to hide, promising to wake her up as soon as the Witch's son had gone past.

So the Princess hid in a cave, and the world went dark once more while the Witch's pale son flew past in the sky. When he had gone, the eagle tried to wake the Princess up, but the blow from the broomstick had made her a bit deaf, and even the eagle with his raucous voice could not wake her. So the eagle asked some sparrows to help him, and they all made as much noise as they could, but still the Princess did not wake up. Eventually the eagle went round all the birds in the neighbourhood and got them all to make as much noise as possible. Finally the Princess awoke, and came out of the cave, lighting the world as she did so.

'Quick!' said the eagle. 'Get on my back – we must be off before the Witch's son comes past again on his broomstick.' So the Princess got on his back again and away they flew, bringing light to the world wherever they went.

And so they continue to this day, for the Princess and the eagle were turned into the sun, and still they ride high up in the sky; and the Witch's son was turned into the moon. And at the end of every day, when the eagle has to rest, the Princess hides while the Witch's son goes past – and if you look up at the moon, you can still see him with his mother's broken broomstick over his shoulder. The Princess is still as beautiful as ever, now she is the sun, but she is also a little deaf, and that is why all the birds sing as hard as they can every morning in order to wake her up.

THE KEY

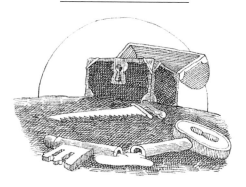

HERE ONCE LIVED A RICH KING whose palace was the largest in the world. On the wall of the palace there hung a huge key that was as long as a man is tall. Now this key was made of pure gold, but it had been made so long ago that no-one could remember what lock it was supposed to open. So the King issued a proclamation that anyone who could discover the lock for which the key had been made should have half his kingdom as a reward.

One day, three brothers came to try their luck.

The eldest one said: 'I am convinced that this is the key to the North Wind.' So the King gave the eldest brother the key, and he rode with it far, far away to the frozen lands, where ice trees grow out of the snow and where even the clouds are hung with icicles. There he found a huge chest lying half-buried in the snow. He tried the key and it fitted the lock but, when he tried to turn it, it was no good. So he loaded the chest on to a cart, and took it back to the King.

Then the second brother said: 'I am sure the key is the key to the South Wind.' So he took the key and rode south to the hot desert, where trees of fire grow out of the burning sands. And there he found a huge door in a mountain. The key fitted the lock perfectly but, when he turned it, it would not work. Just as he was trying it, however, a warm breeze whispered in his ear to look down, and there he found a smaller door which opened when he touched it. So he crept in.

Inside, the mountain was quite hollow right the way across and right the way to the top. The walls were red with the heat, and in the middle was a beautiful Princess, bound with heavy chains.

'Who are you?' asked the second brother.

But the Princess did not reply. She sat looking straight ahead and would not utter a sound.

The second brother tried the great key on the padlock of her chains, but it would not fit. So he placed the Princess on the back of his horse and took her back to the King.

Then the youngest brother said: 'I think the key is the key to the wind that blows sometimes from West to East and sometimes from East to West.' So he didn't ride anywhere. He took the great key and broke it in two, and from inside it came an oil which they poured on to the lock of the chest. Then the lock opened easily, and inside the chest they found a silver saw, whose teeth were all diamonds, and they took the saw and cut through the chains that bound the Princess, and she turned and cried: 'At last! The spell is broken!' and she told them how a wizard had placed a spell upon her in spite, because she would not be his wife, and how she could only be rescued by someone she would love but could not marry.

Then the second brother leapt up and cried: 'I rescued you from the hollow mountain of the South Wind!'

Then the eldest brother leapt up and said: 'But it was the silver saw that freed you from the spell, and *I* brought that back from the frozen lands!'

Finally the youngest brother stood up and said: 'But it was *I* who broke the golden key and, if I had not done that, the chest would not have opened and your chains would never have been cut.'

The Princess looked at all three of them and said: 'The wizard's curse has indeed come true. All three of you have rescued me, and I love you all equally, and it is certain I cannot marry all three of you.'

So the youngest brother took one half of the golden key as his reward, and the second brother took the other half, and the eldest brother took the silver saw with the diamond teeth. And all three were then wealthier than anyone else in the kingdom. But they were never truly happy, for they continued to love the beautiful Princess, and she continued to love all three of them equally, and they could never marry.

And many times they all four sighed together and sometimes they even wished they had left the golden key hanging on the palace wall.

THE WINE OF LI-PO

N THE LAND OF LI-PO THEY MADE a very special wine. It was deep red in colour, it tasted like nectar, and it kept for ever. But it had one other quality which made it more special than any other wine in the world – whoever drank the wine of Li-Po would speak the truth and only the truth as long as its influence lasted.

Now you might think that a wine with such wonderful properties would be in great demand, and that the vineyards of Li-Po would have had difficulty in producing enough grapes. But quite the reverse was true. It seemed that fewer and fewer people dared to drink the wine of Li-Po for fear that they would have to tell the truth, and the cellars became filled with barrels and bottles of the wine that no-one would buy.

At length there was only one wine-maker left in the whole of Li-Po. 'I cannot understand,' he said, 'why everyone is so afraid of the truth. In my father's time, everyone drank the wine and enjoyed it. And if they had to tell the truth for half a day after, it was no matter to them.'

One day, however, the King of a distant country got to hear of the famous wine of Li-Po. So he said to his Lord Chancellor: 'Lord Chancellor, it is time I found out who are my trusty subjects and who are not. I want you to arrange for everyone in my kingdom to drink the wine of Li-Po, and to present themselves to me for questioning.'

When the Lord Chancellor heard this command, he shook with fear, for he had many dark secrets that he dreaded the King might find out. But he smiled and said: 'An excellent idea, Your Majesty. May I be the first to try it out?'

'Good!' said the King. 'See to it straight away.'

So the Lord Chancellor ordered all the barrels of wine in Li-Po to be bought up, and carried in carts over the country to his own land. There the wine was put into bottles, and on every bottle was written somebody's name. Then the bottles were carefully placed in a huge rack in the main market-place, and seven soldiers were put on duty to guard them day and night.

The Lord Chancellor, meanwhile, was racking his brains to think how he could avoid the test himself, for fear that he should reveal any of his own dark and guilty secrets to the King. So too were all the other members of the King's Council, for they *all* had dark and guilty secrets. The same went for all the other lords and ladies and lawyers and doctors and innkeepers and shopkeepers. In fact, every single person in the land was trying his hardest to think how he could avoid drinking the wine of Li-Po and having to tell the truth to the King.

Then the Lord Chancellor hit upon a plan. He had a sleeping potion put into the guards' drink, and then, at dead of night when they had all fallen fast asleep, the Chancellor crept down to the market square, and took the bottle of wine which bore his name, emptied it out, and refilled it with ordinary wine. Then he made his way home, satisfied that when his turn came he would not have to tell the truth.

The same plan had also occurred to the other members of the King's Council, and each one of them crept down to the market square during the nights that followed, and each, unknown to the others, substituted ordinary wine in the bottle which bore his name. It was not long, of course, before word got out that the guards were asleep all night, and very soon all the other lords and ladies had taken the opportunity to do the self-same thing. So too did all the lawyers and doctors and innkeepers and shopkeepers and craftsmen. In short, by the time the day of the tasting came, every one of those bottles of the wine of Li-Po had been emptied and refilled with ordinary wine.

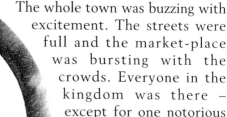

The whole town was buzzing with excitement. The streets were full and the market-place was bursting with the crowds. Everyone in the kingdom was there – except for one notorious robber, who had been hiding up in the hills for several years.

As soon as it was light, the King took his place on his throne, and summoned the Lord Chancellor forward.

'My Lord Chancellor,' he said, 'since you are the most eminent of all my subjects, you shall commence.'

The Lord Chancellor smiled, filled his goblet and drank it down, and said: 'Now I am ready to answer any questions you wish, Your Majesty.'

'Very well,' said the King, 'first tell me: are you a good and loyal subject?'

'Indeed I am!' replied the Lord Chancellor, although at that very moment he was plotting to overthrow the King.

'Secondly', said the King, 'do you think I'm a wise ruler?'

'Indeed I *do*!' exclaimed the Lord Chancellor, although secretly he thought: 'What a fool the king is making of himself!'

'And lastly,' said the King, 'how does the wine of Li-Po taste?'

'It tastes like nectar distilled from all the flowers of heaven!' said the Lord Chancellor.

'Very good,' said the King. 'You may step down.'

The next to drink the wine was the Prime Minister, and the King asked him the same three questions, and the Prime Minister made similar answers – although he was really no better than the Lord Chancellor.

And so they went on through all the King's Council, and all the lords and ladies, and the lawyers and doctors and the townsfolk and all the countryfolk. And, because they had all emptied the wine of Li-Po out of the bottles that bore their names and replaced it with ordinary wine, none of them was afraid of answering any of the King's questions.

Well, the questioning went on all that day and all the next day, and all the day after that, until – just as they were questioning the very last subject of all – some soldiers arrived with the robber, whom they had caught stealing in broad daylight, while everyone was in the city. They hauled him up before the King, and the King ordered him to drink the wine of Li-Po, and then answer the questions that he would put to him.

Now the robber did not know that all the wine of Li-Po had been poured away, and so he took the cup with fear and trembling. But he drank it all the same. Then he faced the King.

'Firstly, are you a good and loyal subject?' asked the King.

'You know me for what I am,' replied the robber. 'I've robbed your kingdom for many years.'

'Shame!' cried all the people.

'Secondly, do you think I'm a wise ruler?' asked the King.

'I've nothing to lose by telling the truth,' replied the robber, 'and the truth is: a wise ruler would decide for himself which of his subjects he could trust.'

'Traitor!' shouted the crowd.

'Lastly,' said the King, 'how does the wine of Li-Po taste?'

'I'm sure I don't know,' replied the robber. 'I've never tasted it, and this is just ordinary wine.'

At which words a silence fell over the market-place, and everyone stared at the ground. And the King rose and said: 'Is this the only person in my kingdom who dares to tell the truth?'

There and then he dismissed the Lord Chancellor, and appointed the robber in his place, saying: 'I would rather be served by a thief than a hypocrite.' And from that day forth, the wine of Li-Po was never seen in his kingdom again, for it had served its purpose – even though not one drop of it had been drunk.

THE ISLAND OF PURPLE FRUITS

 SAILOR WAS ONCE SHIPWRECKED on a strange island. He swam ashore and then turned and watched his ship sink beneath the waves. But he did not despair. 'I will build myself another boat to take me home,' he said. 'And I will also build a great fire that I will light to attract the attention of any ship that passes.' So he got to work, and in the meantime he lived off the fruits and berries that grew there in abundance.

On this island, however, there was one kind of fruit that he could never taste. It was large and purple, and it grew high up on the tallest of all the trees. The trunk of the tree was perfectly smooth and impossible to climb but, as he gazed up at those purple fruits, the sailor said to himself: ' I am sure that those are the most delicious fruits on the island. I am going to taste them, no matter what.'

So he stopped building his boat, and built himself a ladder instead, which he leant up against the tree. Then he climbed to the top, picked a fruit, and ate it. It tasted more delicious than anything else he had ever eaten in his life, and that night he dreamt a wonderful dream. He dreamt he had finished his boat, and that it was a fine vessel with tall sails. On it he sailed back in his dream across the vast ocean to his wife and children, and he was truly happy at last.

When he woke up, he took another bite of the purple fruit, and fell asleep again, and this time he dreamt that he built himself a suit of feathers, and in this suit he flew like a bird over the waters and over his own home, and his wife and children came out and waved up at him, and he flew to the King's palace, and the King gave him jewels and gold and a fine house, where he lived with his family, and they were all truly happy.

When he woke up, it was broad daylight, and there in the bay was a great ship.

'At last!' he cried. 'I'm saved!' And he ran down to the shore and waved, but the ship was already well out to sea, and no-one saw him. So he ran to his fire, but it had gone out and, before he could light it, the ship was but a speck on the horizon.

The poor shipwrecked sailor sat down with his head in his hands in despair. Then he took another bite of the purple fruit, and once more he slept and dreamt that he was truly happy.

Many months passed, and the sailor began to eat nothing but the purple fruit, and he dreamt all the night and most of the day – beautiful dreams in which he was truly happy, and so were his wife and children. Little by little, he forgot about building his boat that was going to take him home, and, whenever the occasional ship passed the island, he never even noticed it, and the fire remained unlit. Thus, although the sailor returned home time and time again in his dreams, the years passed and still he remained on that desert island.

One day, however, a tall ship entered the bay and sent a search party ashore to gather fresh water and fruit. There they came across the ragged figure of the sailor, sleeping happily under a purple fruit tree. They could not wake him, however hard they tried, and so they picked him up and carried him down to the ship. There they placed him in a bed and put to sea once more.

When the sailor eventually awoke and learnt what had happened, his rescuers expected him to leap for joy, but instead he cried out: 'Oh! Now I shall never be truly happy again, for I shall never be able to eat any more of that purple fruit!'

There was no going back, however, and eventually they returned him to his own country. There he made his way home at long last. When he got there, he found it had all changed from his dreams, for he had been away so long that his children had grown up, and the pretty young wife that he had left behind had grown old with work and care.

Nevertheless, he took her in his arms, and said: 'Why! I am as happy now as I was in my dreams on the island of purple fruits!'

But his wife said: 'How can you compare the happiness of a dream with true happiness?'

'But it *was* true happiness,' replied the sailor. 'No-one could be happier than I was in those dreams.'

But his wife looked at him and said: 'In your dreams on the island of purple fruits, did you dream that we were happy too?'

'Indeed I did!' said the sailor. 'And that made my happiness complete.'

'Yet it was just a dream,' said his wife, 'for we were still sad, believing you were dead. But now you have returned to us, you know it's not a dream, and that knowledge – surely – *is* true happiness.'

The sailor kissed his wife and children and after that, although he often thought of the island of purple fruits and the happiness of dreams, he never spoke of either again.

THE BEAST WITH
A THOUSAND TEETH

A LONG TIME AGO, in a land far away, the most terrible beast that ever lived roamed the countryside. It had four eyes, six legs and a thousand teeth. In the morning it would gobble up men as they went to work in the fields. In the afternoon it would break into lonely farms and eat up mothers and children as they sat down to lunch, and at night it would stalk the streets of the towns, looking for its supper.

In the biggest of all the towns, there lived a pastrycook and his wife, and they had a small son whose name was Sam. One morning, as Sam was helping his father to make pastries, he heard that the Mayor had offered a reward of ten bags of gold to anyone who could rid the city of the beast.

'Oh,' said Sam, 'wouldn't I just like to win those ten bags of gold!'

'Nonsense!' said his father. 'Put those pastries in the oven.'

That afternoon, they heard that the King himself had offered a reward of a hundred bags of gold to anyone who could rid the kingdom of the beast.

'Oooh! Wouldn't I just like to win those hundred bags of gold,' said Sam.

'You're too small,' said his father. 'Now run along and take those cakes to the Palace before it gets dark.'

So Sam set off for the Palace with a tray of cakes balanced on his head. But he was so busy thinking of the hundred bags of gold that he lost his way, and soon it began to grow dark.

'Oh dear!' said Sam. 'The beast will be coming soon to look for his supper. I'd better hurry home.'

So he turned and started to hurry home as fast as he could. But he was utterly and completely lost, and he didn't know which way to turn. Soon it grew very dark. The streets were deserted, and everyone was safe inside, and had bolted and barred their doors for fear of the beast.

Poor Sam ran up this street and down the next, but he couldn't find the way home. Then suddenly – in the distance – he heard a sound like thunder, and he knew that the beast with a thousand teeth was approaching the city!

Sam ran up to the nearest house, and started to bang on the door.

'Let me in!' he cried. 'I'm out in the streets, and the beast is approaching the city! Listen!' And he could hear the sound of the beast getting nearer and nearer. The ground shook and the windows rattled in their frames. But the people inside said no – if they opened the door, the beast might get in and eat them too.

So poor Sam ran up to the next house, and banged as hard as he could on their door, but the people told him to go away.

Then he heard a roar, and he heard the beast coming down the street, and he ran as hard as he could. But no matter how hard he ran, he could hear the beast getting nearer . . . and nearer. . . . And he glanced over his shoulder – and there it was at the end of the street! Poor Sam in his fright dropped his tray, and hid under some steps. And the beast got nearer and nearer until it was right on top of him, and it bent down and its terrible jaws went SNACK! and it gobbled up the tray of cakes, and then it turned on Sam.

Sam plucked up all his courage and shouted as loud as he could: 'Don't eat me, Beast! Wouldn't you rather have some more cakes?'

The beast stopped and looked at Sam, and then it looked back at the empty tray, and it said: 'Well . . . they *were* very nice cakes . . . I liked the pink ones particularly. But there are no more left, so I'll just have to eat you. . . .' And it reached under the steps where poor Sam was hiding, and pulled him out in its great horny claws.

'Oh . . . p-p-please!' cried Sam. 'If you don't eat me, I'll make you some more. I'll make you lots of good things, for I'm the son of the best pastrycook in the land.'

'Will you make more of those pink ones?' asked the beast.

'Oh yes! I'll make you as many pink ones as you can eat!' cried Sam.

'Very well,' said the beast, and put poor Sam in his pocket, and carried him home to his lair.

The beast lived in a dark and dismal cave. The floor was littered with the bones of the people it had eaten, and the stone walls were marked with lines, where the beast used to sharpen its teeth. But Sam got to work right away, and started to bake as many cakes as he could for the beast. And when he ran out of flour or eggs or anything else, the beast would run back into town to get them, although it never paid for anything.

Sam cooked and baked, and he made scones and éclairs and meringues and sponge cakes and shortbread and doughnuts. But the beast looked at them and said, 'You haven't made any pink ones!'

'Just a minute!' said Sam, and he took all the cakes and he covered every one of them in pink icing.

'There you are,' said Sam, 'they're *all* pink ones!'

'Great!' said the beast and ate the lot.

Well, the beast grew so fond of Sam's cakes that it shortly gave up eating people altogether, and it stayed at home in its cave eating and eating, and growing fatter and fatter. This went on for a whole year, until one morning Sam woke up to find the beast rolling around groaning and beating the floor of the cave. Of course you can guess what was the matter with it.

'Oh dear,' said Sam, 'I'm afraid it's all that pink icing that has given you toothache.'

Well, the toothache got worse and worse and, because the beast had a thousand teeth, it was soon suffering from the worst toothache that anyone in the whole history of the world has ever suffered from. It lay on its side and held its head and roared in agony, until Sam began to feel quite sorry for it. The beast howled and howled with pain, until it could stand it no longer. 'Please, Sam, help me!' it cried.

'Very well,' said Sam. 'Sit still and open your mouth.'

So the beast sat very still and opened its mouth, while Sam got a pair of pliers and took out every single tooth in that beast's head.

Well, when the beast had lost all its thousand teeth, it couldn't eat people any more. So Sam took it home and went to the Mayor and claimed ten bags of gold as his reward. Then he went to the King and claimed the hundred bags of gold as his reward. Then he went back and lived with his father and mother once more, and the beast helped in the pastry-shop, and took cakes to the Palace every day, and everyone forgot they had ever been afraid of the beast with a thousand teeth.

FAR-AWAY CASTLE

A TRAVELLER ONCE STOPPED TO ASK an old woman the name of a castle that stood on a hill close by.

'Well, nobody rightly knows its name,' said the old woman, 'but round here they do call it Far-Away Castle.'

'That's an odd name,' said the traveller, 'for it doesn't look so very far from here.'

'Ah no,' said the woman, 'it don't look very far, do it?'

'It couldn't take me more than an hour to walk there, could it?' said the traveller.

'I wouldn't know,' said the old woman.

'But you must know how far away it is.'

'Can't say as I do,' said the old woman.

'Well, that's where I'm going,' said the traveller, and he set off, shaking his head at the ignorance of country folk.

Well, he walked for an hour, and he walked for two hours, and he walked for three hours – up hill and down hill. And when he looked up at the castle, it seemed not an inch closer.

'Bless my soul!' said the traveller. 'I must be walking round it in circles, for I'm certainly not getting any nearer!' So he left the road, and headed off across the fields straight for the castle.

Well, he'd been walking for another hour or so when he found himself entering a dark and gloomy forest. He got a firm grip on his staff, and took out his great knife, in case he met with any bears or wolves. Then on he went through the forest.

At first he followed a path, but it soon petered out, and the forest grew thicker and the undergrowth grew denser until he was forced to cut his way through with his knife. At length, however, the forest began to thin out again and he began to see the light shining through the trees once more, and he knew he was getting to the other side. But when he finally stepped out from the forest and looked up, he couldn't believe his eyes: there was the castle on the hill above him, but not one inch closer than it had been before.

The traveller redoubled his efforts, and walked as fast as he could until night fell, and he was still no nearer his goal. Wearily he wrapped himself up in his cloak and lay down to sleep.

Hardly had he shut his eyes, when he heard a voice say: 'You'd better give up, you know.'

He turned round, and found the old woman sitting up in a tree.

'I shan't give up!' cried the traveller. 'I'll reach that castle tomorrow – you'll see!'

'I suppose I shall,' said the old woman, 'but remember what I told you.' And with that she folded up like black paper, into a bat that flew out of the branches and away into the night.

The traveller lay down to sleep again, and he dreamt he could hear elfin music, borne faintly upon the breeze, all the time he slept.

The next day, he woke up, and there, sure enough, was the castle sitting above him on the hill – not very far away at all.

'I can reach that by lunchtime!' he cried, and he seized his staff, put his pack on his back, and walked as hard and as fast as he could. And all the time, he never once took his eyes off that castle.

But lunchtime came, and still he was no nearer. No matter what path he took or how fast he went, it made not a scrap of difference. By supper-time, he was still no nearer the castle.

He sat down with his head between his hands, and heaved a big sigh.

'That castle's enchanted,' he said to himself. 'The old woman was right – I might as well give up trying.' And he got to his feet and walked round the corner, and there – to his amazement – was the castle, and the little old woman was sitting outside it.

'Ah!' she cried. 'So you gave up trying at last, did you? It's the only way to get here, though no-one ever believes it.'

And with that she opened the door of the castle, and the traveller went in.

Dr Bonocolus's Devil

R BONOCOLUS WAS A VERY CLEVER MAN. He lived a long time ago in a distant land. He was very proud of his learning, and he enjoyed performing in public debates, where he could show how much cleverer he was than anyone else.

One day, however, Dr Bonocolus decided to sell his soul to the Devil. He read in a big book a certain number of magic spells, and late that night, he lit a candle in his study, drew some lines on the floor and summoned the Devil to appear before him. There was a flash and a puff of smoke and the smell of brimstone and, for just a moment, he thought he could hear the roaring of hell-fire. But before he could change his mind, there in front of him stood a short gentleman in grey with a pen tucked behind his ear.

'You're not the Devil!' cried Dr Bonocolus.

'Er . . . no,' replied the figure in grey. 'The Devil is extremely busy at this moment in time. I'm his official representative. Now, if you'd just like to give me your details, we can get on with the sale.' And he opened a large leather book that he was carrying.

'Wait a moment!' said Dr Bonocolus. 'I wanted to see the Devil himself! I don't want to sell my soul to some half-witted underling!'

'The Devil *does* apologize, most sincerely,' said the gentleman in grey, 'but it's all a question of feasibility. If you don't want to do the deal with me, that's quite understandable – but we'll just have to let the sale go. We have more than enough to choose from as it is. It's a buyer's market at the moment, you know.'

In the end, Dr Bonocolus agreed to sell his soul to the Devil's representative on what seemed very favourable terms. For thirty years, the Devil would give Dr Bonocolus unlimited wealth, fame and magical powers. At the end of thirty years, Dr Bonocolus would have to sit and play backgammon with the Devil for ever.

Dr Bonocolus made a cut on his arm, and was just about to sign in his own blood when the Devil's representative stopped him. He looked around rather furtively and then lowered his voice and said: 'Look . . . officially, I shouldn't be telling you this, but . . . well, are you quite sure you know what you're doing?'

'Of course I am!' said Dr Bonocolus. 'You forget I'm the cleverest man in the world! I've thought out exactly what I will do with my thirty years, and after that the Devil can torture me as much as he likes. I've worked it out as a mathematical equation and the worst pain he could inflict on me will not outweigh the amount of pleasure I will be able to cram into thirty years!'

'He may *not* torture you,' said the Devil's representative.

'Then so much the better!' said Dr Bonocolus.

'It may be much worse than torture.'

'Impossible!' cried Dr Bonocolus. 'I've thought about every conceivable thing he could do to me, and I'm prepared for anything.'

The Devil's representative glanced over his shoulder and lowered his voice even more. 'Look,' he said, 'I know you're the cleverest man in the world right now but, no matter what you've imagined, I can tell you it will be worse.'

'I can't believe it!' said Dr Bonocolus, and he dipped his pen into the blood from his arm, and signed his name in the big book and on two contracts. Then the Devil's representative went away, and for thirty years Dr Bonocolus became not only the cleverest man in the world, but also the richest and the most respected and the most admired. Naturally he told no-one about his deal with the Devil, and everywhere he was revered for the brilliance of his mind, the sharpness of his wit, and the depth of his understanding. He learnt every language in the world, and there was no branch of science or art at which he did not become a master.

Finally, though, his thirty years were up, and he had to go down to Hell to face the Devil, who was now his master. He had prepared himself well for his ordeal, however. He had studied every existing portrait of the Devil, and had steeped himself in every picture of evil, ugliness and horror in order that he would not be aghast at the Devil's appearance.

As he was taken down into Hell by numerous nasty little creatures who pulled his hair and tugged his clothes, he felt quite cheerful and confident that he could cope with the worst that the Devil could do. To tell the truth, he felt quite proud of himself, for he had been master of the world while he lived, and now he was prepared to submit to one who was greater than himself. Indeed, he flattered himself that the Devil might well appreciate his fine wit and intelligence, and even find some use for his talents.

At length, Dr Bonocolus was brought to the Devil's audience chamber. The Devil's throne was standing there empty, surrounded by a host of ugly creatures so evil in their appearance that even Dr Bonocolus began to feel uneasy.

Then a scaly monster, whose smell was so loathsome that it made the Doctor feel sick, slouched towards the throne, and put out a grasping hand towards the Doctor, so that he suddenly trembled and was gripped by a fear of something unimaginable. And an unearthly voice croaked: 'Dr Bonocolus . . . prepare to meet the Devil himself!'

Even Dr Bonocolus felt a little weak at the knees and a little apprehensive, remembering what the Devil's representative had said to him all those years ago: 'No matter what you've imagined . . . it will be worse.'

Suddenly there was a flash, and the throne was engulfed in smoke. Dr Bonocolus braced himself and then there he was – face to face with the Devil . . . his new master. Dr Bonocolus's jaw dropped, and he went cold with horror. The Devil's representative had been right, of course . . . but it wasn't the hideousness of the Devil's features, nor even the cold brutality of that face that was worse than any torture to Dr Bonocolus. It was the appalling realization, as he gazed into the Devil's eyes, that the Devil was clearly stupid.

'Of course!' cried Dr Bonocolus. 'It's so obvious!' But it was too late. The cleverest man in the world had sold his soul to a fool.

THE BOAT THAT WENT NOWHERE

ONCE UPON A TIME A POOR WIDOW HAD A SON called Tom, whom she loved very much. But she was so poor that there was often not enough food in the house, and young Tom was often hungry.

One day in the middle of winter, when the pond was frozen over and icicles hung from the hedges, Tom's mother went to the larder and said: 'There is nothing at all to eat. Whatever shall we do?' and she sat down and wept.

'Don't cry, Mother,' said Tom, 'I'll go and seek my fortune and bring back enough money so you will never have to worry again.' And he tied his only pair of boots up in a handkerchief and set off to seek his fortune.

He hadn't gone very far before he came to a great house with huge gates and beautiful gardens and fountains. 'There must be a lot of money here,' thought Tom to himself. 'I'm sure I'll be able to earn enough in this place so that my mother will never go short again.' So he walked boldly up to the great house and knocked at the door.

A little old man in black answered the door and said: 'What do you want?' When Tom told him, the little old man looked very angry and said: 'There's no money for you here!' and set a dog on poor Tom that chased him off.

Well, he travelled on until at length he came to a city, where a rich merchant lived. He knocked on the door of the rich merchant's house, and a fat man in a wig asked: 'What do you want?'

'I want to earn some money so that my mother will not go hungry again.'

'Very well, you can work here,' said the fat man, and led Tom out into the garden at the back of the house.

'All you have to do', he said, 'is to climb into the sack that hangs from that tree over there and stay in it for a year and a day.'

'What's the point of that?' asked Tom.

'Never you mind,' said the fat man in the wig. 'I'll pay you more money than you've ever had in your life and feed you well into the bargain.'

'Very well,' said Tom and climbed into the sack. But just as night fell, and Tom was growing very bored and wondering how on earth he was going to last out a whole year in that sack, an owl settled on the branch above him and cried: 'Towit-to-woo, towit-to-woo.' But it seemed to Tom that it was saying: 'You'll sit life through! You'll sit life through!'

'He's right!' cried Tom. 'I won't make my mother happy by wasting my life in this sack! I'll find some better way of getting rich.' And he jumped down from the sack and walked out of the garden into the night.

It was very cold and dark and a little frightening, but he thought to himself: 'I must keep going.' Eventually he saw a fire glowing in the distance. 'Ah, I shall at least be able to warm myself there,' he said.

When he reached the fire, he found it was a roaring furnace, and there was a huge man, stripped to the waist and sweating as he shovelled coal into the furnace as hard as he could.

'May I warm myself by your fire?' asked Tom. The man didn't answer, but he kept on shovelling the coal.

'What are you doing?' asked Tom.

The man paused for a moment and looked at Tom and said: 'I'm earning more money than you've ever set eyes on!'

'May I help you?' asked Tom.

'You can take over just as soon as I finish,' said the man.

'When will that be?' asked Tom.

'Oh, not long,' said the man. 'I just have to finish feeding the fire, and then climb to the top of the chimney, and I'm done.' So

Tom sat down on the grass to wait his turn, and by and by he fell fast asleep.

When he woke up it was broad daylight, and the huge man was still busy shovelling away as hard as ever.

'When do you finish feeding the fire?' asked Tom.

'When it's had enough,' replied the man without stopping.

'But a fire can never have enough!' said Tom, and just then he noticed that the furnace was at the bottom of a chimney that had steps running round and round all the way up the outside. And Tom looked up and up, and he saw that the chimney went straight up into the sky – for ever – as if it had no top.

'I'm afraid I can't wait for you to finish,' said Tom, and he picked up his pack and set off again. And he walked down to the harbour, where the great ships lay at anchor, and he asked to be taken on. But everywhere they told him he was too young and too small to be of any use on a great ship.

At length, however, he came to a queer little boat, smaller than the rest and painted red and white. The captain was leaning over the side, and so Tom said: 'Could you use another hand?'

'Aye,' said the captain.

'Where are you going?' asked Tom.

'Nowhere,' said the captain.

'Well, I'll get nowhere if I stay here, so I might as well go with you,' said Tom and he climbed aboard.

Straight away the captain ordered the sails to be set and the anchor weighed and that little boat set off on the high seas. And the winds blew it along until it was out of sight of land, and they sailed into the setting sun. How many days and how many nights they sailed for, I don't know, but one morning there was a shout: 'Land ahoy!'

And they all looked over the side of the boat and there, sure enough, was a beautiful country with tall mountains. And as they got closer they saw that the mountains were shining white with red tops. And as they got closer still, they saw that they weren't mountains at all, but huge cities reaching up to the clouds.

'Where are we?' cried Tom.

'Nowhere,' said the captain, and they all got out.

Tom couldn't believe his eyes. On each side of them were flowerbeds full of flowers, and each one of their petals was a pound note. In front of them stretched a lawn down to a river of pure silver. When he looked at the trees they were made out of solid gold and the leaves were emeralds, and everywhere piles of precious jewels lay around for the taking. 'We're rich!' he cried.

'You haven't seen anything yet,' smiled the captain, and they all set off for the great city that glittered and shone before them. As they walked, birds flew above them, dropping pearls and rubies into their upturned hats, and wild deer ran up to them and laid golden sticks at their feet.

Eventually they reached the gates of the shining city, and the captain pulled on a golden chain.

A peal of bells rang out in welcome and a boy opened the door wide and said: 'We are glad to see you in the Forgotten City, come in,' and took them into a pure white square, where the sound of laughter echoed all around. And before Tom could blink, a table had been set out for them with all the food they could eat and all the wine they could drink. And the townspeople brought them presents and played them music, and gave up their own beds so that the travellers should sleep well.

And there they stayed for many weeks, until at length Tom said: 'I must go back to my mother.'

The captain said: 'Very well! Take the boat.'

'But what about you and the others?' asked Tom.

'That's all right,' said the captain, 'we can easily get another.' So Tom loaded up the boat with all the gold and silver and jewels he could carry and set off back across the ocean.

Well, he hadn't sailed very far before he was caught in a terrible dark storm. The waters raged and the little boat was tossed here and there until at length it took on so much water that it sank to the bottom of the sea. And Tom went down too, until a dolphin came up and put him on its back and swam with him until they got to the very river that ran past his own home.

Tom was still as poor as ever but, when he saw his mother, he smiled and said: 'Well, I have discovered that nobody with money will part with it, unless I waste my life away, and that those whose *only* desire is wealth will never rest content, and that the only place where there is enough for all and everyone is kind and generous is Nowhere. So, Mother, what shall I do?'

And his mother said: 'Sit by the fire, and I shall make soup from your stories, and we'll have our hopes for bread.'

And that is what they did.

Fantastic Stories

THE SHIP OF FOOLS

A YOUNG BOY NAMED BEN once ran away to sea. But the ship he joined was a very odd one indeed.

The Captain always wore his trousers tied over his head with seaweed. The Bosun danced the hornpipe all day long from dawn to dusk wearing nothing but beetroot juice. And the First Mate kept six families of mice down the neck of his jumper!

'This is a rum vessel, me hearty!' said Ben to one of the sailors, who was at that moment about to put his head into the ship's barrel of syrup.

'It's a Ship of Fools!' grinned the sailor, and he stuck his head in the syrup.

'I suppose you all must know what you're doing,' murmured young Ben, but the sailor couldn't reply because he was all stuck up with syrup.

Just then the Captain yelled: 'Raise the hanky! And sit on the snails!' Although, because he still had his trousers over his head, what it actually sounded like was: 'Gmpf der wmfky! Umf bmfwmf umf wmf!'

'I'm sure he means: "Raise the anchor! And set the sails!" ' said young Ben to himself. But whatever it was the Captain had said, nobody seemed to be taking the slightest bit of notice.

'They must be doing more important things,' said Ben to himself. 'So I suppose *I'd* better obey Captain's orders.'

So Ben raised the anchor by himself, and hoisted the sails as best he could, and the ship sailed off into the blue.

'Where are we heading, shipmate?' Ben asked a sailor who was hanging over the side, trying to paint the ship with a turnip and a pot of lemonade.

'Goodness knows!' exclaimed the sailor. 'It's a Ship of Fools!'

'The Captain will know,' said Ben, and he climbed up to the bridge, where the Captain was standing upside-down at the wheel, trying to steer with his feet.

'I'm almost sure you shouldn't steer a ship like that,' said Ben to himself, 'but then what do I know? I'm just a raw land-lubber getting his first taste of the briney.' But even so, Ben realized that the Captain couldn't see where they were going, because his trousers were still over his eyes. As it happened, the ship was, at that moment, heading straight for a lighthouse! So Ben grabbed the wheel, and said: 'What's the course, skipper?'

'Bmf Bmf Wmf!' replied the Captain.

'Nor' Nor' West it is, sir!' said Ben, and he steered the ship safely round the lighthouse and off for the open sea.

Well, they hadn't sailed very far before a storm blew up.

'Shall I take in the yard-arm and reef the sails, Captain?' yelled Ben. But the Captain was far too busy trying to keep his game of marbles still, as the ship rolled from side to side.

The wind began to howl, and the sea grew angry.

'I better had, anyway,' said Ben to himself, and he ran about the ship, preparing for the storm ahead.

As he did so, the rest of the crew grinned and waved at him, but they all carried on doing whatever it was they were doing. One of them was hanging by his hair from the mainmast, trying to play the violin with a spoon. Another was varnishing his nose with the ship's varnish. While another was trying to stretch his ears by tying them to the capstan and jumping overboard.

'Well . . . I wouldn't have thought this was the way to run a ship!' said young Ben. 'I suppose they know the ropes and I'm just learning. Even so . . . I didn't realize the newest recruit had to do *everything*! But I suppose I'd better get on with it.' And he set about doing what he thought should be done, while the rest of the crew just grinned and waved at him.

The storm gathered force, and soon great waves were lashing across the deck, as the ship rolled and wallowed. Ben rushed about trying to get everyone below decks, so he could batten down the hatches. But as soon as he got one sailor to go below, another would pop up from somewhere else.

And all the time, the ship rolled, and before long it began to take on water.

'Cap'n! We must get the men below decks and batten down the hatches, while we ride out the storm!' yelled Ben.

But the Captain had decided to take his supper on the fo'c'sle, and was far too busy – trying to keep the waves off his lamb chop with an egg whisk – to listen to Ben.

And still the ship took on more water.

'She's beginning to list!' shouted Ben. 'The hold's filling with water!'

'It's OK!' said the Bosun, who had stopped doing the hornpipe, but was still only wearing beetroot juice. 'Look!' and he held up a large piece of wood.

'What's that?' gasped Ben.

'It's the ship's bung!' said the Bosun proudly. 'Now any water will run out through the bunghole in the bottom of the ship!'

'You're a fool!' yelled Ben.

'I know!' grinned the Bosun. 'It's a Ship of Fools!'

'Now we'll sink for sure!' cried Ben.

And, sure enough, the ship began to sink.

'Man the lifeboats!' yelled Ben. But the fools had all climbed up the mast and were now clinging to it, playing conkers and 'I Spy With My Little Eye'.

So Ben had to launch the lifeboat on his own. And he only managed to do it just as the ship finally went down. Then he had to paddle around in the terrible seas, fishing the crew of fools out of the heaving waters.

'I spy with my little eye something beginning with . . . S!' shouted the First Mate, as Ben hauled him into the lifeboat.

'Sea,' said Ben wearily, and rowed over to the next fool.

By the time night fell, Ben had managed to get the Captain and the Bosun and the First Mate and all the rest of the crew of fools into the little lifeboat. But they wouldn't keep still, and they kept shouting and laughing and falling overboard again, and Ben had his work cut out trying to keep them all together.

By dawn the storm had died down, and Ben was exhausted, but he'd managed to save everyone. One of the fools, however, had thrown all the oars overboard while Ben hadn't been watching, so they couldn't row anywhere. And now the First Mate was so hungry he'd started to eat the lifeboat!

'You can't eat wood!' yelled Ben.

'You can – if you're fool enough!' grinned the First Mate.

'But if you eat the lifeboat, we'll all drown!' gasped Ben.

'It's a pity we don't have a little pepper and salt,' remarked the Captain, who had also started to nibble the boat.

'It's salty enough as it is!' said the Bosun, who was tucking into the rudder.

'Urgh!' said the Chief Petty Officer. 'It's uncooked! You shouldn't eat uncooked lifeboat!'

But they did.

By midday, they'd managed to eat most of the lifeboat, and Ben had just given them all up for lost, when, to his relief, he saw land on the horizon.

'Land ahead!' shouted Ben, and he tried to get the fools to paddle with their hands towards it, but they were feeling a bit sick from all the wood they'd just eaten. So Ben broke off the last plank and used that to paddle them towards the shore.

At last they landed, and the fools all jumped ashore and started filling their trousers with sand and banging their heads on the rocks, while young Ben looked for food.

He hadn't looked very far, when a man with a spear suddenly barred his way.

Ben tried to signal that he meant no harm, that he had been shipwrecked, and that he and his crew-mates were in sore distress. Once the man understood all this, he became very friendly, and offered Ben food and drink. But as soon as the two of them returned to Ben's shipmates, the crew of fools all leapt up making terrible faces and tried to chase the stranger off.

'Stop it!' cried Ben. 'He's trying to help us!' But the crew of fools had already jumped on the poor fellow, and started beating and punching him, until eventually he fled back to his village to fetch a war party.

'Now we can't even stay here!' screamed Ben. 'You're all fools!'

'Of course we are!' cried the Captain. 'We keep telling you – it's a Ship of Fools!'

Now I don't know how what happened next came about, or what would have happened to Ben if it hadn't, but it did. And this is what it was.

Young Ben was just wondering what on earth he was going to do, when a sail appeared on the horizon!

But before Ben could shout out: 'There's a ship!', he turned and saw the war party approaching with spears and bows and arrows, while the crew of fools were busy trying to bury the Bosun head-first in the sand.

Ben finally shook his head and said: 'Well you've all certainly taught me one thing: and that's not to waste my time with those I can see are fools – no matter who they are – Captain, Bosun or First Mate!'

And with that, Ben dived into the sea and swam off to join the other boat. And he left the Ship of Fools to their own fate.

THE DRAGON ON THE ROOF

A LONG TIME AGO, in a remote part of China, a dragon once flew down from the mountains and settled on the roof of the house of a rich merchant.

The merchant and his wife and family and servants were, of course, terrified out of their wits. They looked out of the windows and could see the shadows of the dragon's wings stretching out over the ground below them. And when they looked up, they could see his great yellow claws sticking into the roof above them.

'What are we going to do?' cried the merchant's wife.

'Perhaps it'll be gone in the morning,' said the merchant. 'Let's go to bed and hope.'

So they all went to bed and lay there shivering and shaking. And nobody slept a wink all night. They just lay there listening to the sound of the dragon's leathery wings beating on the walls behind their beds, and the scraping of the dragon's scaly belly on the tiles above their heads.

The next day, the dragon was still there, warming its tail on the chimney-pot. And no one in the house dared to stick so much as a finger out of doors.

'We can't go on like this!' cried the merchant's wife. 'Sometimes dragons stay like that for a thousand years!'

So once again they waited until nightfall, but this time the merchant and his family and servants crept out of the house as quiet as could be. They could hear the dragon snoring away high above them, and they could feel the warm breeze of his breath blowing down their necks, as they tiptoed across the lawns. By the time they got half-way across, they were so frightened that they all suddenly started to run. They ran out of the gardens and off into the night. And they didn't stop running until they'd reached the great city, where the king of that part of China lived.

The next day, the merchant went to the King's palace. Outside the gates was a huge crowd of beggars and poor people and ragged children, and the rich merchant had to fight his way through them.

'What d'you want?' demanded the palace guard.

'I want to see the King,' exclaimed the merchant.

'Buzz off!' said the guard.

'I don't want charity!' replied the merchant. 'I'm a rich man!'

'Oh, then in you go!' said the guard.

So the merchant entered the palace, and found the King playing Fiddlesticks with his Lord High Chancellor in the Council Chamber. The merchant fell on his face in front of the King, and cried: 'O Great King! Favourite Of His People! Help me! The Jade Dragon has flown down from the Jade Dragon Snow Mountain, and has alighted on my roof-top, O Most Beloved Ruler Of All China!'

The King (who was, in fact, extremely unpopular) paused for a moment in his game and looked at the merchant, and said: 'I don't particularly like your hat.'

So the merchant, of course, threw his hat out of the window, and said: 'O Monarch Esteemed By All His Subjects! Loved By All The World! Please assist me and my wretched family! The Jade Dragon has flown down from the Jade Dragon Snow Mountain, and is, at this very moment, sitting on my roof-top, and refuses to go away!'

The King turned again, and glared at the merchant, and said: 'Nor do I much care for your trousers.'

So the merchant, naturally, removed his trousers and threw them out of the window.

'Nor,' said the King, 'do I really approve of anything you are wearing.'

So, of course, the merchant took off all the rest of his clothes, and stood there stark naked in front of the King, feeling very embarrassed.

'*And* throw them out of the window!' said the King.

So the merchant threw them out of the window. At which point, the King burst out into the most unpleasant laughter. 'It must be your birthday!' he cried, 'because you're wearing your birthday suit!' and he collapsed on the floor helpless with mirth. (You can see why he wasn't a very popular king.)

Finally, however, the King pulled himself together and asked: 'Well, what do you want? You can't stand around here stark naked you know!'

'Your Majesty!' cried the merchant. 'The Jade Dragon has flown down from the Jade Dragon Snow Mountain and is sitting on my roof-top!'

The King went a little green about the gills when he heard this, because nobody particularly likes having a dragon in their kingdom.

'Well, what do you expect me to do about it?' replied the King. 'Go and read it a bedtime story?'

'Oh no! Most Cherished Lord! Admired And Venerated Leader Of His People! No one would expect you to read bedtime stories to a dragon. But I was hoping you might find some way of . . . getting rid of it?'

'Is it a big dragon?' asked the King.

'It is. Very big,' replied the merchant.

'I was afraid it would be,' said the King. 'And have you tried asking it – politely – if it would mind leaving of its own accord?'

'First thing we did,' said the merchant.

'Well, in that case,' replied the King, ' . . . tough luck!'

Just at that moment there was a terrible noise from outside the palace. 'Ah! It's here!' cried the King, leaping onto a chair. 'The dragon's come to get us!'

'No, no, no,' said the Lord High Chancellor. 'That is nothing to be worried about. It is merely the poor people of your kingdom groaning at your gates, because they have not enough to eat.'

'Miserable wretches!' cried the King. 'Have them all beaten and sent home.'

'Er . . . many of them have no homes to go to,' replied the Chancellor.

'Well then – obviously – just have them beaten!' exclaimed the King. 'And sent somewhere else to groan.'

But just then there was an even louder roar from outside the palace gates.

'*That's* the dragon!' exclaimed the King, hiding in a cupboard.

'No,' said the Chancellor, 'that is merely the rest of your subjects demanding that you resign the crown.'

At this point, the King sat on his throne and burst into tears. 'Why does nobody like me?' he cried.

'Er . . . may I go and put some clothes on?' asked the merchant.

'Oh! Go and jump out of the window!' replied the King.

Well, the merchant was just going to jump out of the window (because, of course, in those days, whenever a king told you to do something, you always did it) when the Lord High Chancellor stopped him and turned to the King and whispered: 'Your Majesty! It may be that this fellow's dragon could be just what we need!'

'Don't talk piffle,' snapped the King. '*Nobody* needs a dragon!'

'On the contrary,' replied the Chancellor, '*you* need one right now. Nothing, you know, makes a king more popular with his people than getting rid of a dragon for them.'

'You're right!' exclaimed the King.

So there and then he sent for the Most Famous Dragon-Slayer In The Land, and had it announced that a terrible dragon had flown down from the Jade Dragon Snow Mountain and was threatening their kingdom.

Naturally everyone immediately forgot about being hungry or discontented. They fled from the palace gates and hid themselves away in dark corners for fear of the dragon.

Some days later, the Most Famous Dragon-Slayer In The Whole Of China arrived. The King ordered a fabulous banquet in his honour. But the Dragon-Slayer said: 'I never eat so much as a nut, nor drink so much as a thimbleful, until I have seen my dragon, and know what it is I have to do.'

So the merchant took the Dragon-Slayer to his house, and they hid in an apricot tree to observe the dragon.

'Well? What d'you think of it?' asked the merchant.

But the Dragon-Slayer said not a word.

'Big, isn't it?' said the merchant.

But the Dragon-Slayer remained silent. He just sat there in the apricot tree, watching the dragon.

'How are you going to kill it?' inquired the merchant eagerly.

But the Dragon-Slayer didn't reply. He climbed down out of the apricot tree, and returned to the palace. There he ordered a plate of eels and mint, and he drank a cup of wine.

When he had finished, the King looked at him anxiously and said: 'Well? What are you going to do?'

The Dragon-Slayer wiped his mouth and said: 'Nothing.'

'Nothing?' exclaimed the King. 'Is this dragon so big you're frightened of it?'

'I've killed bigger ones,' replied the Dragon-Slayer, rubbing his chest.

'Is it such a fierce dragon you're scared it'll finish you off?' cried the King.

'I've dispatched hundreds of fiercer ones,' yawned the Dragon-Slayer.

'Then has it hotter breath?' demanded the King. 'Or sharper claws? Or bigger jaws? Or what?'

But the Dragon-Slayer merely shut his eyes and said: 'Like me, it's old and tired. It has come down from the mountains to die in the East. It's merely resting on that roof-top. It'll do no harm, and, in a week or so, it will go on its way to the place where dragons go to die.'

Then the Dragon-Slayer rolled himself up in his cloak and went to sleep by the fire.

But the King was furious.

'This is no good!' he whispered to the Lord High Chancellor. 'It's not going to make me more popular if I leave this dragon sitting on that man's roof-top. It needs to be killed!'

'I agree,' replied the Lord High Chancellor. 'There's nothing like a little dragon-slaying to get the people onto your side.'

So the King sent for the Second Most Famous Dragon-Slayer In The Whole Of China, and said: 'Listen! I want you to kill that dragon, and I won't pay you unless you do!'

So the Second Most Famous Dragon-Slayer In The Whole Of China went to the merchant's house and hid in the apricot tree to observe the dragon. Then he came back to the palace, and ordered a plate of pork and beans, drank a flask of wine, and said to the King: 'It's a messy business killing dragons. The fire from their nostrils burns the countryside, and their blood poisons the land so that nothing will grow for a hundred years. And when you cut them open, the smoke from their bellies covers the sky and blots out the sun.'

But the King said: 'I want that dragon killed. Mess or no mess!'

But the Second Most Famous Dragon-Slayer In The Whole Of China replied: 'Best to leave this one alone. It's old and on its way to die in the East.'

Whereupon the King stamped his foot, and sent for the Third Most Famous Dragon-Slayer In The Whole Of China, and said: 'Kill me that dragon!'

Now the Third Most Famous Dragon-Slayer In The Whole Of China also happened to be the most cunning, and he knew just why it was the King was so keen to have the dragon killed. He also knew that if he killed the dragon, he himself would become the First Dragon-Slayer In The Whole Of China instead of only the Third. So he said to the King: 'Nothing easier, Your Majesty. I'll kill that dragon straight away.'

Well, he went to the merchant's house, climbed the apricot tree and looked down at the dragon. He could see it was an old one and weary of life, and he congratulated himself on his good luck. But he told the King to have it announced in the market square that the dragon was young and fierce and very dangerous, and that everyone should keep well out of the way until after the battle was over.

When they heard this, of course, the people were even more frightened, and they hurried back to their hiding places and shut their windows and bolted their doors.

Then the Dragon-Slayer shouted down from the apricot tree: 'Wake up, Jade Dragon! For I have come to kill you!'

The Jade Dragon opened a weary eye and said: 'Leave me alone, Dragon-Slayer. I am old and weary of life. I have come down from the Jade Dragon Snow Mountain to die in the East. Why should you kill me?'

'Enough!' cried the Dragon-Slayer. 'If you do not want me to kill you, fly away and never come back.'

The Jade Dragon opened its other weary eye and looked at the Dragon-Slayer. 'Dragon-Slayer! You know I am too weary to fly any further. I have settled here to rest. I shall do no one any harm. Let me be.'

But the Dragon-Slayer didn't reply. He took his bow and he took two arrows, and he let one arrow fly, and it pierced the Jade Dragon in the right eye. The old creature roared in pain, and tried to raise itself up on its legs, but it was too old and weak, and it fell down again on top of the house, crushing one of the walls beneath its weight.

Then the Dragon-Slayer fired his second arrow, and it pierced the Jade Dragon in the left eye, and the old creature roared again and a sheet of fire shot out from its nostrils and set fire to the apricot tree.

But the Dragon-Slayer had leapt out of the tree and onto the back of the blinded beast, as it struggled to its feet, breathing flames through its nostrils and setting fire to the countryside all around.

It flapped its old, leathery wings, trying to fly away, but the Dragon-Slayer was hanging onto the spines on its back, and he drove his long sword deep into the dragon's side. And the Jade Dragon howled, and its claws ripped off the roof of the merchant's house, as it rolled over on its side and its blood gushed out onto the ground.

And everywhere the dragon's blood touched the earth, the plants turned black and withered away.

Then the Dragon-Slayer took his long sword and cut open the old dragon's fiery belly, and a black cloud shot up into the sky and covered the sun.

When the people looked out of their hiding places, they thought the night had fallen, the sky was so black. All around the city they could see the countryside burning, and the air stank with the smell of the dragon's blood. But the King ordered a great banquet to be held in the palace that night, and he paid the Dragon-Slayer half the money he had in his treasury.

And when the people heard that the dragon had been killed, they cheered and clapped and praised the King because he had saved them from the dragon.

When the merchant and his wife and children returned to their house, however, they found it was just a pile of rubble, and their beautiful lawns and gardens were burnt beyond repair.

And the sun did not shine again in that land all that summer, because of the smoke from the dragon's belly. What is worse, nothing would grow in that kingdom for a hundred years, because the land had been poisoned by the dragon's blood.

But the odd thing is, that although the people were now poorer than they ever had been, and scarcely ever had enough to eat or saw the sun, every time the King went out they cheered him and clapped him and called him: 'King Chong The Dragon-Slayer', and he was, from that time on, the most popular ruler in the whole of China for as long as he reigned and long after.

And the Third Most Famous Dragon-Slayer In The Whole Of China became the First, and people never tired of telling and retelling the story of his fearful fight with the Jade Dragon from the Jade Dragon Snow Mountain.

What do you think of that?

THE STAR OF THE FARMYARD

HERE WAS ONCE A DOG who could perform the most amazing tricks. It could stand on its head and bark the Dog's Chorus whilst juggling eight balls on its hind paws and playing the violin with its front paws. That was just one of its tricks.

Another trick it could do was this: it would bite its own tail, then it would roll around the farmyard like a wheel, balancing two long poles on its paws – on top of one of which it was balancing Daisy the Cow and on the other Old Lob the Carthorse – all the while, at the same time, telling excruciatingly funny jokes that it made up on the spot.

One day Charlemagne, the cock, said to Stanislav, the dog: 'Stan, you're wasted doing your amazing tricks here in this old farmyard – you ought to go to the Big City or join the circus.'

Stan replied: 'Maybe you're right, Charlemagne.'

So one bright spring morning, Stanislav the Dog and Charlemagne the Cock set off down the road to seek their fortunes in the Big City.

They hadn't gone very far before they came to a fair. There were people selling everything you could imagine. There was also a stage on which a troop of strolling players were performing.

So Charlemagne the Cock strode up to the leader of the troop and said: 'Now, my good man, this is indeed your lucky day, for you

see before you the most talented, most amazing juggler, acrobat, ventriloquist, comedian and all-round entertainer in the whole history of our – or any other – farmyard . . . Stanislav the Dog!' And Stanislav, who all this time had been looking modestly down at his paws, now gave a low bow.

'Can't you read?" said the leader of the troop. 'No dogs!'

And without more ado, Charlemagne the Cock and Stanislav the Dog were thrown out.

'Huh!' said Charlemagne, picking himself up and shaking the road-dust out of his feathers. 'You're too good for a troop of strolling players anyway.'

Stanislav climbed wearily out of the ditch. He was covered in mud, and he looked at his friend very miserably.

'I'm tired,' he said. 'And I want to go home to my master.'

'Cheer up, my friend!' replied Charlemagne the Cock. 'We're going to the Big City, where fine ladies and gentlemen drip with diamonds, where dukes and earls sport rubies and emeralds, and where the streets are paved with gold. With your talents, you'll take 'em by storm. We'll make our fortunes!'

So the cock and the dog set off once more down the long, dirty road that led to the Big City.

On the way they happened to pass a circus. Charlemagne the Cock strode up to the ringmaster, who was in the middle of teaching the lions to stand on their hind legs and jump through a ring.

'Tut! Tut! Tut! My good man,' said Charlemagne the Cock. 'You needn't bother yourself with this sort of rubbish any more! Allow me to introduce you to the most superlative acrobat and tumbler – who can not only stand on his hind paws, but can jump through fifty such rings . . . backwards and whilst balancing one of your lions on his nose . . . and do it all on the high wire . . . *without a safety net!*'

'I only do tricks with lions,' said the ringmaster.

'But Stanislav the Dog has more talent in his right hind leg than your entire troop of lions!'

'These are the best lions in the business!' exclaimed the ringmaster. 'And they'd eat you and your dog for supper without even blinking. In fact they need a feed right now!' And he reached out his hand to grab Charlemagne the Cock. Stan the Dog saw what was happening, however, and nipped the ringmaster on the ankle.

'Run, Charlemagne!' he yelled.

And Charlemagne ran as fast as he could, while Stan the Dog leapt about – nipping people's ankles – as the entire circus chased them down the road.

'Help!' squawked Charlemagne, as the circus folk got closer and closer and hands reached out to grab him by the neck.

But Stan the Dog ran under everyone's legs and tripped them up. Then he said to Charlemagne: 'Jump on my back! I can run four times as fast as these clowns!'

And so they escaped, with Charlemagne the Cock riding on Stan the Dog's back.

That night they slept under a hedge. Charlemagne the Cock was extremely nervous, but Stan the Dog curled himself around his friend to protect him. Stan himself, however, was not very happy either.

'I'm hungry,' he murmured, 'and I want to go home to my master.'

'Cheer up!' said Charlemagne. 'Tomorrow we'll reach the Great City, where your talents will be appreciated. Forget these country yokels. I'm telling you – fame and fortune await you and . . .'

But his friend was fast asleep.

Well, the next day, they arrived in the Great City. At first they were overawed by the noise and bustle. Many a time they had to leap into the gutter to avoid a cart or a carriage, and on one occasion they both got drenched when somebody emptied a chamber-pot from a window above the street, and it went right over them.

'Oh dear, I miss the farmyard,' said Stan the Dog. 'And nobody here wants to know us.'

'Brace up!' cried Charlemagne. 'We're about to make our break-through! We're going straight to the top!' And he knocked on the door of the Archbishop's palace.

Now it so happened that the Archbishop himself was, at that very moment, in the hallway preparing to leave the palace, and so, when the servant opened the door, the Archbishop saw the cock and the dog standing there on the step.

'Your Highness!' said Charlemagne, bowing low to the servant. 'Allow me to introduce to you the Most Amazing Prodigy Of All Time – Stanislav the Dog! He does tricks you or I would have thought impossible! They are, indeed, miracles of . . .'

'Clear off!' said the servant, who had been too astonished to speak for a moment. And he began to close the door.

But Charlemagne the Cock suddenly lost his temper.

'LISTEN TO ME!' he cried, and he flew at the servant with his spurs flying.

Well, the servant was so surprised he fell over backwards, and Charlemagne the Cock landed on his chest and screamed: 'THIS DOG IS A GENIUS! HIS LIKE HAS NEVER BEEN SEEN OUTSIDE OUR FARMYARD! JUST GIVE HIM A CHANCE TO SHOW YOU!'

And Stan the Dog, who had nervously slunk into the hallway, started to do his trick where he bounced around on his tail, juggling precious china ornaments (which he grabbed off the sideboard as he bounced past) whilst barking a popular Farmyard Chorus that always used to go down particularly well with the pigs.

'My china!' screamed the Archbishop. 'Stop him at once!' And several of the Archbishop's servants threw themselves at Stan the Dog. But Stan bounced out of their way brilliantly, and grabbed the Archbishop's mitre and started to balance a rare old Ming vase on the top of it.

'Isn't he great?' shouted Charlemagne the Cock.

'Grab him!' screamed the Archbishop, and the servants grabbed Charlemagne.

'But look at the dog!' squawked the cock. 'Don't you see how great he is? Do you know anyone else who can juggle like that?'

But just then – as luck would have it – all the butlers and chambermaids and kitchen skivvies and gardeners, who had heard all the noise, came bursting into the Archbishop's hall. They stood there for a moment horrified, as they watched a barking dog, bouncing around on his tail, juggling the most precious pieces of the Archbishop's prize collection of china.

'Stop him!' roared the Archbishop again. And without more ado everybody descended on poor Stan, and he disappeared under a mound of flailing arms and legs. As a result, of course, all the Archbishop's best china crashed to the floor and was smashed into smithereens.

'Now look what you've done!' yelled Charlemagne.

'Now look what *we've* done!' exclaimed the Archbishop. 'Listen to me! You're both filthy, you look as if you slept in a hedge, you stink of the chamber-pot and you dare to burst into my palace and wreck my best china! Well! You're going to pay for it! Throw them into my darkest dungeons!'

And the Archbishop's servants were just about to do so, when suddenly a voice spoke from above them.

'Silence, everybody!' said the Voice.

Everybody froze. Then the Voice continued: 'Don't you know who this is? Archbishop! Shame on you! This is the Voice of God!'

The Archbishop fell to his knees, and muttered a prayer, and everyone else followed suit.

'That's better!' said the Voice of God. 'Now let Stan the Dog go free. He didn't mean no harm.'

So they let go of Stan the Dog.

'And now,' continued the Voice of God. 'Let Charlemagne the Cock go!'

So they let go of Charlemagne the Cock.

'Now shut your eyes and wait for me to tell you to open them again!' said the Voice of God.

So they all shut their eyes, and Stan the Dog and Charlemagne the Cock fled out of the Archbishop's palace as fast as their legs could carry them.

I don't know how long the Archbishop and his servants remained kneeling there with their eyes shut, but I am certain that the Voice of God never told them to open their eyes again. For, of course, the Voice wasn't the Voice of God at all – it was the Voice of Stan the Dog.

'You are, as I say, a very talented dog,' said Charlemagne as they ran down the road. 'But I'd almost forgotten you were a ventrilo-quist as well!'

'Luckily for us!' replied Stan. 'But look here, Charlemagne, I'll always be talented – it's just the way I am. Only I'd rather use those talents where they're appreciated, instead of where they get us into trouble.'

'Stanislav,' said Charlemagne, 'maybe you're right.'

And so the two friends returned to the farmyard. And Stanislav the Dog continued to perform his astounding tricks for the entertain-ment of the other farm animals, and they always loved him.

And even though Charlemagne occasionally squawked a bit at night, and said that it was a waste of talent, Stan the Dog stayed where he was – happy to be the Star of the Farmyard.

THE IMPROVING MIRROR

A MAGICIAN ONCE MADE A MAGICAL MIRROR that made everything look better than it really was.

It would make an ugly man look handsome, and a plain woman beautiful.

'I will bring happiness to a lot of people with this mirror,' said the Magician to himself. And he went to the main city, where he had his invention announced to the public. Naturally everybody was very curious to see themselves more handsome and more beautiful than they really were, and they queued up to see the magical improving mirror.

The Magician rubbed his hands and said: 'I will not only make people happy – I will also make my fortune!'

But before he was able to show the mirror to a single person, a most unlucky thing occurred.

It so happened that the King of that particular country had married a Queen who was bad-tempered, selfish and cruel. The King put up with all her faults of character, however, because she was also very, very beautiful. She also happened to be extremely vain. So when she heard about the improving mirror, she simply couldn't wait to get her hands on it before anyone else.

'But, my dear,' said the King, 'you know you are already the most beautiful lady in the realm. And I should know – I searched the kingdom through and I found no one whose looks surpassed yours. That's why I married you.'

But the Queen replied: 'I must see how even more beautiful I can look in this magical mirror.' And nothing would satisfy her but to be the first to look in the improving mirror.

So the King sent for the Magician with strict instructions that he was to show the mirror to nobody until he had demonstrated it to Queen Pavona.

Well, the Magician entered the audience chamber with a feeling of dread.

'Great Queen!' he said with a low bow. 'You are the most peerless beauty in this land. No one could be more beautiful than you are now. I beg you not to look in my magic mirror!'

But the Queen could not contain her eagerness to see herself in the improving glass, and she said: 'Show me at once! I must see myself even more beautiful than I really am!'

'Alas!' said the Magician. 'I made this mirror for those less fortunate in looks – to give them hope of how they might be.'

'Show me!' cried Queen Pavona. 'Or I will have you executed on the spot!'

Well, the poor Magician saw there was nothing for it but that he must show the Queen the magic improving mirror. So he brought out the special box in which he kept it locked away, but he did so with a heavy heart.

He took the key, which he had tied around his waist, and opened up the lock. The courtiers pressed around, but the King ordered them to stand back, and the box was brought nearer the throne.

Then the Magician lifted the lid, and the Queen peered in. There she saw the magic mirror – lying face down.

'Your Majesty!' said the Magician. 'I fear only evil will come of your looking in my magic mirror.'

'Silence!' shouted the Queen, and she seized the mirror and held it up to her face.

For some moments she did not speak, nor move, nor even breathe. She was so dazzled by the reflection before her. If her eyes had been dark and mysterious before, now they were two pools of midnight. If her cheeks had been fair and rosy before, now they were like snow touched by the dawn sun. And if her face had been well-shaped before, now it was so perfect that it would carry away the soul of anyone who gazed upon it.

For what seemed a lifetime, her eyes feasted on the image before her. And everyone in the court waited with bated breath.

Eventually the King spoke: 'Well, my dear? What do you see?' he asked.

Slowly the Queen came to her senses. As she did so, the Magician trembled in his shoes, and humbled himself on the floor before her.

'Does it make you more beautiful?' asked the King.

Queen Pavona suddenly hid the mirror in her sleeve, glared around the court and cried: 'Of course not! It's just an ordinary mirror! Have this charlatan thrown into the darkest dungeon!'

So the poor Magician was carried off down to the darkest dungeon.

Meanwhile the King turned to Queen Pavona and said: 'Perhaps it will work for me, since I am less well-favoured than you . . .'

'I tell you it's just an ordinary mirror!' cried the Queen. 'I shall use it in my chamber.'

And with that, she went straight to her room, and hid the magic mirror in her great chest.

Now the truth of the matter is that the moment Queen Pavona had looked into the magic mirror and seen herself even more beautiful than she really was, she had been consumed with jealousy. She could not bear the thought that there was a beauty greater than hers – even though it was that of her own reflection! So she locked the mirror away, resolving that no one should ever look in it again.

None the less, she could not forget what she had seen in that looking-glass, and – despite her resolve – she found herself drawn to it, and time and again she would creep into her room and steal a look in the magic glass. Before long, she was spending many hours of the day alone in her chamber, gazing into that mirror, trying to see what made her reflection so much more beautiful than she already was.

As the weeks passed, Queen Pavona began to try and make herself more like her reflection in the magic looking-glass. But, of course, it was no use. For no matter how beautiful she made herself, her reflection became even more beautiful still.

The more she tried, the more she failed, and the more she failed to be as beautiful as her reflection in the magic mirror, the more time she spent alone in her room, gazing into it. Until eventually

she hardly ever came out of her room – not even to eat or to dance
or to make merry with the rest of the court.

Meanwhile the King grew more and more anxious about his
wife, for she never explained to him what kept her in her room
from morn till night, and whenever he entered the chamber, she
always took care to hide the magic mirror.

One night, however, after Queen Pavona had been poring all day
over her reflection in the fatal looking-glass, she fell asleep with it
still in her hand.

It so happened that some time later the King entered her chamber to kiss her goodnight, as was his custom.

The King had, long ago, guessed that the magic mirror was the cause of his wife's strange behaviour, and he too had long been curious to see just what was so special about it. So when he found her fast asleep on her couch, with the magic mirror still in her hand, he couldn't resist. He lifted it slowly to her face and gazed into it. And there he saw for the first time his Queen's reflection in the magic looking-glass.

The King had believed he would never find another woman more beautiful to his sight than Queen Pavona. But now he saw in the magic mirror the reflection of someone who was three times as beautiful, and he let out a cry as if he had been stabbed to the heart.

At that, the Queen woke up with a scream of rage, and she struck the King with the mirror – so hard that he fell over.

'How dare you look in this mirror!' she cried, her face all screwed up with anger. Well, of course, when the King looked at her now with her face distorted by rage, he thought that Queen Pavona was almost ugly compared to her reflection.

'How dare you strike me!' cried the King. And he strode out of the Queen's chamber, resolving that he would put up with her ill-temper no longer.

From that day on, the King scarcely spoke to his Queen, or even set eyes on her. But he could not forget the vision of loveliness that he had seen in the magic glass.

Now all this while, the poor Magician had been languishing in the darkest dungeon. And every day he cursed himself for making the improving mirror.

Then one day, in the midst of his misery, the door of his cell was flung open and in strode the King!

The Magician fell at his feet and cried: 'Mercy, O King! Have you come to release me? You know I've done nothing wrong.'

'Well . . . That's as maybe,' replied the King. 'But if you want to get out of this dungeon, there is something you must do for me.'

'Anything that is within my power!' exclaimed the Magician.

'Very well,' said the King. 'I want you to change the Queen, my wife, for her reflection in your magic looking-glass.'

'But Your Majesty!' cried the Magician. 'That would be a cruel thing to do to your wife!'

'I don't care!' replied the King. 'I am sick of her evil temper, her selfishness and her cruelty. And now I have seen her reflection – which is so much more beautiful than she ever can be – I am no longer even satisfied by her looks. Can you change her for her reflection?'

'Alas!' cried the Magician. 'Is this the only way I can gain my freedom?'

'If you can't do it, then you can rot in here until you die – for all I care!' said the King.

'Then I shall do it,' said the Magician. 'But we shall both suffer for it.'

And so the King released the Magician from his dungeon, and the Magician was led into the Queen's chamber.

The Queen was standing as usual in front of the magic glass, staring at her reflection. 'What do you want?' she cried as the King entered.

'You wish you were more like your reflection, my dear?' said the King. 'Then so do I!'

At which the Magician threw a handful of magic dust into the air, and for a few moments it filled the chamber so that no one could see. Then, as the dust cleared, a most extraordinary thing happened.

There was a flash and a groan, and suddenly the mirror rose up into the air – but the Queen's reflection stayed where it was! Then the mirror turned over several times in the air, before landing over the Queen herself.

And so the King had his wish.

From that time on, Queen Pavona's beautiful reflection became his wife, and the real queen was trapped for ever in the mirror. But, just as the Magician had promised, the King lived to regret the change. For even though she was now his wife, the Queen's reflection was still only a reflection, and – when the King tried to touch her beautiful skin – he found it was as cold as glass.

What's more, he soon discovered that the Queen's reflection was not only more beautiful than the real Queen, it was also more heartless, more selfish and even more ill-tempered. And many a time he longed for the Magician to change them back.

But the Magician had long since fled the country, and now lived in miserable exile, swearing that he would never make another magic mirror that could so inflame the vanity of those who were already vain enough.

THE MERMAID WHO
PITIED A SAILOR

HERE WAS ONCE A MERMAID who pitied the sailors who drowned in the windy sea.

Her sisters would laugh whenever a ship foundered and sank, and they would swim down to steal the silver combs and golden goblets from the sunken vessels. But Varina, the mermaid, wept in her watery cave, thinking of the men who had lost their lives.

'What in the sea is the matter with you?' her sisters would exclaim. 'While we are finding jewels and silver, you sit alone and grieve. It's not our fault if their ships are wrecked! That is the way the sea goes. Besides, these sailors mean nothing to us, sister, for they are not of our kind.'

But Varina the mermaid replied: 'What though they are not of our kind? Their hopes are still hopes. Their lives are lives.'

And her sisters just laughed at her, and splashed her with their finny tails.

One day, however, a great ship struck the rocks near by and started to sink. All the other mermaids stayed sitting on the rocks where they had been singing, but Varina slipped away into the sea, and swam around and around the sinking ship, calling out to see if any sailors were still alive.

She saw the Boatswain in his chair, but he had drowned as the ship first took water. She saw the First Mate on the poop deck, but he had drowned, caught in the rigging. She saw the Captain, but he too was lifeless, with his hands around the wheel.

Then she heard a tap-tap-tapping, coming from the side of the sunken ship, and there was the frightened face of the Cabin Boy, peering through a crack.

'How are you still alive, when your ship-mates are all drowned?' asked Varina.

'I'm caught in a pocket of air,' replied the Cabin Boy. 'But it will not last, and we are now so deep at the bottom of the ocean, that unless I can swim as fast as a fish through the ship's hold, through the galley and up onto the deck, I shall drown long before I can make my way up to the waves above.'

'But I swim faster than forty fishes!' exclaimed the mermaid. And without more ado, she twitched her tail, and swam to the deck, and down through the galley and along through the ship's hold to the place where the Cabin Boy was trapped in the pocket of air.

Then she took his hand and said: 'Hold your landlubberly breath!' And back she swam, faster than forty fishes, back through the ship's hold, back through the galley and up to the deck and then up and up and up to the waves above.

There the Cabin Boy got back his breath. But the moment he turned to the mermaid, it left his body again, for he suddenly saw how beautiful she was.

'Thank you!' he finally managed to say. 'Now I can swim to the shore.' But the mermaid would not let go of his hand.

'Come with me to my watery cave,' she said.

'Oh no!' cried the Cabin Boy. 'You have saved my life, and grateful I am more than six times seven, but I know you mermaids are not of our kind and bring us poor sailors only despair.'

But still the mermaid would not let go of his hand, and she swam as fast as forty fishes, back to her watery cave.

And there she gave the Cabin Boy sea-kelp and sargassum, bladder-wrack and sea-urchins, all served up on a silver dish. But the Cabin Boy looked pale as death and said:

'Your kindness overwhelms me, and grateful I am more than six times sixty, but you are not of my kind, and these ocean foods to me are thin and savourless. Let me go.'

But the mermaid wrapped him up in a seaweed bed and said: 'Sleep and tomorrow you may feel better.'

The Cabin Boy replied: 'You are kind beyond words, and grateful I am more than six times six hundred, but I am not of your kind, and this bed is cold and damp, and my blood runs as chill as sea-water in my veins.'

Finally the mermaid said to the Cabin Boy: 'Shut your eyes, and I shall sing you a song that will make you forget your sorrow.'

But at that, the Cabin Boy leapt out of the bed and cried: 'Oh no! That you must not! For don't you know it is your mermaids' singing that lulls our senses and lures us poor sailors onto the rocks so that we founder and drown?'

When the mermaid heard this, she was truly astonished. She swam to her sisters and cried out: 'Sisters! Throw away those silver combs and throw away those golden goblets that we have stolen from the drowned sailors – for it is our songs that lull these sailors' senses and lure them onto the rocks.'

When they heard this, the mermaids all wept salty tears for the lives of the men who had been drowned through their songs. And from that day on the mermaids resolved to sit on the rocks and sing only when they were sure there was no ship in sight.

As for Varina, she swam back to her watery cave, and there she found the Cabin Boy still waiting for her.

'I could not leave,' he said taking her hand. 'For though we are of different kind, where shall I find such goodness of heart as yours?'

And there and then he took the mermaid in his arms and kissed her, and she wrapped her finny tail around him, and they both fell into the sea.

Then they swam as if they were one creature instead of two – fast as forty fishes – until, at last, they reached the land the Cabin Boy had left, many years before. And there they fell asleep upon the shore – exhausted and sea-worn.

When the Cabin Boy awoke, he looked and he found Varina still asleep beside him. And as he stared at her, all the breath once again went from his body, for her finny tail had disappeared, and there she lay beside him – no longer a mermaid, but a beautiful girl, who opened her eyes and looked at him not with pity but with love.

FORGET-ME-NUTS

A LONG, LONG TIME AGO in a very distant land, there once lived a king with a very bad conscience. But he didn't let his conscience trouble him one little bit, because in that land there also happened to grow a very rare and peculiar fruit. It was known as the forget-me-nut. And whenever King Yorick felt bad about something he'd done, or something he hadn't done, he would chew a forget-me-nut, and whatever it was that was worrying him would simply vanish from his mind.

One cold winter's day, for example, King Yorick was being carried home to his palace in his specially heated chair, when he noticed a poor man dressed in rags with his wife and three small children shivering under a wall.

'Oh dear,' said King Yorick, when he got back to his palace. 'I really ought to do something about all the poor people who have nowhere to live in this bitter cold weather. I suppose I ought to convert one of my palaces into a home for them . . . '

'Oh! But Your Majesty!' said his Chancellor. 'You've only got sixteen palaces! If you were to lose one of them, you'd have one less than King Fancypants of Swaggerland – and that wouldn't do, would it?'

'Good gracious no! That wouldn't do at all,' replied King Yorick.

'Best go to bed and chew one of those delightful forget-me-nuts,' said his Chancellor.

'Yes, perhaps you're right,' sighed King Yorick.

So he put himself to bed with a hot-water bottle, chewed a forget-me-nut, and had soon forgotten all about the poor family, who were freezing outside in the ice and snow.

But, of course, the poor man and his family outside didn't have any forget-me-nuts to chew on. Forget-me-nuts were worth their weight in gold – far too rare and expensive for the likes of them.

And even if they could have found one, it wouldn't have done them any good, for, you see, forget-me-nuts only helped you to forget your conscience – they didn't help you to forget that you were cold or hungry or homeless.

As a matter of fact, the forget-me-nuts didn't really help King Yorick that much either, for even though he chewed on one most days – and sometimes two or three – he was always pretty miserable, though he never quite knew why.

'Perhaps if I had another palace built so I had one *more* than King Fancypants of Swaggerland – I'd feel happier?' said King Yorick.

'Exactly so,' said the Lord Chancellor (whose brother got all the building contracts).

And so King Yorick had yet another palace built. It was opened with great celebrations and fantastic fireworks and a lavish feast that went on for three whole days. Then the new palace stood empty for the rest of the year like all the other palaces.

Now the poor man, whose family the King had seen shivering in

the midst of winter, had a son whose name was Tim. And one day, Tim said to his father: 'Father! I cannot bear to see you so unhappy! I'm going to bring King Yorick to his senses!'

Whereupon Tim's father exclaimed: 'But what on earth can you do, Tim? You're so small.'

'You'll see!' said Tim. And there and then he set off for the King's palace.

When he reached it, he found the doors shut tight against the freezing winter and the walls too high to climb.

'What *am* I going to do?' thought Tim to himself. 'I'll never even get into the palace – let alone bring the King to his senses!'

But he didn't give up. He sat on a stone outside the palace and waited to see what would happen. And as he sat there, the sky grew dark and the world grew quiet, as if it too were waiting to see what would happen. Then finally it started to snow. And the snow fell on Tim's head and shoulders. But still he just sat there, watching the King's palace.

Well, after a while, Tim saw a face at one of the windows. And all the while the snow fell thicker and faster, until it quite covered Tim's head and his shoulders. Yet still Tim just sat and waited to see what would happen.

Before long, the window opened, and a boy stuck his head out and called to Tim: 'Aren't you cold?'

Now Tim was so used to being cold that he scarcely thought about it any more. But, now he came to think about it, he realized he was so cold he couldn't even speak.

'You'd better come in and get warm,' said the boy at the window.

But Tim found he could neither speak nor move. He was frozen fast and completely covered in snow like a snowman.

So the boy climbed out of the window, brushed the snow off Tim, and lifted him in through the window. (For, truth to tell, Tim was extremely small and light because he'd never really had enough to eat all his life.)

Well, it didn't take Tim long to thaw out and explain what he was doing.

'That's odd!' replied the boy. 'I was wondering what I could do to make *my* father happier too.'

'But your father's the king!' exclaimed Tim, who had already guessed that the boy was King Yorick's son. 'He must have every-thing he could ever want!'

'That's right,' replied the Prince. 'But he's miserable from morn till night. I try and cheer him up, but he doesn't even seem to notice I exist. He just sits and chews forget-me-nuts.'

When Tim heard this, he sat and stared into the fire.

'How on earth are we going to help our fathers to be happier?' he said.

No sooner had he spoken these words than a most extraordinary thing happened. The fire began to move, and, as the two boys watched, the red-hot coals turned over and around until they formed themselves into a face that spoke and said:

'The Key of Memory is the only thing that will bring your fathers happiness. But be warned – it will also bring grief as well.'

'Where do we find the Key of Memory?' asked Tim.

'Go with your consciences . . .' replied the fire.

'What?' said the Prince.

'What?' said Tim.

But the coals in the fire shifted around again, and didn't say another word.

Then suddenly there was a noise like thunder. Tim and the Prince rushed to the window and looked out into the freezing black night. They could see two points of light coming towards them fast.

'What d'you think they are?' asked Tim.

'Perhaps they're our consciences,' said the Prince.

'Don't be daft!' said Tim.

And the two points of light got nearer and nearer, until suddenly two huge black stallions, breathing fire out of their nostrils, burst out of the night, leapt over the palace wall, and reared up to a halt underneath the window.

Tim looked at the Prince, and the Prince looked at Tim, and Tim shrugged and said: 'Well, I don't know . . . maybe you're right . . . '

And without another word they leapt onto the backs of those stallions and galloped off into the night.

The next morning, when King Yorick found that his son had vanished, he wrang his hands in despair.

'What shall I do? My only son has run away . . . I should have loved him more! I should have been a better father!'

'Don't make such a fuss!' said his Chancellor. 'Just chew a forget-me-nut, and you'll soon feel better.'

So the King ate a forget-me-nut, and, after a while, he forgot all about it. But when he went to bed that night, he found the Queen crying into her pillow.

'What on earth's the matter with you?' he asked.

The Queen looked at him in anger and exclaimed: 'What! Have you already forgotten that our son has run away?'

'Oh, don't make such a fuss,' said the King. 'Have a forget-me-nut.' And he offered the bowl of nuts to the Queen, but she seized it from his grasp and threw the entire thing on the fire.

'Don't!' cried the King. 'Those are worth their weight in gold!' But it was too late. The nuts burst into flame as soon as they touched the fire, and the smoke went up the chimney.

Meanwhile, Tim and the Prince were riding through the frozen Northlands on the backs of their fire-breathing stallions.

By and by, they saw a cloud on the horizon, and the stallions redoubled their speed. And, by and by, they reached the cloud and found it was a pall of smoke, under which their stallions came to a halt. When Tim and the Prince looked down, they saw they were on the edge of a sheer cliff that dropped straight down a thousand feet into a lake of fire.

But they didn't have time to be frightened, for – to their horror – their stallions reared up, pawed the air, and then leapt straight off the cliff and plunged down towards the fiery lake.

The two boys shut their eyes, convinced that their last moment had come, but, as they reached the surface of the burning lake and they felt the fire licking up around their stallions' bellies, suddenly the flames seemed to separate, and they found themselves plummeting down into a black hole until they disappeared below the surface of the lake of fire.

For a moment, their eyes were filled with smoke, and they couldn't see a thing, but when they opened them again, they found they had landed in a vast cavern. And there in the centre of the cavern was a great forge, with flames shooting up and feeding the fiery lake above. At the forge worked a huge blacksmith, with iron bands on his arms and fire coming from his nostrils.

The two stallions reared in the air once more, and Tim and the Prince fell off onto a pile of straw.

When he saw them, the huge blacksmith stopped his work and laughed. And every time he laughed, the flames shot out from his nostrils and set fire to his beard, so he had to keep running to the water-butt to put it out.

Meanwhile Tim had got to his feet and said: 'We have come for the Key of Memory.'

'Have you now?' roared the blacksmith, and this time he laughed so hard that he set fire to his hood, and he had to plunge his whole head into the water-butt.

'We've been told it is the only thing that will bring our fathers happiness,' said the Prince.

'And grief!' roared the blacksmith, and he laughed again so long and loud that he set fire to his jerkin, and he had to jump into the water-butt right up to his neck.

'Is the Key of Memory here?' asked Tim.

The blacksmith lay there, half in the water, and roared: 'I've just finished making it! It's on the anvil.'

The two boys turned and saw a huge key lying on the anvil and glowing red-hot.

'Take a pair of tongs,' said the blacksmith, 'and drop it in this water butt.'

So the Prince took a long pair of tongs, lifted up the red-hot key and dropped it into the water-butt, where the giant blacksmith was still sitting. Immediately the blacksmith disappeared in a cloud of steam, and when the steam had cleared away, the blacksmith had gone, and there was an old woman, whose face was red like the coals of the fire. The old woman turned to the Prince and said:

'Prince! In the unhappiest part of your father's kingdom, you will find a chest filled with your father's memories. This is the only key that will unlock it.'

Then the old woman seemed to fall into pieces, and sank like glowing embers down into the water-butt.

So Tim and the Prince took the key, and looked for their black stallions, but they had disappeared too.

162

'Well,' said Tim. 'It looks as if we've got to walk home.'

The two boys searched until eventually they found the entrance to the cavern, and they were able to climb up and escape. When they reached the world above, however, they found that the lake of fire was just an ordinary lake. And there at the water's edge were two grey horses – just ordinary horses.

They rode back through the frozen Northlands, but what had taken a few minutes on the marvellous stallions now took days. And what had taken hours now took weeks.

But eventually they arrived back in the land of King Yorick.

'Where shall we find the unhappiest part of my father's kingdom?' asked the Prince.

'I know where that is!' said Tim, and he led the Prince to the place where forty beggars slept under a bridge, but they couldn't find the chest there.

Then Tim led the Prince to a shed, where twenty robbers were hiding for fear of being caught. But they didn't find the chest there.

Finally Tim led the Prince to the place where his own mother and father and brother and sister were huddled around a poor fire, beneath the wall. But when they saw Tim, their faces burst into smiles of happiness, and they didn't find the chest there.

'Well, it beats me,' said Tim. 'I don't know where else to look.'

So the Prince returned to the palace, and Tim went with him. There they found the King sitting under a nutmeg tree with tears in his eyes.

The Prince stood in front of his father, and said: 'What is the matter? You're the King! You have seventeen palaces and everything your heart could desire! Why are you unhappy?'

The King looked at his son without recognizing him and said: 'I forgot to love my son, and he ran away. And now I've even forgotten what he looks like!'

At that moment, Tim noticed that the King was sitting on a rusty old iron chest. He handed the key to the Prince and the Prince tried it in the lock. It fitted exactly.

'Father,' said the Prince. 'I've come back in hope of bringing you happiness.'

With that, he unlocked the chest, and at once the lid flew open and a million black thoughts flew into the air and blotted out the sun for a moment.

The King gave a roar of grief, as the black cloud suddenly melted into his mind, and he looked into the Prince's eyes and said:

'My son, I fear this is not happiness you have brought me, for I now remember everyone who has gone hungry – even for a day. I now remember every poor mother who cannot feed her children. I now remember every poor father who cannot clothe his family nor provide a roof to keep the rain and snow from their heads. I now remember everyone whose sufferings I have ignored, and my heart is overcome with grief.'

'But, Your Majesty!' cried Tim. 'Why don't you give up just one of your seventeen palaces to house the hungry?'

King Yorick looked at Tim and, for the first time in years, he smiled: 'I'll do better than that!' he said.

And then and there King Yorick became the first king to give up living in a palace. Instead he lived in a comfortable house, that was just roomy enough for himself and his family and also for Tim and his mother and father and brother and sister. King Yorick opened up every one of his seventeen palaces so that from that day on there was not one single homeless person in the kingdom.

The Lord Chancellor left in disgust, and went to work with King Fancypants of Swaggerland. And so did the Chancellor's brother.

Then King Yorick ordered his gardeners to cut down all the orchards of forget-me-nut trees. This they did. And from that day on everyone forgot that there was ever such a thing as a forget-me-nut.

EYES-ALL-OVER

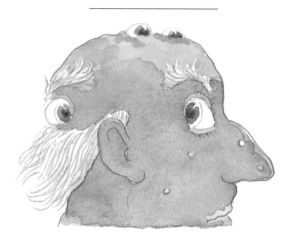

THERE WAS ONCE AN OLD MAN whose name was Eyes-All-Over, because that's what he had. He had eyes in the back of his head, eyes on the top of his head, eyes on his elbows, and eyes on his knees. He even had one eye on the bottom of each foot.

'Nobody ever catches me out!' chuckled old Eyes-All-Over. And it was true, because each of his eyes could see different things.

The eyes in the back of his head could see things that happened yesterday. The eyes on the top of his head could see things that happened a long way away. The eyes on his elbows could see everyone else's mistakes. The eyes on his knees could see everyone else's hopes. And the eyes on the soles of his feet could see things that would never happen.

Now the only thing in the whole world that old Eyes-All-Over really cared for was a pot of gold that he kept under the floorboards in his bedroom. Every night he would close all the shutters, draw the curtains, take out his pot of gold and count it – just to make sure it was all there.

And as he counted it, the eyes on the top of his head looked around to make sure no one was peeping in – while the eyes in the back of his head made sure the coins were the same as they were yesterday.

Every week his pot of gold would get larger, because, whenever he went to market, the eyes in his elbows spotted everyone else's mistakes – so, if someone were selling a pig for a pound that was really worth three, old Eyes-All-Over would snap it up and sell it again as quick as fat in the frying-pan!

And, of course, old Eyes-All-Over never warned anybody they were making a mistake or that they'd lose their money. Oh no! He was far too busy thinking about adding all those golden guineas to his pot of gold.

Well, one day, Eyes-All-Over was sitting at home, counting through his pot of gold as usual, when suddenly there was a knock on the door.

'Burglars!' he exclaimed to himself. Then he thought: 'No . . . wait a minute . . . burglars wouldn't knock on the door. They'd just climb down the chimney.'

So he carefully hid away his pot of gold, and then he opened the door – just a crack.

There on the step stood a thin girl who said: 'I'm hungry and I have nowhere to live. May I do some work for you to earn a slice of bread and dripping?'

'Bread and dripping!' exclaimed old Eyes-All-Over. 'D'you think I'm made of money?'

'I could clean your house or chop your wood for you,' said the girl.

'Listen!' said Eyes-All-Over. 'The eyes in my knees can see what you're hoping – you're hoping to be rich one day and live in a nice house like this! Why, you'd probably cut my throat while I'm asleep! Be off with you!'

'Oh no!' said the poor girl. 'I'd never do a thing like that!'

Well, old Eyes-All-Over slyly slipped off a shoe and looked at the girl with one of the eyes in the soles of his feet – the eyes that could see things that would never happen. He saw at once that she would never do anything to harm anyone.

'Hmm! Very well,' he said. 'I do need some firewood chopping.'

So the girl chopped some firewood, and he gave her a piece of bread (without any dripping) and let her sleep that night in the woodshed.

The next day, old Eyes-All-Over woke up to find his house clean and neat and a breakfast of beans and ham waiting for him on the table. For the girl (whose name was May) had been up working hard for several hours already.

So Eyes-All-Over gave her another piece of dry bread and said: 'You can stay another day.'

Well, May stayed and worked for old Eyes-All-Over for some

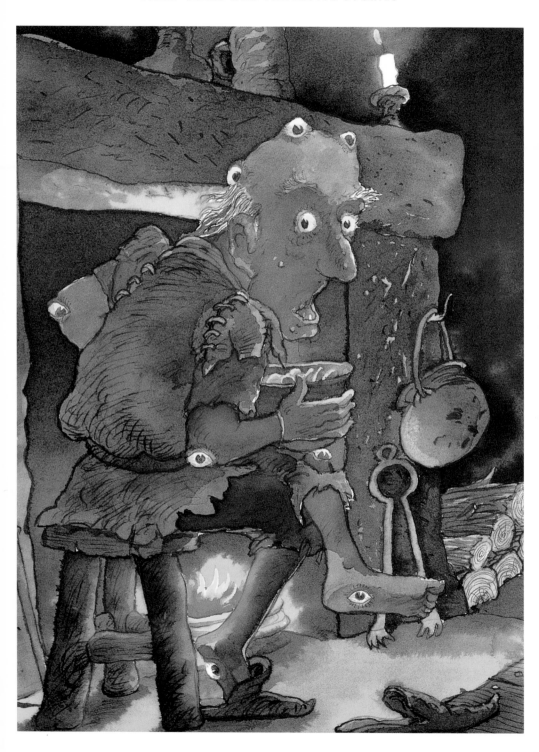

years. In return he let her sleep in the woodshed and allowed her to eat one piece of bread in the morning and one bowl of soup at night. 'Eh, eh!' he used to grin to himself. 'She costs me nothing and she works as hard as six men. What a bargain!'

One day, however, a stranger was riding past the house, when he caught sight of May digging the cabbage patch. She was still dressed in the same rags she'd been wearing when she first arrived (for it never occurred to old Eyes-All-Over that she might need new clothes) and she was exhausted from all her hard work, but even so May looked so beautiful that the young man fell in love with her on the spot. And, not long after, she fell in love with him.

So the young man went to Eyes-All-Over and told him that he wanted to marry May.

Now old Eyes-All-Over saw at once that he must be a rich young fellow. 'Eh, eh!' he thought, 'I can make a good bargain out of this business!'

But he put on a sad face and said: 'Oh no! You can't take young May away from me! She cooks my breakfast every morning!'

'Very well,' said the young man, 'take this.' And he handed old Eyes-All-Over a ruby ring. 'With that you can hire the finest cook in the world to make your breakfast every day!'

But old Eyes-All-Over slyly looked at the young man with the eyes in the back of his head – the eyes that could see things that had happened yesterday – and he could see that only yesterday the young man had bought a fine fur coat. So old Eyes-All-Over screwed up his face and looked very sad and said: 'Oh, young sir, you don't really mean to take young May away from me? Don't you know she cuts my wood every day and makes my fire . . . I'd need a fine fur coat to keep me warm, if you were to take her away from me.'

So the young man went and fetched the fine fur coat, which he had actually bought for his father, and gave it to old Eyes-All-Over.

'There,' he said. 'Now may I marry May?'

But old Eyes-All-Over looked with the eyes on the top of his head – the eyes that could see things that were happening far away – and he could see that the young man's father, who was waiting for his return, lived in a fine palace, surrounded by fabulous wealth.

So Eyes-All-Over took out his hanky, and pretended to cry salty tears into it.

'Oh, good sir!' he said. 'You cannot possibly want to take young May away from me! She works so hard and keeps my house so neat and clean. Why! She's worth her weight in gold!'

So the young man rode off and returned, some time later, with a chest filled with gold pieces that altogether weighed exactly the same as young May.

'Now,' he said, 'May and I must go and be married.'

But old Eyes-All-Over hadn't finished yet. 'I can still screw even more out of this bargain!' he said to himself. Then he looked at the young man with the eyes in his knees – the eyes that could see people's hopes – and he could see that the young man had hopes, one day, to be a king – for he was, in fact, a prince.

So old Eyes-All-Over clutched his heart and said: 'Ah! Good sir! Would you take this child from me? She has been like a daughter to me these many years. I would not part with her for half a kingdom!'

'Very well,' said the Prince, and there and then he signed away half his kingdom to old Eyes-All-Over. Then he lifted May up onto his horse, and they rode off together – to be married with great feasting and merry-making in his father's palace.

As they rode away, old Eyes-All-Over rubbed his hands with glee.

'What a bargain!' he said to himself. 'I get all those years of work out of that thin stick of a girl, and then I sell her off for jewels, furs, gold and half a kingdom! I certainly am the sharpest chap around!'

But, at that very moment, he looked at himself with the eyes in his elbows – the eyes that saw people's mistakes – and he saw, to his horror, that he himself had made a big mistake, though he didn't know what.

As he got his lonely breakfast, however, and sat by his lonely fire, he began to realize what it was, for he found himself longing to hear May's voice singing in the garden and to see her face across the room. Soon he found himself thinking that he would give back everything just to have May give him one of her smiles.

But, when he looked at himself with the eyes in the soles of his feet – the eyes that saw things that would never happen – he knew she would never smile at him again.

And this time, old Eyes-All-Over cried real tears, for he suddenly realized that – when he gave May away – he'd given away the only thing he'd ever really loved.

And he cursed himself that – all the time she'd lived with him – he'd given her nothing but hard words and hard work, and had never given her any reason to care for him.

And old Eyes-All-Over then saw – clearer than anything he'd ever seen in his life – that despite having eyes all over, he had really been quite, quite blind.

THE SNOW BABY

N OLD WOMAN ONCE WISHED she had a child. But she had never married, and now she lived all alone in a bare cottage beside a dark wood.

One day, however, around Christmas time, when the sky was yellow and heavy with snow, she looked out of the little window by her bed, and thought she saw the evening star.

'That's strange,' she said to herself, 'to see the evening star on such a stormy night. It must be a lucky star.'

So there and then she made a wish. I can't tell you what she wished for, because she never told anyone, but I think I can guess – can't you?

Now, as it happened, the light that the old woman had seen was not the evening star – in fact it was not a star at all, but a firefly. The firefly overheard the old lady's wish, and felt very sorry for her. So it flew to the place where all fireflies go to fetch their lights, and told its comrades what it had heard. And they all agreed to try and help her.

Well that night it began to snow from the black sky onto the black ground, until – as if by magic – the ground turned white, and the morning broke over a different world.

The old woman woke up and put on her shawl. Then she took a shovel and cleared away the snow from her door.

When she looked at the pile of snow she'd made, she smiled to herself and said: 'I don't think the evening star has granted my wish – so I'll make myself my own baby.'

And she spent the morning making the pile of snow into a snow baby.

That night, she sat in her cottage and felt very lonely. So she went to the door, and looked out at her snow baby.

'Tomorrow is Christmas Day,' she said to her snow baby. 'And here am I all alone in the world, and nobody cares whether I'm alive or dead – except you. And you'll be gone when the snows thaw.'

Then she climbed into her bed, and put out her candle.

A moment later she woke up and looked out of her window. She could hear a sound like tiny bells jingling far, far away, and she could see a strange yellow light all around her cottage. She could not see, but above her all the fireflies in the world were gathered together on her roof. The last one had just arrived, and now they all flew together to form one single ball of light.

The next moment, the old woman couldn't believe her eyes as she watched a glowing ball of light descend onto the heap of snow that she had shaped like a baby. The light landed where the baby's heart would be. Then it poured into the snow baby and filled it top to toe!

The instant it did, the snow baby opened its eyes and looked around.

'What are you doing out there in the cold?' said the old woman. 'Come in at once.'

So the snow baby stepped unsteadily down from its little mound, and toddled towards the cottage door.

The old woman rushed to the door, flung it open and lifted her snow baby up in her arms. She kissed it and held it tight.

'Now,' she said, 'I will not be alone this Christmas.'

Then she tucked the snow baby up in her own bed, and bustled about the cottage to make everything ready.

The next morning the snow baby awoke to find a stocking hanging at the end of the bed.

'You must look in your stocking and see what St Nicholas has brought you,' said the old woman.

So the snow baby opened its stocking. Inside there was a chocolate medal, a wooden man on a trapeze, an old doll with one eye missing, a mince pie and an apple in the toe.

173

When the snow baby had opened all its presents and played with its toys, the old woman said: 'Now we must have our breakfast.'

So she sat her snow child on the other side of the table, and they both ate a little toast and drank a little warm milk.

Just then they heard the church bell sounding across the snow. 'Now,' said the old woman, 'it's time we went to church.'

So she dressed the snow baby up in a woollen hat and muffler and a knitted woollen coat, and off they went, through the snow to the little church on the hill.

No one noticed the old woman and her snow baby, as they slipped into the back of the church while everyone else was on their knees. The two of them sat close together in the very back pew, holding hands. When the moment came, they stood up and sang the carols. Then, before the end of the service, they stole out again, before anyone else saw them.

Then the old woman and her snow baby ran back through the snow, laughing and shouting and throwing snowballs at each other.

When they finally got back to the cottage, there was a good smell coming from the old woman's oven.

'Now we must eat our Christmas pudding and mince pies,' said the old woman. 'I'm afraid I haven't got a goose or a ham pie to offer you.'

But the snow baby didn't seem to mind at all. They both sat down and ate the happiest Christmas dinner that the old woman could remember since she was a child.

As they finished, night began to fall, and the snow baby grew tired, and the light with which it was filled grew dimmer – for the truth is that the fireflies needed to fetch new lights.

The old woman looked rather sadly at her snow baby.

'Must you go?' she asked. And the snow baby nodded. 'Well, thank you for keeping me company this Christmas,' said the old woman. 'I wish it could have gone on longer . . . but there it is . . .'

And then the first wonderful thing happened. The snow baby got up from its chair and came across to the old woman and kissed her.

And then the second wonderful thing happened. It spoke. 'Goodbye,' it said.

Then it went out of the door, and the old woman watched from her window, as the snow baby climbed back onto its little mound of snow. Then the fireflies came out, one by one, and flew off dimly into the night to fetch new lights.

And the old woman fell asleep, nodding to herself as she remembered all the things she'd done that Christmas Day with her snow baby.

The next day, the sun shone, and the snows had gone. The old woman lit a fire and bustled about her little cottage. And when she felt brave enough, she went out of her door, and swept away the last heap of snow that had been – for a short time – her very own snow baby.

HOW THE BADGER
GOT ITS STRIPES

N THE GREAT LONG-AGO, the Badger was pure white all over.

'How sorry I feel for Bear with his dull brown coat,' the Badger would say. 'And who would want to be like leopard – all covered in spots? Or – worse still – like Tiger, with his vulgar striped coat! I am glad that the Maker Of All Things gave me this pure white coat without a blemish on it!'

This is how the Badger would boast as he paraded through the forest, until all the other creatures were thoroughly sick and tired of him.

'He always looks down his nose at me,' said the Rabbit, 'because only my tail is white.'

'And he sneers at me,' said the Field Mouse, 'because I'm such a mousy colour.'

'And he calls me an eye-sore!' exclaimed the Zebra.

'It's time we put a stop to it,' they said.

'Then may I make a suggestion?' asked the Fox, and he outlined a plan to which all the other animals agreed.

Some time later, the Fox went to the Badger and said:

'O, Badger, please help us! You are, without doubt, the best-looking creature in the Wild Wood. It's not just your coat (which is exceedingly beautiful and without a blemish) but it is also . . . oh . . . the way you walk on your hind legs . . . the way you hold your head up . . . your superb manners and graceful ways . . . Won't you help us humbler animals by giving us lessons in how to improve our looks and how to carry ourselves?'

Well, the Badger was thrilled to hear all these compliments and he replied very graciously: 'Of course, my dear Fox. I'll see what I can do.'

So the Fox called all the animals to meet in the Great Glade, and said to them: 'Badger, here, has kindly agreed to give us lessons in how to look as handsome as he does. He will also instruct us in etiquette, deportment and fashion.'

There were one or two sniggers amongst the smaller animals at this point, but the Badger didn't notice. He stood up on his hind legs, puffed himself up with pride, and said: 'I am very happy to be in a position to help you less fortunate animals, and I must say I can see much room for improvement. You, Wolf, for example, have such a shabby coat . . .'

'But it's the only one I've got!' said the Wolf.

'And I pity you, Beaver,' went on the Badger, 'such an ordinary pelt you have . . . and as for that ridiculous tail . . .'

'Er, Badger,' interrupted the Fox, 'rather than going through all our short-comings (interesting and instructive though that certainly may be), why don't you teach us how to walk with our noses in the air – the way that makes you look so distinguished and sets off your beautiful unblemished white coat so well?'

'By all means,' said the Badger.

'Why not walk to the other end of the Glade, so we can see?' said the Fox.

'Certainly,' said the Badger. And so, without suspecting a thing, he started to walk to the other end of the Glade.

Now if the Badger had not been so blinded by his own self-satisfaction, he might have noticed the Rat and the Stoat and the Weasel smirking behind their paws. And if he had looked a little closer, he might have noticed a twinkle in many an animal's eye. But he didn't. He just swaggered along on his hind legs with his nose right up in the air, saying:

'This is the way to walk . . . notice how gracefully I raise my back legs . . . and see how I am always careful to keep my brush well ooooooooaaaaarrrggggghhhup!'

This is the moment that the Badger discovered the Fox's plan. The Fox had got all the other animals to dig a deep pit at one end of the Great Glade. This they had filled with muddy water and madder-root, and then covered it over with branches and fern.

The Badger, with his nose in the air, had, of course, walked straight into it – feet first. And he sank in – right up to his neck.

'Help!' he cried. 'Help! My beautiful white coat! Please pull me out someone! Help!'

Well, of course, all the animals in the Glade laughed and pointed at the poor Badger, as he struggled to keep his head out of the muck. Eventually he had to pull himself out by his own efforts.

When the Badger looked down at his beautiful white coat, stained with mud and madder-root, he was so mortified that he ran off out of the forest with a pitiful howl. And he ran and he ran until he came to a lake of crystal water.

There he tried to clean the stuff off his coat, but madder-root is a powerful dye, and no matter what he did, he could not get it off.

'What shall I do?' he moaned to himself. 'My beautiful white coat . . . my pride and joy . . . ruined for ever! How can I hold my head up in the forest again?'

To make matters worse, at that moment, a creature whom the Badger had never seen before swam up to him and said: 'What are you doing – washing your filthy old coat in our crystal-clear lake? Push off!'

The badger was speechless – not only because he wasn't used to being spoken to like this, but also because the creature had such a beautiful coat. It was as white and unblemished as the Badger's own coat used to be.

'Who are you?' asked the Badger.

'I'm Swan of course,' replied the Swan. 'Now shove off! We don't want dirty creatures like you around here!' And the Swan rose up on its legs and beat its powerful wings, and the badger slunk away on all fours, with his tail between his legs.

For the rest of that day, the Badger hid himself away in a grove overlooking the crystal lake. From there he gazed down at the white swan, gliding proudly about the lake, and the Badger was so filled with bitterness and envy that he thought he would burst.

That very night, however, he stole down to the Swan's nest, when the Swan was fast asleep, and very, very gently, he pulled out one of the Swan's feathers and then scuttled back to his hiding-place.

He did the same thing the next night, and the next and the next, and each night he returned to the grove, where he was busy making himself a new coat of white feathers, to cover up his stained fur.

And, because the Badger did all this so slowly and slyly, the Swan never noticed, until all but one of his feathers had disappeared.

That night the Swan couldn't sleep, because of the draught from where his feathers were missing, and so it was that he saw the Badger creeping up to steal the last one. As he did so the Swan rose up with a terrible cry. He pecked off the Badger's tail and beat him with his wings and chased him off.

Then the Swan returned to the crystal lake, and sat there lamenting over his lost feathers.

When the Maker Of All Things found the Swan – that he had made so beautiful – sitting there bald and featherless, he was extremely surprised.

But he was even more surprised when he went to the Wild Wood, and found the Badger parading about, looking quite ridiculous in his stolen feather coat!

'Badger!' exclaimed the Maker Of All Things. 'I knew you were vain, but I didn't know you were a thief as well!'

And there and then he took the feathers and gave them back to the Swan.

'From this day on,' he said to the Badger, 'you will wear only your coat stained with madder-root. And, if you're going to steal, I'd better give you a thief's mask as well!'

And the Maker Of All Things drew his fingers across the Badger's eyes, and left him with two black stripes – like a mask – from ears to snout.

The Badger was so ashamed that he ran off and hid, and to this very day all badgers avoid company. They live in solitude, stealing a little bit here and there, wherever they can. And each and every badger still wears a mask of stripes across its eyes.

OLD MAN TRY-BY-NIGHT

LD MAN TRY-BY-NIGHT prowls round the house after dark. He rattles a window here, and he bangs a door there – just to see if anyone's left one open. And, if anyone has, this is what he does.

Old Man Try-By-Night slips right in and makes himself at home. He spreads marmalade on the doormat, puts his dirty feet up on the kitchen table, and has a little snack.

He doesn't eat all the doormat – in fact you'd scarcely notice he's been at it – he just nibbles a little bit here and a little bit there. Then he takes out the sugar bowl and empties just a little sugar into his smelly old trousers so they crackle when he sits. He likes that. Then Old Man Try-By-Night pads around, putting his dirty fingers here and making muddy footmarks there. Then, once he's quite satisfied that everybody is fast asleep, do you know what he does? He slips right out again, and bangs the door so that every-one wakes up!

Oh yes! And there's something else that he does, but I can never remember what it is . . .

Well, one night, a small boy named Tom was lying in bed, when he thought he could hear Old Man Try-By-Night rattling the doors and windows downstairs.

'He's not going to keep me awake!' said Tom, and he jumped out of bed and crept downstairs.

Now, nobody has ever seen Old Man Try-By-Night, because he doesn't like to be seen in his dirty old galoshes and his old torn overcoat. So he always makes himself scarce as soon as anyone stirs.

But young Tom was known to be the quietest boy in his school. He was always very, very quiet. And tonight, creeping downstairs to try and catch Old Man Try-By-Night, Tom was quieter than he'd ever been ever before in his life.

Well, he was so quiet that not even Old Man Try-By-Night, with his sharp ears, heard him.

Tom stood as still as a chimney, peering round the kitchen door. He could see Old Man Try-By-Night peering in at the kitchen window, and he saw him grin and give it just a little rattle. Then he watched as Old Man Try-By-Night tried the back-door handle. He rattled it once. He rattled it twice. Then he looked up to see if he'd woken anybody up yet, but nobody seemed to be stirring. And young Tom just stood in the shadows, still as stone.

Old Man Try-By-Night gave a chuckle, and turned the door handle, and – to Tom's horror – it opened! His mother must have forgotten to lock the back door!

Tom's heart jumped into his throat, as he watched Old Man Try-By-Night slip through the door and stand there in the kitchen – large as life – looking around with that chuckly grin still on his face, and a big, dirty red handkerchief hanging from his overcoat pocket.

Before Tom could take another breath, Old Man Try-By-Night was padding across the floor towards him! For a moment, Tom thought he'd been spotted and that Old Man Try-By-Night was going to come and grab him with his grimy hands, and tie that filthy old red hanky round his eyes to stop him watching. But the Old Man hadn't even so much as noticed a whisper of Tom – he was simply padding over to the broom that stood in the corner. Old Man Try-By-Night looked at the dirty bristles and licked his lips. Then he padded round to the pantry and opened a jar of chocolate spread with his grimy fingers. Next he stuck the dirty broom into it and got a good dollop of chocolate on the bristles. Then he sat down, put his filthy old galoshes up on the kitchen table, and started to nibble on the broom.

And he only stopped in order to wipe his chocolatey mouth on his filthy sleeve.

All this time, Tom stood there, peering round the kitchen door, as still and as silent as the clock on the kitchen wall that had stopped nine years ago – before Tom was born.

But Tom said to himself: 'That's too much! It's one thing to keep us awake at night rattling the windows and doors, but nibbling my mother's best broom is really downright rude!'

So Tom suddenly stepped into the kitchen and said: 'Hey! Old Man Try-By-Night! Stop that!'

Well, of course, Old Man Try-By-Night leaps to his feet and drops the broom and bangs his head on the cupboard that Tom's father always bangs his head on and keeps meaning to move.

'Ow!' shouts Old Man Try-By-Night, and he makes for the back door as fast as his muddy old galoshes can take him. But Tom gets there first, and he locks it and throws the key into the sink.

'Oh! Please let me out!' whimpers Old Man Try-By-Night. 'I'm only doing a bit of broom-nibbling!'

But young Tom stands his ground and says: 'Now listen here, Old Man Try-By-Night! I'm fed up with your keeping me awake at night, rattling doors and windows. If I let you out of here, you must promise me you'll stop it.'

'I promise,' says Old Man Try-By-Night. 'But just unlock the door and let me out, for I hate being seen in my dirty old galoshes and my old torn overcoat.'

'Very well,' says young Tom. 'But look at the mess you've made of the kitchen. You've put your grimy fingermarks on the pantry door, you've got mud-marks on the kitchen table, and you've got chocolate on the broom! Before I let you out, you must clean it all up!'

'Very well,' sighs Old Man Try-By-Night, and he gets out his dirty old red handkerchief, and starts to rub his fingermarks off the pantry door.

But everywhere he goes, his filthy old galoshes make more mud-marks on the floor, and everywhere he wipes, his dirty old red handkerchief just smears the grime across and leaves everything twice as dirty as before.

'You're putting on more dirt than you're taking off!' exclaims Tom.

'I'm doing my best!' whimpers Old Man Try-By-Night, and he rubs the pantry door with his mucky sleeve, and leaves a great smear of chocolate right across it. Then he kneels down on the floor and tries to wipe up the muddy marks from his filthy old galoshes, but his knees are covered in grease and his hands are covered in chocolate and the floor gets worse and worse wherever he goes.

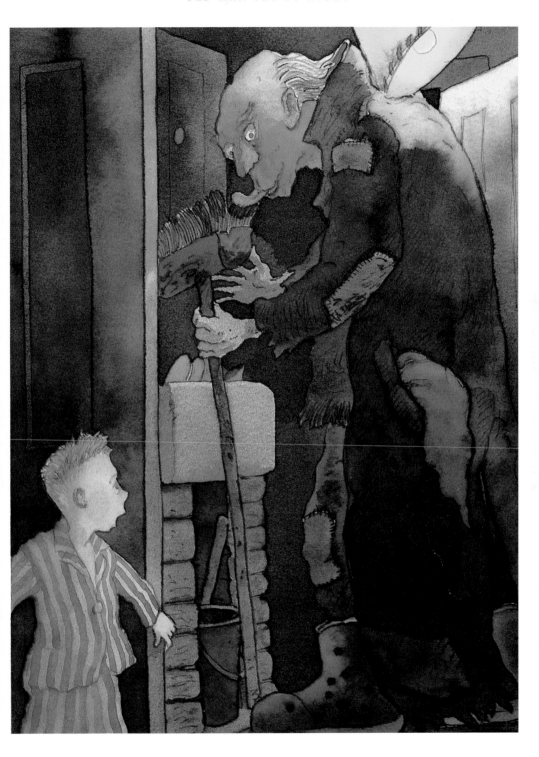

'Stop it! Stop it!' cries Tom. 'I'll have to clear up myself!' And he grabs a bucket and a scrubbing brush, and goes round after the old man, cleaning up and cleaning up . . . And Tom starts feeling tired and sleepy . . . but the kitchen's still covered in mud and chocolate, and the more Old Man Try-By-Night tries to clean it up, the worse it gets. Tom just can't keep up with his bucket and scrubbing brush, and just as he's beginning to think maybe he should unlock the back door and get rid of Old Man Try-By-Night once and for all, he suddenly finds it's gone dark and he can't see.

Tom's blood runs cold, for he's just realized that Old Man Try-By-Night has crept up behind him, while he was busy scrubbing, and has tied that dirty old red handkerchief over his eyes . . .

And Old Man Try-By-Night is saying: 'This is what happens if you go prowling around the house at night, when you ought to be asleep. You never wake up in the morning!'

Tom twists from side to side, and tries to pull the dirty old red handkerchief away from his eyes, when he suddenly realizes that it's not the dirty old red handkerchief but Old Man Try-By-Night's grimy hand round his eyes! Tom manages to pull it away, but then he notices a strange thing: Old Man Try-By-Night's hand isn't grimy at all!

Then Tom looks up and he sees that it isn't even Old Man Try-By-Night! It's his father! And the morning light is streaming in through the bedroom window, and Tom is safe and sound in his own bed.

'You see? This is what happens if you go prowling round the house at night,' his father is saying. 'You never wake up in the morning!'

'But Old Man Try-By-Night . . .' says Tom. 'He's made such a mess in the kitchen!'

And Tom's father says: 'Tom, I think you've been dreaming.'

Oh yes! That's the other thing that Old Man Try-By-Night does that I can never remember. After he's woken everybody up by rattling the windows and banging the doors, he takes out his dirty old red handkerchief, and he opens it up, and there – inside – are all manner of dreams. And before he goes, Old Man Try-By-Night chooses one or two for us, and leaves them on the doorstep – to keep us company through the night.

TOBY TICKLER

OBY HAD A TICKLE. It was a really good tickle. He could tickle anybody – even the most unticklish sort of person – and make them laugh.

Now it just so happened that His Lordship The Royal Treasurer Of The Realm was exactly that sort of person – extremely unticklish. In fact, he hadn't laughed for twenty years.

'Oh, for goodness' sake, Franklin,' the King would say to him. 'It's so gloomy having you around. Why don't you smile sometimes?'

'I smile exactly as often as is necessary,' said His Lordship The Royal Treasurer Of The Realm, and he demonstrated his smile to the King.

'If that's a smile,' said the King, 'I'm a left-handed corkscrew!'

'I beg your pardon?' said the Royal Treasurer.

'Smiling isn't like gold, you know,' said the King. 'You can't use it up or run out of it!'

'I don't care to squander anything unnecessarily, Your Majesty,' replied the Royal Treasurer, and went off to organize the day's business.

Now at the very moment that the Prime Minister was saying this to the King, Toby Tickler's mother was saying something very different to her son.

'Toby, my son,' she said. 'You are as dear to me as any son can be to his mother. If only love could make you fat, you'd be the plumpest boy in the whole kingdom. But look at you! You're just skin and bones, and I haven't enough money to feed us. I can't even pay the rent, and unless I do, we'll be thrown out of our house tomorrow morning.'

'Don't worry, Mother,' said Toby Tickler. 'I'll earn some money!'

'How are you going to do that?' replied his mother. 'You're too small and puny to work. All you can do is tickle people and make them laugh.'

'Very well,' said Toby, 'I'll make them laugh and then perhaps they'll give me a job.' And with that, he set off into town.

First he went to the Brickmaker and tickled him behind the right ear. Sure enough, the Brickmaker burst out laughing. In fact, he laughed so hard that he dropped his bricks. But when he'd stopped laughing, he turned on Toby Tickler and said: 'Look what you've done! I've broken my bricks! Get out of here!'

So then Toby went to the Bootmaker, and he tickled him behind the left ear. Well, the Bootmaker threw down his hammer and nails and started to laugh, and he couldn't stop laughing for forty minutes. When he did stop, however, he turned on Toby Tickler and shouted: 'Look what you've done! You've made me waste forty precious minutes! I don't want any ticklers around here!'

So then Toby went to the Bellmaker, and tickled him on the back of his neck. The Bellmaker laughed and laughed so much that he cracked the bell he was casting. Whereupon he chased Toby Tickler out of his shop, even though he was still laughing as hard as ever.

Finally, Toby went to the palace kitchen, where he found the Cook cutting up the bacon. Toby thought he'd better not tickle him, so instead he said: 'Please let me work here. I have to earn some money – otherwise my mother and I will be thrown out of our house.'

But the Cook replied: 'It's a hard life, working in the King's kitchen, and you're all skin and bones. You'd never last a day!' And he went on cutting the bacon.

Well, of course, Toby looked at the eggs being boiled for the King's breakfast, and the bread being buttered, and his mouth began to water, as he began to remember that it was two days since he had last eaten anything.

He tried to leave, but he just couldn't take his eyes off all that food.

Suddenly he felt a hand on his shoulder. He looked up into the face of one of the pantrymaids.

'Dearie me!' she said. 'You're as pale as pork and as thin as breadsticks! You'd better come in and have something to eat, before you go anywhere else, young man.'

And she sat him at the pantry table, and brought him plates of porridge and hunks of bread and a little strawberry jam.

Now, it just so happened that the Princess's favourite place in the whole palace was the pantry. She would come down every morning to spend an hour with Polly the Pantrymaid. So, of course, when she came down on this particular morning, who should she find but Toby Tickler, licking his porridge plate clean.

'You've got to earn some money somehow,' agreed the Princess, when she'd heard his story. 'Isn't there anything you're good at?'

Toby shook his head gloomily. 'There's only one thing I'm good at,' he said, 'and that just gets me into trouble.'

'What about sums?' asked the Princess. 'Perhaps my father would give you a job in the counting-house?'

So the Princess took Toby's hand, and led him to the King, who was still eating his breakfast (it used to take him most of the morning). But the King shook his head. 'You don't look serious enough for the counting-house, I'm afraid. His Lordship The Royal Treasurer Of The Realm would never approve.'

Just at that moment the Royal Treasurer came in, looking very solemn.

'Your Majesty!' he said in his gravest manner.

'Oh dear,' muttered the King. 'Here comes Cheerful Charlie . . .'

'There are three men at the door,' continued the Royal Treasurer, looking more and more solemn, 'who wish you to hear their complaints.'

'Oh dear, do I really have to?' sighed the King.

'It's a most serious matter!' exclaimed the Royal Treasurer.

'I thought it would be,' said the King. 'Very well, show them in.'

So the Royal Treasurer Of The Realm showed in the three men. They were the Brickmaker, the Bootmaker and the Bellmaker. As soon as they saw Toby Tickler, of course, they all three pointed at him and cried:

'That's him!'

'That's who?' asked the King.

'He made me laugh,' exclaimed the Brickmaker, 'so hard that I dropped a whole tray of new-baked bricks and broke them. I demand a good penny for the bricks I broke!'

'Well, he made me laugh so hard,' said the Bootmaker, 'that I wasted forty precious minutes. I demand a silver sixpence for the boots I could have made in that time.'

'And I demand a golden guinea!' exclaimed the Bellmaker, 'for the bell I cracked when he made me laugh.'

'Is this right?' demanded His Lordship The Royal Treasurer Of The Realm. 'You made all these people laugh?'

'It's right enough, and I'm sorry enough,' said Toby Tickler.

'Then,' said the Royal Treasurer, 'you must pay for every single thing – or I'll have you thrown into jail by your ears!'

'I can't pay anybody for anything!' cried Toby Tickler. 'My mother and I haven't even enough to pay our rent or buy our food.'

'That's your lookout!' shouted the Royal Treasurer. 'Guards! Seize this boy by the ears, and throw him in jail!'

As the guards came forward to arrest Toby Tickler, the Royal Treasurer put his face right up against Toby's and said: 'Perhaps this will teach you that there is a time and a place for everything.'

Well, I don't really know why it was, but His Lordship The Royal Treasurer Of The Realm looked so serious and so solemn that Toby Tickler just couldn't help himself . . . Just as the guards were grabbing him by the ears, he reached out his hand and tickled His Lordship under the chin.

Of course, the Royal Treasurer burst out laughing. In fact, he fell on the floor and rolled around, laughing and laughing and laughing.

'Amazing!' exclaimed the King. 'I haven't seen him laugh in twenty years! Did you just do that?'

'I'm afraid it's the only thing I can do,' sighed Toby Tickler, as the guards dragged him off by the ears.

'Then you're hired!' shouted the King after him. 'Bring that boy back here!' For, by this time, the guards had already dragged Toby out of the breakfast room and halfway down the steps to the dungeon, so they promptly turned about and dragged him all the way back again – still by his ears. (It was very painful).

Some time later, the King explained Toby's duties to him: 'There certainly is a time and place for everything – especially laughter,' he said. 'You are hereby engaged to make His Lordship The Royal Treasurer Of The Realm smile at least thirty times every day and laugh out loud at least once!'

Well, that's how Toby Tickler found a job at last, and saved his mother and himself from being thrown out of their house.

As a matter of fact, it turned out that he was good at sums after all, so when His Lordship The Royal Treasurer Of The Realm retired, Toby got his job. Although by that time he didn't really need a job any more, because he'd already married the Princess. You see . . . she sometimes liked Toby to tickle her too!

THE CAT WITH TWO TAILS

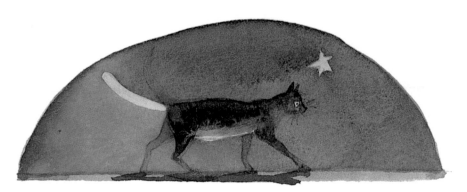

N THE OLDEN DAYS ALL CATS had two tails – one for the daytime and one for the night. During the day they kept their long, thick daytime tail curled around themselves and slept tight and snug. But when it grew dark – ah! then each cat would go to a secret place and there it would reach in its paw and pull out a bundle wrapped in mouse-fur. Then it would wait until it was sure . . . absolutely sure . . . that nobody and nothing . . . absolutely nothing . . . was looking. (For cats, you must know, are crafty as only cats can be.) And then it would unwrap the bundle of mouse-fur, and there, inside, would be its own – its very own – night-time tail.

Its night-time tail was an ordinary length and an ordinary thickness, but it would twitch as it lay there in the bundle of mouse-fur. And although it was only an ordinary length and an ordinary thickness, it was nevertheless a very remarkable tail indeed.

Can you guess why? Well . . . I'll tell you . . . it shone – as bright as day. And every cat would *off*! with its daytime tail in the twinkling of an eye, and *on*! with its shining night-time tail. And they'd hold their tails above their heads, and light the night as bright as day, and all the mice would tremble in the darkest corners of their holes.

When the cats stepped out, the badgers and the foxes would stop whatever they were doing to watch and clap. But every family of mice huddled together deeper in their holes, and their whiskers shook.

192

When the cats stepped out, the weasels and the stoats would stand on each others' shoulders to get a better view, but the mouse babies crept closer into their mothers' arms.

Now one day, a certain mouse said: 'I've had enough!'

And his wife replied: 'You're always right, of course, my dear. But enough of what? We haven't had anything to eat for days.'

'That's right!' said the mouse. 'We've had nothing to eat because those cats sleep outside our holes all day, wrapped up in their long, thick daytime tails. And at night, just when you'd think it would be safe to tiptoe out and steal a piece of cheese . . .'

'Just *one* piece of cheese!' twittered all his children.

'Those cats put on their night-time tails, and light the night as bright as day!'

'You never spoke a truer word, my dear,' said his wife. 'Those cats are crafty as only cats can be . . .'

'*That's* why I've had enough!' exclaimed the mouse, and he banged his paw on the nest. And his children felt very frightened – as they always did whenever their father got cross.

'So, since nobody else seems to be doing anything, I, Frederick Ferdinand Fury-Paws The Forty-Fourth, intend to do something about it!'

'Oh, do be careful!' twittered his wife, who was always alarmed when her husband used his full name. 'Don't do anything rash, my dear! Don't let your strength and size lead you to do things you might regret!'

But before you could say 'cheesefeathers!' that mouse had scuttled off to the Father Of All Things, and made his complaint.

The Father Of All Things listened with his head on one side. And then he listened with his head on the other side.

Then he turned to the Mother Of All Cats, who was pretending to be asleep nearby, and said: 'Well, Mother Of All Cats? It doesn't seem fair that you should have two tails when every other creature has only one.'

'Oh, I don't know,' replied the Mother Of All Cats. 'Some creatures have two legs, some creatures have four legs, some creatures have six legs and some – like the ungrateful centipede – have a hundred! So why shouldn't us cats have two tails?'

'Because,' said the mouse, 'it's unfair to us mice. You can see us by day *and* by night! We don't stand a chance.'

194

And so they argued all day long, until the Father Of All Things said: 'Enough! All creatures have only one head. And as it is with the head, so it should be with the tail.'

At this all the mice cheered. But the Mother Of All Cats twitched her crafty whiskers and smiled and said: 'Very true. Therefore let us cats have only one tail in future – but do you agree to let us choose which sort of tail?'

The Father Of All Things turned to the mouse and asked: 'Do you agree to this?'

And the mouse replied: 'Yes! Yes! But only the one tail!'

So the Father Of All Things said: 'Very well, you may choose.'

'Then,' said the Mother Of All Cats, giving her tail a crafty flick, 'please take note that we cats choose the sort of tail that is thick and long to keep us warm (like our daytime tails) *and* shining bright to light the night (just like our night-time tails) – both at the same time.'

'That reply was crafty as only a cat's can be,' said the Father Of All Things.

And all the other mice turned on Frederick Ferdinand Fury-Paws The Forty-Fourth and said: 'There! Now see what your meddling's done! It'll be twice as bad as it was before!'

The mouse bent his whiskers to the floor and cried out: 'Oh, please, Father Of All Things, don't allow the cats to have tails that are like their daytime tails *and* like their night-time tails both at the same time, or, I fear, we mice will all be destroyed!'

But the Father Of All Things replied: 'I cannot go back on my word.' And he turned to the Mother Of All Cats, who was sitting sleek and crafty as only cats can be, and he said:

'Mother Of All Cats, do you promise to be satisfied if I give you a tail that is like your daytime tail and like your night-time tail – both at the same time?'

And the Mother Of All Cats smiled a crafty smile, and said: 'I agree.'

And all the cats and stoats and weasels cheered, and the baby mice crept even further into their mothers' arms and their fathers wrung their paws in despair.

'Then, from this day forth,' said the Father Of All Things, 'let all cats' tails be like their night-time tails – ordinary in size, neither thick nor long. And let them be also like their daytime tails – not shining bright to light the night – but just ordinary tails.'

And no sooner had the Father Of All Things said this, than there was a crack and a whizz, and all the cats' tails turned into ordinary tails, very much like they are today.

When they saw that, all the mice cheered, and the cats blew on their whiskers and slunk off into the forest.

But now I have to tell you a terrible thing, which goes to show that cats really are as crafty as only cats can be.

That very night – the mouse said to his wife: 'My dear, now it is dark, let us go for a promenade, for – thanks to my efforts – it is now perfectly safe to walk abroad at eventide, since cats no longer have tails that are shining bright to light the night, and they will not be able to see us.'

And his wife said: 'As always, my dear, you know best.'

And so they put on their best summer coats and frocks, and they stepped out of their hole and at once were pounced upon by the cat. For cats, of course, have all got special night-time eyes, and have always been able to see as perfectly well by night as they can by day – with or without their shining tails.

They really are as crafty as only cats can be . . .

THE FLYING KING

HERE WAS ONCE A DEVIL in Hell named Carnifex, who liked to eat small children. Sometimes he would take them alive and crush all the bones in their bodies. Sometimes he would pull their heads off, and sometimes he would hit them so hard that their backs snapped like dry twigs – Oh! There was no end to the terrible things he could do. But one day, Carnifex got out of his bed in Hell to find there was not a single child left.

'What I need is a regular supply,' he said to himself. So he went to a country that he knew was ruled by an exceedingly vain king. He found him in his bathroom (which contained over a hundred baths) and said to him: 'How would you like to fly?'

'Very much indeed,' said the King, 'but what do you want in return, Carnifex?'

'Oh . . . nothing very much,' replied Carnifex, 'and I will enable you to fly as high as you want, as fast as you want, simply by raising your arms like this,' and he showed the King how he could fly.

'I should indeed like to be able to do that,' thought the King to himself. 'But what is it you want in return, Carnifex?' he asked aloud.

'Look! Have a try!' replied Carnifex. 'Put out your arms – that's right, and now off you go!'

The King put out his arms, and immediately floated into the air. Then he soared over the roofs and chimney-pots of the city. He went higher and higher, until he was above the clouds, and he flew like a bird on a summer's day. Then he landed back beside the devil and said:

'But what is it you want in return, Carnifex?'

'Oh, nothing very much,' replied Carnifex. 'Just give me one small child every day, and you shall be able to fly – just like that.'

Now the King was indeed very anxious to be able to fly – just like that – but he knew the terrible things that Carnifex did to small children, so he shook his head.

'But there are thousands of children in your kingdom,' replied Carnifex. 'I shall only take one a day – your people will hardly notice.'

The King thought long and hard about this, for he knew it was an evil thing, but the idea of walking anywhere, now he'd tasted the thrill of flying, seemed to him so slow and dull that in the end he agreed. And from that day on he could fly – just like that.

To begin with all his subjects were very impressed. The first time he took to the air, a great crowd gathered in the main square and stood there open-mouthed as they watched their king spread out his arms, rise into the air, and then soar up beyond the clouds and out of sight. Then he swooped down again and flew low over their heads, while they all clapped and cheered.

But after a few months it became such a common sight to see their king flying up over the city that they ceased to think anything of it. In fact some of them even began to resent it. And every day some poor family would find that one of their children had been taken by Carnifex the devil.

Now the King's youngest daughter had a favourite doll that was so lifelike that she loved it and treated it just as if it were a real live baby. And she was in the habit of stealing into the King's bathroom (when he wasn't looking) to bath this doll in one of his baths. Well it so happened that she was doing this on the very day that the King made his pact with Carnifex, and thus she overheard every word that passed between them.

Naturally she was terrified by what she had heard, but because girls were not reckoned much of in that country in those days, and because she was the least and most insignificant of all his daughters, she had not dared tell anyone what had happened.

One day, however, Carnifex came and took the King's own favourite son.

The King busied himself in his counting-house, and would not say a word. Later that day he went off for a long flight, and did not return until well after dark. But the boy's mother was so overcome with grief that she took to her bed and seemed likely to die.

Then the youngest daughter came to her, as always clutching her favourite doll, and told her all she knew.

At once the Queen's grief turned to anger against the King. But she was a shrewd woman, and she knew that if she went to the King and complained, he would – as like as not – have her head chopped off before she could utter another word. So, instead, she dressed herself as a beggarwoman, and, taking her youngest daughter with her, crept out of the palace at dead of night.

Then she went about the kingdom, far and wide, begging her way. And everywhere she went, she got her youngest daughter to stand on a stool, still clutching her favourite doll (which everyone thought was real) and tell her story. And everyone who heard the tale said: 'So that's how the King can fly!' And they were all filled with anger against the King.

Eventually all the people from all the corners of the realm came to the King to protest. They gathered in the main square, and the King hovered above them looking distinctly uneasy.

'You are not worthy to be our king!' the people cried. 'You have sacrificed our very children just so that you can fly!'

The King fluttered up a little higher, so he was just out of reach, and then he ordered them all to be quiet, and called out: 'Carnifex! Where are you?'

There was a flash and a singeing smell, and Carnifex the devil appeared, sitting on top of the fountain in the middle of the square.

At once a great cry went up from the crowd – something between fear and anger – but Carnifex shouted: 'Listen! I understand how you feel!'

The people were rather taken aback by these words, and one or two of them began to think that perhaps Carnifex wasn't such a bad fellow after all. Some of the ladies even began to notice that he was quite handsome – in his devilish sort of way . . . But the King's youngest daughter stood up on her stool, and cried out: 'He's a devil! Don't listen to him!'

'Quite, quite,' said Carnifex, licking his lips at the sight of the little girl still clutching her favourite doll. 'But even I can sympathize with the tragic plight of parents who see their own beloved offspring snatched away in front of their very eyes.'

'Well, fancy that!' said more than once citizen to his neighbour.

'Whoever would have thought he would be such a gentleman . . .' whispered more than one housewife to her best friend.

'Don't listen!' shouted the King's youngest daughter.

'So I'll tell you what I'll do,' said Carnifex, never taking his beady eyes off the little girl clutching what he thought was a small baby. 'I'll give you some compensation for your tragic losses. I will let you *all* fly – just like that!' And he pointed to the King, who flew up and down a bit and then looped-the-loop, just to show them all what it was like.

And there was not a single one of those good people who wasn't filled with an almost unbearable desire to join him in the air.

'Don't listen to him!' shouted the little girl. 'He'll want your children!'

'All I ask,' said Carnifex in his most wheedling voice, 'is for one tiny . . . weeny . . . little child a day. Surely that's not too much to ask?'

And, you know, perhaps there were one or two there who were so besotted with the desire to fly that they might have agreed, had not a remarkable thing happened. The King's youngest daughter suddenly stood up on tiptoe, and held up her favourite doll so that all the crowd could see, and she cried out: 'Look! This is what he'll do to your children!' And with that, she hurled the doll, which she loved so dearly, right into Carnifex's lap.

Well, of course, this was too much for the devil. He thought it was a real live baby, and he had its head off and all its limbs torn apart before you could say 'Rabbits!'

And when the crowd saw Carnifex apparently tearing a small baby to pieces (for none of them knew it was just a doll) they came to their senses at once. They gave an angry cry, and converged on Carnifex where he crouched, with his face all screwed up in disgust, spitting out bits of china and stuffing.

And I don't know what they would have done if they'd laid hold of him, but before they could, Carnifex had leapt from the fountain right onto the back of the flying king, and with a cry of rage and disappointment, he rode him down to Hell where they both belonged.

And, after that, the people gave the youngest daughter a new doll that was just as lifelike as the previous one, and she was allowed to bath it in the King's bathroom any day she wanted.

As for Carnifex, he returned every year to try and induce the people to give up just one child a day to him. But no matter what he offered them, they never forgot what they had seen him do that day, and so they refused, and he had to return empty-handed.

And all this happened hundreds and hundreds of years ago, and Carnifex never did think of anything that could persuade them.

But listen! You may think that Carnifex was a terrible devil, and you may think that the flying king was a terrible man for giving those poor children to Carnifex just so that he could fly. But I shall tell you something even more astonishing, and that is that in this very day, in this very land where you and I live, we allow not one . . . not two . . . not three . . . but twenty children to have their heads smashed or their backs broken or to be crushed alive every day – and not even so that we can fly, but just so that we can ride about in things we call motor cars.

If I'd read that in a fairy tale, I wouldn't have believed it – would you?

THE DANCING HORSE

A FARMER WAS WALKING DOWN THE ROAD one day, when he saw the most extraordinary sight. One of his horses, who should have been grazing in the field with all the other horses, was dancing.

The farmer rubbed his eyes, and then he looked again, as the horse skipped around the field on two legs, turning pirouettes and wheeling and bowing and curtsying around and around the field.

Eventually the farmer yelled to the horse: 'Hey! What do you think you're doing?'

And the horse replied: 'I hear this music in my head that makes me want to dance.'

And on it went, round and around the field.

Well, the farmer said to himself: 'People would pay a lot to see such an extraordinary sight as a dancing horse!'

So he took the horse to market, and charged people a penny to come and see it. When everyone had assembled, the town fiddler played a jig on his fiddle, and the farmer led out his dancing horse.

But the horse just stood there and didn't dance a single step.

Well, of course, the audience booed and the farmer had to give

them their money back. And when they'd gone, he turned on the horse and said: 'What's the matter? Why didn't you dance?'

'I didn't feel like it,' replied the horse. 'I couldn't hear the music in my head.'

'Didn't *feel* like it!' exclaimed the farmer. 'Listen here! You've made me a laughing-stock! I'll not feed you again – not so much as a single oat – until you dance!'

Then he took a stick and beat the horse.

Then, once again, the farmer gathered a crowd, and they each paid a penny to see the wonderful dancing horse. Once again the fiddler played a jig, but once again the horse didn't dance a single step. It was so miserable, it just stood there all the time the fiddler played.

Well, of course, the farmer was more furious than ever. He turned on the horse and shouted at it: 'Listen to me! Either you dance, or I'll sell you to the glue factory, where you'll be boiled up to make glue!'

The horse was naturally very frightened by this. And so, when the farmer once again summoned the crowd, and they'd paid their pennies, and the fiddler played his jig, the poor horse tried to dance. But its heart was so heavy that its feet were like lead, and the noise of the fiddler's jig blotted out all the sound of the music in its head.

Pretty soon the crowd started jeering again.

'Call that a dancing horse?'

'My cat dances better than that!' they yelled, and demanded their money back.

The farmer turned on the horse, white with anger, for he'd never touched so much money before, and now he was having to give it all back.

'You lazy, ungrateful creature!' he shouted at the horse. And there and then he took it and sold it to the glue factory.

Now it so happened that the day was Sunday and the glue factory was not working until the next morning. So the horse was put into a field to wait.

When it found itself back in a field of grass, it was so happy to be away from all those staring faces and its cruel owner, that it

When it found itself back in a field of grass, it was so happy to be away from all those staring faces and its cruel owner, that it started to hear the music in its head once more. And once again it started to dance around the field – a sad but graceful dance.

And there, I believe, it is still dancing to this day, for the owner of the glue factory happened to look out of his window and saw the horse dancing so beautifully in the field below. And he said to himself: 'Clearly this is a mare that dances for love not money.'

And he let her dance in that field as long as she lived and heard the music in her head.

MACK AND MICK

NCE UPON A TIME THERE WERE TWO BROTHERS who could never agree about anything. They argued about what to have for breakfast. They argued about what to have for lunch. They even argued about which side of the bed they should sleep on.

One day Mack said to Mick: 'I can't stand living with you another day. I'm leaving!'

'No you're not!' exclaimed Mick. 'I can't stand living with *you* another day. *I'm* the one that's leaving!'

Well, they argued and they argued and they argued about which one of them was to leave, but they just couldn't agree. So, in the end, they both left.

They marched along the road that led to the great wide world, and when they reached the crossroads, Mick turned to Mack and said: 'Goodbye, Mack. I'm taking this road that leads to the sea.'

'No you're not!' shouted Mack. 'That's my road! You'll have to take the road to the hills.'

Well, they stood there arguing for about an hour, but they couldn't agree about which road the other was taking. So in the end, they both set off along the same road. And pretty soon they came to the sea.

'Ah!' said Mick. 'I can't wait to put an ocean between us two.'

'Neither can I,' said Mack.

When they got to the harbour, however, they found there was only one ship due to sail.

Could they agree which of them was to take it? No, of course they couldn't.

'I was the first to say I wanted to put an ocean between us,' said Mick.

'But I was the first to say I wanted to leave!' exclaimed Mack. So they stood on the quay, and they argued and they argued and they argued – until they saw the ship weighing its anchor, and they both had to leap aboard – otherwise they'd both have missed it.

As soon as they got on board they started arguing again, and they didn't stop once.

Their crewmates quickly grew tired of them.

'Don't you two ever agree about anything?' the other sailors asked.

'No,' said Mack and Mick together. 'Never!' And they carried on arguing about which of them felt the more seasick.

Eventually the Captain could stand it no longer, and he made them sleep down in the hold of the ship, away from the rest of the crew.

But, even down in the hold, the entire ship's company could still hear Mack and Mick arguing and arguing and arguing as bad as ever.

So the Captain hauled them up on deck in front of the whole crew, and said: 'We are all sick and tired of your constant bickering. It sets our teeth on edge all day, and it keeps us awake all night. So here's what I'm going to do. Either you two stop arguing, or I'm going to throw you off the ship at the next desert island we come to.'

Mack immediately turned to Mick. 'See?' he said. 'This is all your fault.'

'What are you talking about?' exclaimed Mick. 'I wouldn't be arguing if it weren't for you! It's all *your* fault.'

And they were taken down into the hold again still arguing and arguing.

Well, the ship sailed on for seven days and seven nights, until one morning the lookout shouted: 'Land ahead!'

The Captain looked through his telescope and saw a desert island on the horizon. Once again he summoned Mack and Mick up onto the deck in front of the whole crew, and he said: 'I'll give you

one last chance. If you can keep yourselves from arguing as long as that desert island is in sight, you can stay on board. But if you have so much as one argument, I'll throw you overboard, and you'll have to live out the rest of your lives on that island.'

Well, Mack looked at Mick, and Mick looked at Mack. Then Mack said: 'Well, Mick, if anyone starts an argument – it'll be you.'

'That's a laugh, Mack!' exclaimed Mick. 'You're much more like-ly to start an argument than I am!'

And with that, of course, they started arguing again, and they didn't stop until the ship reached the desert island, and the two of them were thrown overboard and they had to swim for the shore.

Mack and Mick stood on the shore of the desert island, and watched their ship disappear over the horizon.

'Well this is a pretty how's yer father!' said Mack. 'We try to get away from each other . . .'

'And we end up marooned together on a desert island,' said Mick.

'Exactly,' said Mack.

There wasn't much to eat on that desert island. For breakfast they managed to find two clams, so they ate one each. For lunch they managed to catch a dodo (I'm afraid it was the last one). Normally they would have argued about whether to roast or boil it, but as they didn't have any pots or pans they had no choice. They stuck it on a stick, and held it over the fire. And it tasted pretty good.

As night began to fall, they broke branches off a tree and made themselves a rough shelter by the beach. There they sat together, looking out into the night sea, hoping their ship would return to pick them up. But it didn't. And they fell asleep, trying to remem-ber the names of the flowers that grew in their garden back home.

The next day, they searched the island and found a sparkling stream of fresh water. There they decided to build a house. Then they lit a fire at the top of the nearby hill to attract the attention of any ship that might pass by.

'We must make sure we keep it burning . . .' said Mick.

'Day and night,' said Mack.

But that night, as they sat down to a meal of fresh fish, they heard the wind begin to blow.

'Looks like there's going to be a storm,' said Mick.

'You're right,' said Mack. 'We'd better tie the roof on.'

So they tied the roof down with creepers from the forest, as the wind blew stronger and fiercer. Then the rain began to lash the island. Before long, Mick and Mack were cowering in their little log house, listening to the thunder breaking over their heads, and watching the bolts of lightning striking out of the sky.

Suddenly there was a terrible noise and the sound of breaking branches.

'Run!' cried Mick

'I am!' cried Mack.

And they ran as hard as they could out into the storm, just as a huge tree came crashing down on their log house, smashing it to pieces.

Still the wind blew even fiercer, and the rain lashed across their backs, and the water ran down their faces like sheets of tears.

'We must find shelter!' said Mick.

'Over there!' cried Mack. And they started running towards a cave. They reached the cave just as the wind began to turn into a hurricane. It blew away the remnants of their house as if it had been matchwood.

The lightning hit tree after tree, and fire swept across the island. Mack and Mick trembled, holding onto each other in the safety of the cave.

As day broke, the storm subsided, but as it did, their troubles redoubled. They awoke to a roar that made their blood run cold.

Mack and Mick both sat bolt upright, and stared in horror, for there in the mouth of the cave was a huge monster with a head as big as its own body. When it opened its jaws and roared again, both Mack and Mick thought they were going to tumble into it – its throat seemed so vast and deep.

The monster advanced into the cave, and looked from Mack to Mick and from Mick to Mack.

Mack backed away towards one side of the cave, and Mick backed towards the other, as the terrible creature took another step further into the cave. First it turned towards Mick and showed its razor-sharp teeth. Then it turned towards Mack and stretched out a razor-sharp claw.

'It can't make up its mind which of us looks tastiest!' cried Mick.

'Well let's not give it the chance to find out!' shouted Mack.

'Ready?' shouted Mick.

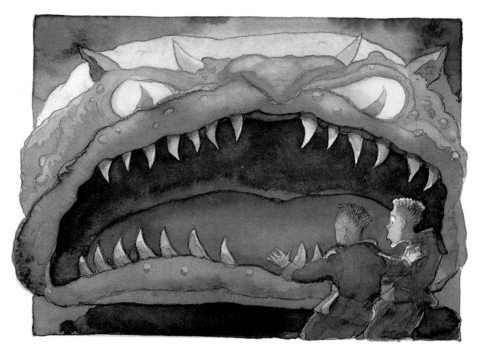

'Ready!' screamed Mack. And they both together sprinted for the entrance of the cave as fast as fear could take them. First the monster darted towards Mick, then it turned towards Mack, but by then Mack was out of the cave, and so was Mick!

'See you on the other side of the island!' shouted Mick.

'Right!' yelled Mack. And they both ran off in opposite directions, and the monster stood roaring in the cave mouth, hopping from one foot to the other, unable to decide whether to chase after Mick or chase after Mack.

So it was that Mack and Mick found themselves on separate sides of the island.

Mack found himself amongst quicksands and deep dark bogs that nearly sucked him down on several occasions . . . until he had the idea of tying branches to his feet so that he didn't sink in.

Mick found himself in a dark forest, infested with wild wolves. He armed himself as best he could with a stout stick and a knife, and pursued his way. But he could hear the wolves following him, and he could see their eyes glinting in the blackness of the forest.

Mick wished he had Mack with him to give him courage. And Mack wished he had Mick with him to help him every time he fell into a bog.

At length, however, they met up together on the other side of the island.

'Thank goodness!' cried Mick.

'It's good to see you!' cried Mack.

But no sooner had they hugged each other and done a little dance of joy, than an even worse calamity befell them!

They heard a terrible explosion above, and they looked up – in time to see the top blow off the volcano in the centre of the island and flames begin to shoot up into the sky. A great cloud of soot shot up into the air and covered the sun. The next minute, they saw molten rock bubbling up over the rim of the crater and down the sides of the mountain towards them.

'The sea!' cried Mack.

'Here we go again!' yelled Mick, and they both plunged into the sea, and started to swim . . . But even as they hit the water, the white-hot molten lava flowed over the shore.

And they had swum no further than the shadow of the mountain at mid-morn, when the lava reached the sea. The air was filled with an ear-splitting hiss, and the island disappeared in a cloud of steam, as the water started to bubble.

'Help!' yelled Mick. 'The sea's boiling!'

'We'll be cooked – like the ogre in the next story!' cried Mack. And they both swam as hard as they could, until – as fate would have it – they reached cooler water. But the smiles on their faces quickly disappeared as they looked around them:

'Sharks!' screamed Mick.

'I don't believe it!' screamed Mack. But sure enough, they could see sharks circling all around them.

'Look out!' screamed Mack. 'Here comes one!'

'What a way to go!' yelled Mack. 'After all we've been through!'

But, just at very that moment, white-hot ash started to fall out of the sky.

'Dive!' yelled Mick. And the two brothers dived, while the hot ash fell on the sharks, and the sharks were so confused they thrashed the sea, and then turned on their tails and swam off.

Some time later, Mack and Mick found themselves clinging to a tree trunk, on which they drifted for two days and two nights. On the third day, however, the breeze blew them onto a little sandy island with two trees in the middle of it.

They lay there gasping, and wondered what else could possibly happen to them, until they both fell asleep from exhaustion, and didn't wake up until the next day.

When they opened their eyes they blinked and looked again, but – sure enough – they could see something on the horizon.

'It's a sail!' exclaimed Mick.

'We're saved!' exclaimed Mack. And the two of them jumped around the little island for joy.

But as the sail got closer, they began to realize it was a very strange sail indeed. In the first place it was big – bigger than any sail either of them had ever seen. The second strange thing about it was that it appeared to be made out of fish-skins, for one side was plain and the other was covered in silver scales. But – without a shadow of doubt – the very strangest thing about the sail was the fact that there was no ship under it. It was simply a giant sail of fish-skins, flying across the water.

And when it reached the island, something even stranger happened. It blew over the heads of Mack and Mick, until it reached

214

half-way across the little island, and there the two trees caught it in their palms – as if they'd been hands – and held it tight.

The sail of fish-skins billowed out as the wind filled it once more, and then *the strangest thing of all happened* . . . The island itself began to move . . . It started to glide across the water like a ship – blown by the wind caught in its fish-skin sail.

Mack and Mick were so surprised and so terrified all at the same time that they held onto each other tight.

Well, the wind blew the sail, and the island sped through the seas until finally they saw ahead of them the shoreline of their own country. As they approached, the wind died down, and the little island started to sink beneath the waves, so Mack and Mick both had to swim for it, until they arrived back at the harbour from which they had first set out.

Mack and Mick crawled ashore, and as they did so they heard a voice. There, standing on a rock, was the Captain of the ship in which they'd first sailed.

'Well?' he said. 'What happened to you?'

Mack and Mick looked at each other and said: 'We've been *bored stiff!*'

And they told the Captain their adventures.

'What!' exclaimed the Captain, when they'd finished. 'Your house was destroyed by a typhoon! You were attacked by a monster! Beset by quicksands and wild beasts! You were caught under an erupting volcano! Attacked by sharks! And brought home by a magic sail! How can you possibly call that "boring"?'

'Tell him,' said Mack.

'No, you tell him.' said Mick.

'Well,' they both said together, 'we were so hard put to it that we didn't have time for a single argument!'

'But that's marvellous!' exclaimed the Captain.

'No it isn't!' replied Mack and Mick. 'Because the one thing we learnt is that we *like* arguing!'

And with that, the two brothers took their leave of the Captain, and made their way back home.

There they continued arguing to their hearts' content.

After all, the world would be a very dull place indeed if we all agreed about absolutely everything, wouldn't it?

THE SLOW OGRE

HERE WAS ONCE AN OGRE who loved to eat . . . CABBAGES! And he loved to eat . . . SAUSAGES! And he loved to eat . . . RADISHES! But best of all . . . absolutely best of all . . . he loved to eat . . . PEOPLE!

But there's nothing so extraordinary about that, because that's what ogres do. None the less, he was a very extraordinary ogre – and I shall tell you why. He was very . . . very . . . very . . . incredibly . . . unbelievably . . . wonderfully SLOW!

When he got up in the morning, it took him eight hours to get out of bed. It would take him nine hours to walk downstairs, and then it would take him ten hours to boil his breakfast of human heads and gentlemen's socks. Then it would take him fifteen hours to eat it. It would take him twenty hours to get up from the table, burp, and put on his Ogres' Boots (which are, by the way, very expensive). And it would take him another twenty-three hours to walk to his front door.

Now, as I expect you know, there are only twenty-four hours in a day, so it had already taken him three days, and all he'd done was get up and have breakfast.

He was, as you can see, a very slow ogre indeed.

Being so slow was a slight problem when it came to stealing . . . CABBAGES! out of people's gardens.

And being so slow was a slight problem when it came to snitching

216

... SAUSAGES! out of butchers' shops. And being so slow made it quite difficult when it came to rustling . . . RADISHES! out of people's salad bowls. But you may well wonder how on earth . . . how on *earth* . . . such a slow ogre could . . . even in a thousand years . . . ever manage to catch *people* to put in his breakfast stew.

Well, here's this Ogre getting up this morning. It's already taken him six days to put his coat on and leave his lair. It's taken him three weeks to walk down the road, and he's just arrived at the house of a very rich gentleman.

It's taken him half a day to knock at the gates. In the meantime nobody has come in or gone out, because . . . well you wouldn't, would you, if you had an ogre as tall as three men standing outside your gates?

But now the Gatekeeper shouts through the letterbox: 'Go away! We don't want any ogres around here, thank you very much.'

'Oh! I'm not an ogre,' says the Ogre. 'I'm just a poor fellow who has grown too big through eating . . . CABBAGES! and eating . . . SAUSAGES! and eating . . . RADISHES! and . . .'

'And?' asks the Gatekeeper.

'And nothing else,' replies the Ogre.

'I don't believe you,' cries the Gatekeeper.

'But look at me,' says the Ogre. 'I'm so slow, how could I possibly be an ogre?'

So the Gatekeeper looks out of the window, and he sees the Ogre moving so slowly . . . so extraordinarily slowly . . . that he barely seems to be moving at all.

'Anybody could run away from me before I'd got the chance to grab 'em and rip off their heads and boil 'em up for a delicious breakfast stew . . . I mean a disgusting breakfast stew,' says the Ogre.

'That's true,' says the Gatekeeper. 'Maybe I'll open the gate.'

But the Gatekeeper's Daughter says: *'Daddy! Don't let him in!'*

So the Gatekeeper shouts back to the Ogre: 'But before I open the gate, first tell me what you want.'

And the Ogre replies: 'Oh! I just want to do an honest day's work, in return for a dinner of . . . CABBAGES! and . . . SAUSAGES! and . . . RADISHES! and . . .'

'And?' says the Gatekeeper.

'And absolutely nothing else at all,' replies the Ogre.

'Honestly?' asks the Gatekeeper.

'Honestly,' replies the Ogre.

'Well, in that case, maybe I'll open the gate,' says the Gatekeeper. 'We could use someone as big as you to put up the Christmas holly.'

But the Gatekeeper's Daughter cries: *'Daddy! Don't let him in!'*

'I'll tell you what,' says the Ogre. 'I'll put up the Christmas holly and I'll put on a show for all the little kiddies.'

'Well that would be very nice,' says the Gatekeeper, 'but maybe I should just check with the Master of the House.'

So he goes to the Master of the House, and the Master of the House says: 'He sounds like an ogre to me.'

'But he says he'll put up the holly and put on a nice Christmas show for the children,' says the Gatekeeper.

'Oh! That would be very nice,' says the Master of the House. 'Maybe we should let him in after all.'

But the Gatekeeper's Daughter yells: 'Looks like an ogre – *is* an ogre! *Daddy! Don't let him in!*'

'What's she doing here?' cries the Master of the House. 'I don't want to be told what I can and can't do in my own house!' And he has the Gatekeeper's Daughter trussed up like a turkey and locked in the Tall Tower.

Then he and the Gatekeeper go to the gate and look through the letterbox.

'Hmm,' says the Master of the House. 'He may put on a very nice show for the children, but he's as tall as three men and he's got razor-sharp ogre's teeth. Maybe we shouldn't let him in after all.'

'Oh,' says the Ogre. 'I'm only big because I eat . . . CABBAGES! and . . . SAUSAGES! and . . . . RADISHES! and . . . '

'And?' says the Master of the House.

'Absolutely nothing else at all,' says the Gatekeeper.

'That's right,' says the Ogre. 'And my teeth are only razor-sharp because I like whistling!' And he whistled a little tune.

'Well, in that case, maybe we'll let you in,' says the Master of the House.

But the Gatekeeper's Daughter shouts down from the window in the Tall Tower: *'Daddy! Don't let him in!'*

Meanwhile the Mistress of the House has come out to see what all the shouting's about. She looks out through the letterbox and says:

'Well, he may put on a very nice show for the children, and he may put up the holly very tastefully, but he still looks like an ogre to me.'

'But he's so slow,' says the Master of the House.

'He'd never be able to catch any of us,' says the Gatekeeper.

'That's right,' says the Ogre.

'Well, in that case,' says the Mistress of the House, 'maybe he can come in.'

And, from right up in the Tall Tower, comes the voice of the Gatekeeper's Daughter: '*DADDY! DON'T LET HIM IN!*'

But the Gatekeeper has already drawn back the first bolt on the gate. And, because she's up in the Tall Tower, the Gatekeeper's Daughter can see the Ogre, on the other side of the gate, starting to lick his chops. So she yells down: 'He's going to boil your heads for his breakfast stew!'

'Fiddle-de-dee!' says the Ogre.

'Fiddle-de-dee!' says the Master of the House.

'Fiddle-de-dee!' says the Mistress of the House.

And the Gatekeeper draws back the second bolt.

Now the Gatekeeper's Daughter can see the Ogre starting to drool and slobber at the mouth.

'He's going to catch you all and pull off your heads!' she cries.

'Oh! Somebody shut her up!' says the Mistress of the House. 'Even if he were an ogre – he'd never be able to catch any of us.'

'That's right,' says the Ogre, licking his lips.

'That's right,' says the Gatekeeper. 'I'm looking forward to the Christmas show.' And he pulls back the third bolt.

Now all that separates them from the Slow Ogre is one small latch. And the Gatekeeper's Daughter can't shout out anything, because someone's tied a neckerchief round her mouth. But she's thinking: '*Daddy! Don't let him in!*'

And the Ogre's drooling and slobbering and licking his lips, and the Gatekeeper's just about to lift the latch, when he stops and says: 'Wait a minute! My daughter's a very smart girl. She's usually right about most things.'

'But she's only a child,' says the Master of the House.

'And she's still got her hair in braids,' says the Mistress of the House.

'That's true,' says the Gatekeeper, and he lifts the latch, and the Ogre bursts in and grabs everybody in the house – except for the Gatekeeper's Daughter, because she's locked up in the Tall Tower. Then he stuffs them all into the big black bag that he always carries, and races off back to his lair – for you must know that the Slow Ogre can move *surprisingly* quickly when it's a question of making his breakfast stew.

Now, the Gatekeeper's Daughter is still trussed up like a turkey, but she manages to wriggle free. She rips the neckerchief from her mouth. Then she takes the rope with which she'd been tied, hangs it out of the window and slides down it . . . right to the ground.

Then she runs back into her father's bedroom, stuffs all his smelliest old socks into a pillowcase, and races off to the Ogre's lair.

The Ogre's got a cauldron of water coming up to the boil, and he's got all the people locked up in his great iron meat-safe. And they're all moaning and crying and blaming each other for not having taken more notice of the Gatekeeper's Daughter.

The Gatekeeper's Daughter, meanwhile, has marched straight up to the Ogre's front door and knocked on it. (That's a very brave thing to do, and I don't think even she would have done it if she hadn't had a very good plan.)

The Ogre's just thinking: 'Hm! The water's coming to the boil, so I can pop in a few heads . . . but first I need a bit of seasoning. I'd better borrow some of the gentlemen's socks . . .' (I hope you haven't forgotten that he always liked gentlemen's socks in his breakfast stew – the smellier the better.)

So he's just about to open the meat-safe and grab all the gentlemen to see who's got the smelliest socks, when he hears the knock on the door.

'S'funny!' says the Ogre to himself. 'Nobody likes me. Nobody ever comes to visit me. Nobody ever knocks on my door.'

But he goes to the door anyway (only it takes him an hour or so because he's starting to get a bit slower again) and he opens it.

There's the Gatekeeper's Daughter, holding the pillowcase full of her father's smelliest socks.

'Something smells good!' exclaims the Ogre. And he's just going to grab the Gatekeeper's Daughter to pop her into his mouth as a pre-breakfast snack, when she opens up the pillowcase, and the Ogre can't help sticking his head inside, because the Gatekeeper's socks smell so good.

Then, quick as a flash, she ties the pillowcase around his neck with the rope. And the Ogre starts flailing around, going: 'Oh! I can't see! It's all gone dark! Oh! But it's so delicious! The smell is like . . . it's like . . . heaven . . . yum, yum, yum . . .'

And while he's blundering around, getting slower and slower, unable to decide whether to take the pillowcase off his head, so he can see, or to keep it on his head, so he can go on smelling the socks, the Gatekeeper's Daughter - quick as a flash – opens up the Ogre's meat-safe and lets everyone out. They all dash for the door and run off as far away as possible from the Ogre's lair.

The Ogre, meanwhile, has decided to sit down in his favourite cosy chair, while he takes the pillowcase off his head – only he's moving *much* slower by this time. The Gatekeeper's Daughter sees what he's going to do, and – in the time it takes him to get over to his favourite cosy chair and start to sit down – she's switched it, so that instead of sitting down in his favourite cosy chair, the Ogre sits down right in the cauldron of boiling water!

By the time the Ogre's realized what's happened, and before he can get the pillowcase off his head and get himself out again . . . he's cooked – right through! And so are the socks!

When the Gatekeeper's Daughter gets home, her father makes a great fuss of her and says: 'In future, Chloë, we'll always listen to you.' And the Master of the House and the Mistress of the House all nod in agreement. And Chloë looks at them all smiling down at her and she says to herself: 'Hmm! I wonder if you will?'

THE FAST ROAD

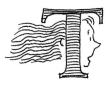HERE USED TO BE ONE ROAD that got you to wherever you wanted to go much quicker than any other road. It looked like a perfectly ordinary road. But the moment you stepped onto it, you got wherever it was you wanted to go to . . . That is if you knew where you wanted to go. Unfortunately most folk weren't absolutely sure. They liked the idea of getting somewhere so much that they often stepped onto the road before they'd really decided where it was that they wanted to end up.

And – when you did that – this is what would happen:

You'd step on the road and start walking. For a moment it would seem just like walking along any old road, but then, as you walked on a bit further, you'd find the countryside slipping past as though you were running – even though you were still just walking. The next minute, the countryside would be speeding past – as if you were galloping on a horse, and before you knew where you were, there would be just a blur on either side of you, as the world flashed past quicker than the eye could see . . .

And if you didn't know where you were going, it would just go on getting faster and faster and faster until . . . all of a sudden! It would stop.

And when you looked around you, you would see this:

Nothing.

Nothing to your left. Nothing to your right. Nothing in front of you. Nothing behind you. Nothing . . . Nothing, that is, except for people wandering around quite lost.

Well, here is the story of a girl, named Poppy, who stepped onto the Fast Road, and who didn't have the first clue where she was heading.

The moment she stepped onto the Fast Road, she had an idea that something was going to happen, but she couldn't imagine what.

To begin with, of course, it was just like walking along any other road, but very soon she noticed the countryside slipping past faster than she was walking. Then, before she could work out what was happening, she found the countryside whizzing past her – as if she were galloping on a horse! And the next minute, it was all a blur – flashing past her on both sides – so fast that she couldn't make out anything. The fields were just a blur of green. Cows and sheep were like stripes of brown and white. It all went faster and faster and faster until . . . all of a sudden! . . . It stopped.

Poppy almost fell over herself, it was so sudden. But she shook her head, and looked around. And do you know what she could see? That's right . . .

Nothing.

Nothing to her left. Nothing to her right. Nothing in front of her. Nothing behind her. There were plenty of people wandering around, but she could see they were quite lost.

Poppy picked herself up and said: 'Well, I wonder where I am?' Then she stepped off the road and walked across the flat nothing-ness towards the horizon.

After a while, she saw something in the distance, and as she got nearer, she saw that it was a strange building. It was as tall as a mountain and it was full of people. But the really extraordinary thing was that the building didn't have an inside! It was all outside!

At the bottom, was a man behind a desk.

'Can you tell me where I am?' asked Poppy.

'This is Nowhere In Particular,' replied the man. 'Would you like to sign the Guest Book?'

'I'll not sign the book,' said Poppy, 'because I'm not stopping, but is it all right if I look around?'

'Help yourself,' said the man. 'There's nothing particular here.'

So Poppy climbed the stairs that led all round the outside of the building.

On the first floor, she met a family who were sitting on stools looking at a stone.

'What on earth are you doing?' asked Poppy.

'We're stone-watching,' replied the whole family, without taking their eyes off the stone.

'Stone-watching?' said Poppy. 'I've never heard of such a thing. Isn't it extremely boring?'

'Oh no!' exclaimed the father.

'But stones don't *do* anything,' said Poppy.

'But this one *might!*' exclaimed the mother.

'And we'll be the first to see it when it does!' exclaimed the children. 'Why don't you come and join us?'

But Poppy shook her head. 'I may not know where I'm going,' she said, 'but you'll not catch me watching stones!'

And on she climbed, up the staircase that wound around the outside of the strange building.

A little further up, she found a man with a broom, sweeping the floor as hard as he could.

'Excuse me,' said Poppy, 'can you tell me where I'm going?'

'I'll tell you just as soon as I've finished getting this room clean,' he said, without once raising his head.

'But it's already as clean as clean can be!' exclaimed Poppy.

'Oh no!' said the man with the broom. 'Look! There's another speck of dust there!'

'Well,' said Poppy, 'I can't wait around for you to finish making a clean room clean.'

'But look!' exclaimed the man. 'If you took that other broom, we'd get it done in half the time!'

'Sorry,' said Poppy. 'Half of never is still never!'

And with that she climbed on her way, up the staircase that led around the outside of the strange house.

Well, up she went, up and up, until finally she reached a place that was full of people lying on their backs with their mouths wide open.

'Excuse me!' said Poppy. 'I'm trying to find out where I'm going. Can you help me?'

But the people just lay on their backs, and they didn't close their mouths for a minute. But one of them said: ' 'Ooee 'ank 'elk 'oo. 'Orry.'

' 'Ooee 'ank 'elk 'oo?' said Poppy. 'Oh! You mean "We can't help you!"'

' 'At's 'ight,' said the man.

'Well, just tell me what you're doing, and then I'll get on my way,' said Poppy.

' 'Ooee're 'atching grocks og 'ain 'orter,' said the man.

' ''Ain 'orter?' said Poppy. 'Oh! Rain water! But it's not raining.'

' 'Ick 'ill 'oon,' said the man.

'Not today,' said Poppy.

'It's 'udderly 'orter!' said the man.

'I'm sure it's lovely water,' replied Poppy, 'but I'm on my way.'

Well, she didn't need to climb much further, before she suddenly found herself right on the top of the strange building. And from there she could see for miles and miles around. And right in the very far distance, she could see a little house, where a woman was working in the kitchen.

'Wait a minute! That's where I'm going!' she exclaimed.

And she ran down that building as fast as she possibly could, past the Mouths-Wide-Open, past the Man with the Broom, past the Stone-Watchers, and past the Man at the Gate. Then she ran and she didn't stop until she'd reached the Fast Road.

'I'm going home!' she shouted, and she started to walk. And before she'd taken a couple of steps . . . there she was – home!

'Well,' said Poppy, as she helped her mother prepare supper, 'at least I know where I'm going in future – I'm only going where I can do something useful! And I'll tell you another thing . . . I also know where I'm not going! And – what's more – I'm never taking the Fast Road to either place!'

THE SONG THAT BROUGHT HAPPINESS

 WANDERING MINSTREL once composed a magical song that made everyone who heard it glad. No matter how many cares weighed them down, this song made them forget them. No matter how miserable their lives, all those who listened to this song felt happy again. But the happiness, of course, only lasted as long as the song. As soon as the song ceased, everyone's cares returned.

The minstrel wandered around from country to country, singing his magical song, and bringing happiness to people for as long as he sang it. One day, however, he sang it at the court of an evil old king, who made all his subjects as miserable as he was himself. Well, the moment the minstrel began to sing his magical song, it was as if a shadow had been lifted from the entire court. Everyone forgot the injustices and humiliations that were daily heaped upon them by the evil old King, and felt a happiness that they had forgotten existed. Even the old King himself started to smile at those around him, and for the first time in years he felt peace in his shrivelled old heart.

As soon as the song stopped, however, the deepest gloom returned to the palace.

The minstrel bowed and began to take his leave of the company, but the evil old King stopped him.

'Play that song again!' commanded the King.

'Excuse me, Your Majesty,' replied the minstrel. 'Nothing would give me greater pleasure, but I have a rule that I only play my songs once – lest I outstay my welcome.'

'I order you to play that song again,' said the King. 'Otherwise I will have you thrown into prison.'

So there was nothing for it – the minstrel had to play the song once more, and once more the gloom lifted from the palace, and everyone felt happy.

When he had finished, the minstrel once again began to take his leave, but again the old King stopped him.

'Keep singing!' he ordered. 'I will tell you when you may stop.'

So the poor minstrel was forced to go on singing the magical song that made everyone happy, over and over again, until everyone started to grow sleepy. Heads nodded and fell onto the tables, and finally the old King himself fell asleep over his plate.

Then the minstrel tried to leave once more, but the guards barred his way.

'The King has not said you can stop singing yet,' they said, and they showed him the sharp blades of their swords.

So, once again, the minstrel had to sing the magical song, over and over again, and carry on – even though weary himself – until everyone in the palace had fallen asleep. Then he tried to steal out of the great hall.

But, as luck would have it, just as he was closing the door behind him, the old King awoke.

'Come back!' roared the King. 'I never want to feel miserable again! You must carry on playing that magical song for me, day and night!' And he appointed guards to stand by the minstrel to see that he did.

And so the wandering minstrel was compelled to remain in the palace, continually singing his magical song that made everyone feel happy.

But the minstrel did not feel happy himself. 'I cannot carry on singing this song over and over again,' he said to himself. 'I must stop to eat . . . besides, my voice will grow hoarse.'

But day and night the guards stood over him, and he had no choice but to go on singing.

Well, this went on for three days and three nights. On the fourth day, a string on his harp broke.

'I cannot play the song any more,' the minstrel said to the King. 'I don't have all the notes.'

'Carry on!' ordered the King.

On the fifth day, the minstrel's voice went hoarse, so that he could only croak, and all the magic went from the song.

'Your Majesty!' gasped the poor minstrel. 'Now surely you will let me stop.'

'Play on!' growled the King.

So the poor minstrel had to play on – even though he could no longer play the right notes nor sing the song, and everyone grew heartily sick of the dreadful noise he was making. Yet still the King would by no means allow him to stop.

In the end, the minstrel could stand it no longer. He flung his harp at the King's head, and it struck him right on the temple, so that he fell down dead. As soon as he did, of course, the guards drew their swords and cut down the unfortunate minstrel, and the magical song was lost for ever.

So it was that the song that brought happiness ended up bringing misery – all through one man's greed.

TOUCH THE MOON

 LONG, LONG TIME AGO, a king once decided to build a tower. 'I shall build this Tower so high,' he said, 'that from its topmost battlements – if you stand on tiptoe – you will be able to touch the moon.'

'I fear,' said his Chief Architect, 'that there will not be enough stone in the whole country to build a tower so high.'

'Nonsense!' said the King. 'Get building.'

'I am afraid,' said his Chancellor, 'that there won't be enough gold in the Treasury to pay for such a building.'

'Nonsense!' said the King. 'Get taxing.'

'What is the point of being able to touch the moon?' asked his daughter.

But the King didn't hear her – he was far too busy organizing the laying of the foundations, the raising of the finances and the knocking-down of half his capital city to make way for the Tower.

The city itself was divided in two about the building of the Tower. Half the citizens thought it was a wonderful project. 'It is vital,' they said, 'that we are able to touch the moon before any of our rivals can.'

But the other half of the city (who were losing their homes and shops to make way for the Tower) were, naturally, much less enthusiastic. But even they were not against building the Tower altogether – they were just against building it in their half of the city.

'It will indeed be marvellous when we can touch the moon – just by standing on tiptoe,' they said. 'But it would make much more sense to build it on the other side of the city – the ground's higher there for a start!'

'But what is the point of touching the moon at all?' asked the King's Daughter again. But she might as well have been talking to a lump of wood. As a matter of fact, she was talking to a lump of wood! You see, the Princess had a secret . . . but I can't tell you what it was. Not just yet.

Well, they knocked down half the city, and, in its place, they started to build the gigantic Tower. The citizens who'd lost their homes had to camp outside the city wall, and they suffered in the cold winter. But no one was allowed to rebuild their house, because all the stone was needed for the Tower.

All the stone quarries in the land were ordered to send every stone they produced to help build the Tower. And the King's builders worked day and night – all through that winter and all through that summer, and, by the time winter came again, they'd built the first storey.

'The work must go faster than this!' exclaimed the King. 'Or we'll never be able to touch the moon – not even by standing on tiptoe!'

So the King gave orders that the work had to go twice as fast. No one was to take lunch breaks or tea breaks, and the mules pulling the carts had to walk twice as quickly.

And on they built – all through that winter. Soon the quarries ran out of stone, and they began digging new quarries in fields where animals used to graze.

And on they built, until by the end of that year, they'd finished the second storey.

'Loafers! Do-nothings! Time-wasters! Afternoon farmers!' exclaimed the King. 'We'll never be able to touch the moon at this rate!'

Then he gave orders that half of his subjects must give up their usual jobs, and work instead upon the Tower. And on the building went.

The countryside began to disappear as quarries took the place of farms. Food became scarce, and everybody in the land suffered.

'This is CRAZY!' shouted the King's Daughter. 'My dad's gone loony! He's ruining his own kingdom, and for what? Just so some idiots can stand on tiptoe and touch the moon!'

But the lumps of wood she was talking to didn't reply. They just lay there, the way that lumps of wood do.

'You've got more sense than my dad!' she exclaimed. 'And you're just two short planks!'

Meanwhile the building went on and on. The citizens suffered more and more each day, but they kept telling each other that it would be all worth it, once they could touch the moon.

Eventually they completed the third storey. But the King's coffers were now empty, there was scarcely any food, and life was miserable.

By the time the fourth storey had been completed, most of the kingdom had been carried away in carts as stone for the building. The green fields had disappeared, the woods and forests had all been chopped down, and all that was left was the Tower.

And now even the citizens themselves began to complain. They sent some representatives to the King, who fell on their knees in front of him, and said:

'O, King! Of course we all know the vital importance to our country of being able to touch the moon, but we have hardly anything left to eat, the kingdom has been turned into one vast quarry, and life has become intolerable. Please may we stop?'

But the King just became furious, and he ordered his army to compel every single person in the kingdom to work on the Tower.

And so they built the fifth storey.

It was at this moment that the King's Daughter, who was, by this time, a fine young girl of sixteen, said:

'I am going to put a stop to this nonsense once and for all.'

And now the time has come when I must tell you the Princess's secret. Only you mustn't tell anyone else because . . . well . . . she liked doing something that Princesses aren't really supposed to like doing. In fact, it was something which she only did if she was sure – absolutely sure – that nobody else, except her most trusted chambermaid, was around. I wonder if you can guess what it was? Well . . . I suppose I'd better tell you . . . The Princess was very keen . . . very keen indeed . . . on carpentry!

Now, in those days, the only people who normally did carpentry were carpenters, and it was considered a pretty lowly job. But the Princess loved oak and chestnut and boxwood. She loved sawing it and planing it and making things from it.

Of course, if her father had found out, he'd have probably jumped through the hole in his crown with rage, because it was such an unprincess-like thing to do. But he never did find out, until . . . well hang on! That's jumping to the end of the story.

Now the Princess was not only very keen on carpentry, she was also very good at it. So she built herself a flying boat, and attached six white-necked swans to it. Then she stood in the market square, disguised as a lunatic, and called out: 'Who wants to touch the moon?'

Well, of course, she pretty soon had a crowd of people around her, all laughing and making fun of her and pretending they wanted to touch the moon. So she invited them into her flying boat, and they all piled in, still joking and smiling and thinking the Princess was just some poor lunatic.

Then – to everyone's surprise – she cracked her whip, and the swans flew up into the air, pulling the flying boat up with them. Up and up they rose, until they were as high as the moon, and everyone leaned out and touched it. Just like that.

When they returned to the earth, however, they found the King in a terrible rage, surrounded by his guards.

'Arrest that lunatic!' screamed the King.

But the Princess flew above the King and his guards, and called down:

'What's the matter? I thought you wanted to touch the moon? Jump aboard and I'll fly you there!'

But the King screamed with rage. 'There's only one way to touch the moon!' he cried. 'And that's from the battlements of my Tower – standing on tiptoe!'

'But we've already touched it,' cried the citizens, who'd flown in the flying boat. 'Look! You can see our fingermarks all over it!'

The King looked up, and he could indeed see their fingermarks all over the moon – like little smudges. (For you must know that

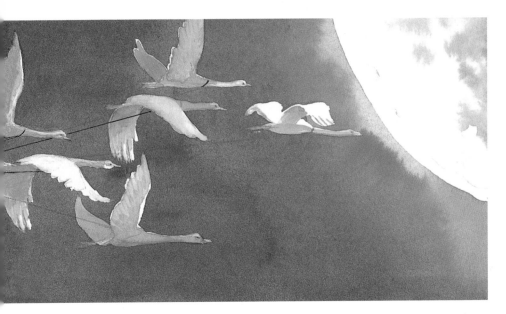

up until that time the moon had been just plain white, and had no markings at all.)

'Fly with her!' pleaded all the citizens. 'Touch the moon! And then we can all stop building this wretched Tower that has destroyed our kingdom!'

But the King went purple with rage. 'No one will stop me building my Tower!' he cried. And he ordered his archers to shoot the six white-necked swans, so the flying boat came crashing down to earth, and the King's Daughter with it.

When the citizens ran to her side, they found her disguise had fallen off, and they recognized the Princess. They turned to the King and said: 'Now see what you've done! You've killed your own daughter!'

Whereupon the King knelt down by her side, and grief swept over him like a hand wiping a slate clean. 'I've been mad!' he cried. 'I have been obsessed – not with touching the moon – but with my own power and glory.'

And there and then he ordered his workmen to destroy the Tower, and start to rebuild his kingdom and his people's homes.

At this moment, the Princess stirred – for she had not been killed by the fall, only stunned – and she murmured:

'Why touch the moon? It looks best as it is.'

And from that day on, no one in that land ever thought of touching the moon again.

But, you know, it still has their fingermarks all over it, and, if you look up at it on a clear night, you will see them – like a face crying out: 'Don't touch me!'

TOM AND THE DINOSAUR

 SMALL BOY NAMED TOM once noticed strange noises coming from the old woodshed that stood at the very bottom of his garden. One noise sounded a bit like his Great Aunt Nelly breathing through a megaphone. There was also a sort of scraping, rattling noise, which sounded a bit like someone rubbing several giant tiddlywinks together. There was also a rumbling sort of noise that could have been a very small volcano erupting in a pillarbox. There was also a sort of scratching noise – rather like a mouse the size of a rhinoceros trying not to frighten the cat.

Tom said to himself: 'If I didn't know better, I'd say it all sounded exactly as if we had a dinosaur living in our woodshed.'

So he climbed onto a crate, and looked through the woodshed window – and do you know what he saw?

'My hat!' exclaimed Tom. 'It's a Stegosaurus!'

He was pretty certain about it, and he also knew that although it looked ferocious, that particular dinosaur only ate plants. Nevertheless, just to be on the safe side, he ran to his room, and looked up 'Stegosaurus' in one of his books on dinosaurs.

'I knew I was right!' he said, when he found it. Then he read through the bit about it being a vegetarian, and checked the archaeological evidence for that. It seemed pretty convincing.

'I just hope they're right,' muttered Tom to himself, as he unlocked the door of the woodshed. 'I mean after sixty million years, it would be dead easy to mistake a vegetarian for a flesh-eating monster!'

He opened the door of the woodshed *very* cautiously, and peered in.

The Stegosaurus certainly looked ferocious. It had great bony plates down its back, and vicious spikes on the end of its tail. On the other hand, it didn't look terribly well. Its head was resting on the floor, and a branch with strange leaves and red berries on it was sticking out of its mouth. The rumbling sound (like the volcano in the pillarbox) was coming from its stomach. Occasionally the Stegosaurus burped and groaned slightly.

'It's got indigestion,' said Tom to himself. 'Poor thing!' And he stepped right in and patted the Stegosaurus on the head.

This was a mistake.

The Stegosaurus may have been just a plant-eater, but it was also thirty feet long, and as soon as Tom touched it, it reared up onto its hind legs – taking most of the woodshed with it.

If the thing had looked pretty frightening when it was lying with its head on the floor, you can imagine how even more terrifying it was when it towered thirty feet above Tom.

'Don't be frightened!' said Tom to the Stegosaurus. 'I won't hurt you.'

The Stegosaurus gave a roar . . . well, actually it wasn't really a roar so much as an extremely loud bleat: 'Baa**a** - ba**a**a - baa**a**!' it roared, and fell back on all fours. Tom only just managed to jump out of the way in time, as half the woodshed came crashing down with it, and splintered into pieces around the Stegosaurus. At the same time, the ground shook as the huge creature's head slumped back onto the floor.

Once again, Tom tried to pat it on the head. This time, the Stegosaurus remained where it was, but one lizard-like eye stared at Tom rather hard, and its tummy gave another rumble.

'You must have eaten something that disagreed with you,' said Tom, and he picked up the branch that had been in the dinosaur's mouth.

'I've never seen berries like that before,' said Tom. The Stegosaurus looked at the branch balefully.

'Is this what gave you tummy-ache?' asked Tom.

The Stegosaurus turned away as Tom offered it the branch.

'You don't like it, do you?' said Tom. 'I wonder what they taste like?'

As Tom examined the strange red berries, he thought to himself: 'No one has tasted these berries for sixty million years . . . Probably no human being has *ever* tasted them.'

Somehow the temptation to try one of the berries was over-whelming, but Tom told himself not to be so stupid. If they'd given a huge creature like the Stegosaurus tummy-ache, they could well be deadly to a small animal like Tom. And yet . . . they looked so . . . *tempting* . . .

The Stegosaurus gave a low groan and shifted its head so it could look at Tom.

'Well, I wonder how you'd get on with twentieth-century veg-etables?' said Tom, pulling up one of his father's turnips. He prof-fered it to the dinosaur. But the Stegosaurus turned its head away, and then – quite suddenly and for no apparent reason – it bit Tom's other hand.

'Ouch!' exclaimed Tom, and hit the Stegosaurus on the nose with the turnip.

'Baaa!' roared the Stegosaurus, and bit the turnip.

Finding a bit of turnip in its mouth, the Stegosaurus started to chew it. Then suddenly it spat it all out.

'That's the trouble with you dinosaurs,' said Tom. 'You've got to learn to adapt . . . otherwise . . . '

Tom found himself looking at the strange red berries again.

'You see,' Tom began again to the Stegosaurus, 'We human beings are ready to change our habits . . . that's why we're so suc-cessful . . . we'll try different foods . . . in fact . . . I wonder what fruit from sixty million years ago tastes like? Hey! Stop that!'

The Stegosaurus was butting Tom's arm with its nose.

'You want to try something else?' asked Tom, and he pulled up a parsnip from the vegetable patch. But before he could get back to the Stegosaurus, it had lumbered to its feet and started to munch away at his father's prize rose-bushes.

'Hey! Don't do that! My dad'll go crazy!' shouted Tom. But the Stegosaurus was making short work of the roses. And there was really nothing Tom could do about it.

He hit the Stegosaurus on the leg, but it merely flicked its huge tail, and Tom was lucky to escape as the bony spikes on the end missed him by inches.

'That's a deadly tail you've got there!' exclaimed Tom, and he decided to keep a respectable distance between himself and the monster.

It was at that moment that Tom suddenly did the craziest thing he'd ever done in his life. He couldn't explain later why he'd done it. He just did. He shouldn't have done, but he did . . . He pulled off one of the strange red berries and popped it into his mouth.

Now this is something you must never ever do – if you don't know what the berries are – because some berries, like Deadly Nightshade, are *really* poisonous.

But Tom pulled off one of the sixty-million-year-old berries, and ate it. It was very bitter, and he was just about to spit it out, when he noticed something wasn't quite right . . .

The garden was turning round. Tom was standing perfectly still, but the garden . . . indeed, as far as he could see, the whole world . . . was turning around and around, slowly at first, and then faster and faster . . . until the whole world was spinning about him like a whirlwind – faster and faster and faster and everything began to blur together. At the same time there was a roaring noise – as if all the sounds in the world had been jumbled up together – louder and faster and louder until there was a shriek! . . . And everything stopped. And Tom could once again see where he was . . . or, rather, where he wasn't . . . for the first thing he realized was that he was no longer standing in his back garden . . .or, if he was, he couldn't see the remains of the woodshed, nor his father's vegetable patch nor his house. Nor could he see the Stegosaurus.

There was a bubbling pool of hot mud where the rose-bushes should have been. And in place of the house there was a forest of the tallest trees Tom had ever seen. Over to his right, where the Joneses' laundry line had been hanging, there was a steaming jungle swamp.

But to Tom by far the most interesting thing was the thing he found himself standing in. It was a sort of crater scooped out of the ground, and it was ringed with a dozen or so odd-shaped eggs.

'My hat!' said Tom to himself. 'I'm back in Jurassic times! 150 million years ago! And, by the look of it, I'm standing right in a dinosaur's nest!'

At that moment he heard an ear-splitting screech, and a huge lizard came running out of the forest on its hind legs. It was heading straight for Tom! Well, Tom didn't wait to ask what time of day it was – he just turned and fled. But once he was running, he realized it was hopeless. He had about as much chance of out-running the lizard creature as he had of teaching it Latin (which, as he didn't even speak it himself, was pretty unlikely).

Tom had run no more than a couple of paces by the time the creature had reached the nest. Tom shut his eyes. The next second he knew he would feel the creature's hooked claws around his neck. But he kept on running . . . and running . . . and nothing happened.

Eventually, Tom turned to see his pursuer had stopped at the nest and was busy with something.

'It's eating the eggs!' exclaimed Tom. 'It's an egg-eater . . . an Oviraptor! I should have recognized it!'

But before he had a chance to kick himself, he felt his feet sinking beneath him, and an uncomfortably hot sensation ran up his legs. Tom looked down to see that he'd run into the bog.

'Help!' shouted Tom. But the Oviraptor obviously knew as little English as it did Latin, and Tom felt his legs sliding deeper into the bubbling mud.

Tom looked up, and saw what looked like flying lizards gliding stiffly overhead. He wished he could grab onto one of those long tails and pull himself up out of the bog, but – even as he thought it – his legs slid in up to the knee. And now he suddenly realized the mud was not just hot – it was *boiling* hot!

His only chance was to grab a nearby fern frond. With his last ounce of strength, Tom lunged for it and managed to grab the end. The fern was tougher and stronger than modern ferns, but it also stung his hand. But he put up with it, and slowly and painfully, inch by inch, he managed to claw his way up the fern frond until he finally managed to pull himself free of the bog.

'This isn't any place for me!' exclaimed Tom, and, at that moment, the sky grew red – as if some distant volcano were erupting.

'Oh dear!' said Tom. 'How on earth do I get out of this?'

The moment he said it, however, he took it back, for the most wonderful thing happened. At least, it was wonderful for Tom, because he was particularly interested in these things.

He heard a terrible commotion in the forest. There was a crashing and roaring and twittering and bleating. A whole flock of Pterodactyls flew up out of the trees with hideous screeching. The lizard creature stopped eating the eggs and turned to look.

From out of the middle of the forest came the most terrible roar that Tom had ever heard in his life. The ground shook. The lizard thing screamed, dropped the egg it was devouring and ran off as fast as it could. Then out of the forest came another dinosaur,

followed by another and another and another. Big ones, small ones, some running on four legs, some on two. All looking terrified and screeching and howling.

Tom shinned up a nearby tree to keep out of the way.

'Those are Ankylosaurs! Those are Pterosaurs! Triceratops! Iguanadons! Oh! And look: a Plateosaurus!'

Tom could scarcely believe his luck. 'Imagine seeing so many different kinds of dinosaur all at the same time!' he said to himself. 'I wonder where they're going?'

But the words were scarcely out of his mouth before he found out.

CRASH! Tom nearly fell out of the tree. CRASH! The ground shook, as suddenly – out of the forest – there emerged the most terrible creature Tom had ever seen or was ever likely to see again.

'Crumbs!' said Tom. 'I should have guessed! Tyrannosaurus Rex! My favourite dinosaur!'

The monster stepped out into the clearing. It was bigger than a house, and it strode on two massive legs. Its vicious teeth glowed red in the flaming light from the sky.

The curious thing was that Tom seemed to forget all his fear. He was so overawed by the sight of the greatest of all dinosaurs that he felt everything else was insignificant – including himself.

The next moment, however, all his fear returned with a vengeance, for the Tyrannosaurus Rex stopped as it drew level with the tree in which Tom was hiding. Its great head loomed just above Tom and the tree, and made them both quiver like jelly.

Before Tom knew what was happening, he suddenly saw the Tyrannosaurus reach out its foreclaws and pull the tree over towards itself. The next second, Tom found that the branch to which he was clinging had been ripped off the tree, and he was being hoisted forty feet above the ground in the claws of the Tyrannosaurus Rex!

Tom was too terrified to be frightened. A sort of calm hit him as the creature turned him over and sniffed him – as if uncertain as to whether or not Tom was edible.

'He's going to find out pretty soon!' exclaimed Tom, as he felt himself lifted up towards those terrible jaws.

'I bet,' thought Tom, 'I'm the only boy in my school ever to have been eaten by his own favourite dinosaur!'

He could feel the monster's breath on his skin. He could see the glittering eye looking at him. He could sense the jaws were just opening to tear him to pieces, when . . . There was a dull thud.

The Tyrannosaurus's head jerked upright, and it twisted round, and Tom felt himself falling through the air.

The branch broke his fall, and as he picked himself up, he saw that something huge had landed on the Tyrannosaurus's back. The Tyrannosaurus had leapt around in surprise and was now tearing and ripping at the thing that had landed on it.

And now, as Tom gathered his wits, he suddenly realized what it was that had apparently fallen out of nowhere onto the flesh-eating monster. I wonder if you can guess what it was? . . . It was Tom's old friend the Stegosaurus – complete with bits of the garden woodshed still stuck in its armour plates, and the branch of red berries sticking out of its mouth.

'It must have given up eating my dad's roses and gone back to the berries!' exclaimed Tom. And, at that very moment, Tom could have kicked himself. 'I'm an idiot!' he cried. For he suddenly noticed that the tree he'd climbed was none other than the very same magical tree – with its odd-shaped leaves and bright red berries.

But even as he reached out his hand to pick a berry that would send him back again in time, he found himself hurtling through the air, as the Tyrannosaurus's tail struck him on the back.

'Ba**aa**!' bleated the Stegosaurus, as the Tyrannosaur clawed its side and blood poured onto the ground.

'R**aaaa**!' roared the Tyrannosaur as the Stegosaurus thrashed it with the horny spikes on its tail.

The monsters reared up on their hind legs, and fought with tooth and bone and claw, and they swayed and teetered high above Tom's head, until the Tyrannosaur lunged with its savage jaws, and ripped a huge piece of flesh from the Stegosaurus's side. The Stegosaurus began to topple . . . as if in slow motion . . . directly onto where Tom was crouching.

And Tom would most certainly have been crushed beneath the creature, had he not – at that very instant – found that in his hand he already had a broken spray of the red berries. And as the monster toppled over onto him, he popped a berry into his mouth and bit it.

Once again the world began to spin around him. The clashing dinosaurs, the forest, the bubbling mud swamp, the fiery sky – all whirled around him in a crescendo of noise and then . . . suddenly! . . . There he was back in his own garden. The Joneses' washing was still on the line. There was his house, and there was his father coming down the garden path towards him looking none too pleased.

'Dad!' yelled Tom. 'You'll never guess what's just happened!'

Tom's father looked at the wrecked woodshed, and the dug-up vegetable patch and then he looked at his prize roses scattered all over the garden. Then he looked at Tom:

'No, my lad,' he said, 'I don't suppose I can. But I'll tell you this . . . It had better be a *very* good story!'

*   *   *

NOTE: If you're wondering why the magical tree with the bright red berries has never been heard of again, well the Stegosaurus landed on it and smashed it, and I'm afraid it was the only one of its kind.

Oh! What happened to the Stegosaurus? Well, I'm happy to be able to tell you that it actually won its fight against the Tyrannosaurus Rex. It was, in fact, the only time a Stegosaurus ever beat a Tyrannosaur. This is mainly due to the fact that this particular Tyrannosaur suddenly got a terrible feeling of *déjà-vu* and had to run off and find its mummy for reassurance (because it was only a young Tyrannosaurus Rex after all). So the Stegosaurus went on to become the father of six healthy young Stegosauruses or Stegosauri, and Jurassic Tail-Thrashing Champion of what is now Surbiton!

Nicobobinus and the Doge of Venice

THIS IS THE STORY of the most extraordinary child who ever stuck his tongue out at the Prime Minister. His name was Nicobobinus [*Nick-Oh-Bob-In-Us*]. He lived a long time ago, in a city called Venice, and he could do anything.

Of course, not everybody knew he could do anything. In fact only his best friend, Rosie, knew he could, and nobody took any notice of anything Rosie said, because she was always having wild ideas anyway.

One day, for example, Rosie said to Nicobobinus: 'Let's put a rabbit down the Doge's trousers!'

'Don't be silly,' said Nicobobinus. 'The Doge doesn't wear trousers.'

'Yes he does,' said Rosie. '*And* we ought to boil his hat up and give it to the pigeons.'

'Anyway, who *is* the Doge?' asked Nicobobinus.

'How d'you know he doesn't wear trousers if you don't know who he is?' exclaimed Rosie (not unreasonably in my opinion).

Nicobobinus peered across the water and muttered: 'He doesn't live in the Doge's palace, does he?'

'Gosh!' said Rosie. 'I've never been fishing with a real genius before.'

'But he's the most important man in Venice!' exclaimed Nicobobinus.

248

'They've got universities for people like you, you know,' said Rosie, and she yanked a small carp out of the canal.

'What have you got against him?' asked Nicobobinus, as he watched her pulling out the hook with a well-practised twist.

'He's just extended his palace,' said Rosie, looking at her fish. It was about nine inches long.

'So?' said Nicobobinus, wondering why *he* never caught anything longer than his nose – which wasn't particularly long anyway.

'Well, he extended it all over my granny's house. That's what!' said Rosie.

'And now your poor old gran hasn't got anywhere to live?' asked Nicobobinus sympathetically.

'Oh yes she has! She's living with us, and I can't stand it!' replied Rosie.

Nicobobinus pretended, for a moment, that *he* had a bite. Then he said: 'But how will putting a rabbit down the Doge's trousers help?'

'It won't,' said Rosie. 'But it'll make me feel a lot better. Come on!'

'You don't really mean it?' gasped Nicobobinus.

'No,' said Rosie. 'We haven't got a rabbit – so it'll have to be a fish.'

'But that's our supper!' said Nicobobinus. 'And anyway, they've got guards and sentries and dogs all over the Doge's palace. We'd never get in.'

Rosie looked Nicobobinus straight in the eyes and said: 'Nicobobinus! It's *fun!*'

Some time later, when they were hiding under some nets on one of the little fishing boats that ferried people from the Giudecca to St Mark's Square, when the weather was too bad for fishing, Nicobobinus was still less certain.

'My granny says that where her kitchen used to be, they've built this fancy balcony,' Rosie was whispering, 'and she reckons any thief could climb in by day or night.'

'They drown thieves in the Grand Canal at midnight,' groaned Nicobobinus.

'They'll never catch us,' Rosie reassured him.

'Who's that under my nets?' shouted a voice.

'Leg it!' yelled Rosie, and she and Nicobobinus jumped overboard!

'Lucky we'd reached the shore!' panted Nicobobinus as the two sprinted across St Mark's Square.

'Hey! You two!' yelled the fisherman and gave chase.

Some time later, as Nicobobinus was standing on Rosie's shoulders pulling himself onto the balcony of the Doge's palace, he was even less certain.

'Have you got the fish?' hissed Rosie, as he pulled her up after him.

Nicobobinus could feel it wriggling inside his jerkin.

'No,' he replied. 'It was so unhappy I set it free. It said it didn't want to get caught by the Doge's guards in the company of two completely out-of-their-basket idiots like . . .'

'Look!' said Rosie. 'Do you see where we are?'

Nicobobinus peered into the room with Rosie and caught his breath. It was a magnificent room, with lacquered gold furniture and elegant paintings on the wall. But that wasn't what caught the attention of Rosie and Nicobobinus.

'Do you see?' exclaimed Rosie.

'Toys!' breathed Nicobobinus.

'We're in the nursery!' said Rosie, and she was. She had just climbed in.

Back at home Nicobobinus had just one toy. His uncle had made it for him, and, now he came to think about it, it was more of a plank than a toy. It had four wooden wheels, but the main part of it was definitely a plank. Rosie thought about her two toys, back in the little bare room where she slept with her sisters and her mother and her father and now her granny. One was moth-eaten (that was the doll that had been handed down from sister to sister) and the other was broken (that was a jug that she used to pretend was a crock of gold). But the Doge's children had: hoops, spinning tops, hobby horses, dolls' houses, dolls, toy furniture, masks, windmills, stilts (of various heights), rattles, building blocks, boxes, balls and a swing.

'There's only one thing,' whispered Rosie.

'What's that?' asked Nicobobinus as he picked up one of the hoops.

'The Doge hasn't got any children,' said Rosie, but before she could say anything else, one of them walked in through the door.

'Hasn't he?' said Nicobobinus.

'Well I didn't think he had,' said Rosie.

During this last exchange, the little girl who had just walked in through the door had turned pale, turned on her heel, and finally turned into a human cannonball, that streaked off back the way it had come.

'Quick!' cried Rosie. 'She'll give the alarm!'

NICOBOBINUS AND THE DOGE OF VENICE

And before Nicobobinus could stop her, Rosie was off in pursuit. So Nicobobinus followed . . . What else could he do?

Well, they hadn't got more than half-way across the adjoining room, when they both noticed it was rather full of people.

'Hi, everyone!' yelled Nicobobinus, because he couldn't think of anything else to say.

'That's torn it!' muttered Rosie. And on they dashed into the next chamber.

The Doge, who had been one of the people the room was full of, sat up in bed and said: 'Who are *they?*'

'I'll have them executed straightaway,' said the Prime Minister.

'No, no! *Apprehend* them,' said the Doge.

'At once,' said the Chief of the Guards.

'My clothes!' said the Doge, and sixteen people rushed forward with sixteen different bits of the Doge's clothing. Getting out of bed for the Most Important Person In Venice in 1545 was a lot more elaborate than it is for you or me . . . at least, it's more elaborate than the way I get up – I don't really know about you.

Anyway, by this time, Nicobobinus and Rosie had bolted through six more rooms, down a flight of stairs and locked themselves in a cupboard.

'Phew!' said Rosie. 'Sorry about this.'

'That's all right,' said Nicobobinus.

'Please don't hurt me,' said a third voice. Nicobobinus and Rosie looked at each other in astonishment (although, as it was pitch-dark in the cupboard, neither of them realized they did).

'Who's that?' asked Nicobobinus.

'I'm not allowed to play with other children,' said the voice. 'My nurse says they might hurt me or kidnap me.'

'Don't be daft!' exclaimed Rosie. 'Children don't kidnap other children.'

'Don't they?' said the other occupant of the cupboard.

'No. And *we're* not going to hurt you,' said Nicobobinus.

'Then why are you here?'

'A lark,' said Rosie.

'What's that?' asked the girl.

'You know . . .' said Nicobobinus, 'fun.'

'Fun?' said the little girl. 'What's that?'

'Oh dear,' muttered Rosie.

'Stick with us and you'll see,' said Nicobobinus.

'All right,' said the girl. 'My name's Beatrice.'

But before either Nicobobinus or Rosie could tell Beatrice their names, there was a thundering as dozens of people went storming and clattering past the cupboard shouting things like: 'There they are!' and 'No! That's not them!' and 'Ow! Take that spear out of my ear!' and 'Quick! This way!' and 'Look in there!' and 'Help me! I've fallen over!' and so on.

When they'd all finally gone and it was quiet again, Nicobobinus, Rosie and their new friend stuck their heads out of the cupboard. The coast was clear, except for the guard who had fallen over.

'Give me a hand would you?' he asked. 'This armour's so heavy that once you fall over it's very difficult to get back on your feet again.'

'Doesn't that make it rather hard to fight in?' said Nicobobinus as they helped him to stand upright.

'Hopeless,' admitted the guard. 'But it *is* very expensive. Now, have you seen two children go past here?'

'Yes,' said Beatrice. 'They went that way!'

'Thanks!' said the guard and ran off as fast as his expensive armour would allow him. He'd got round the corner before he must have realized he'd made a mistake, for there was a crash and a muffled curse, as he tried to stop and turn, but fell over again instead.

'Come on!' yelled Rosie.

'Is this fun?' asked Beatrice, as they ran up another staircase and onto a long balcony and looked out over a narrow street.

'Are you enjoying it?' asked Nicobobinus.

'So-so,' said Beatrice.

'Then it's probably fun,' said Nicobobinus.

'Oh! Stop wittering, you two!' exclaimed Rosie. 'And help me down off here!' Rosie was already climbing over the balustrade and hanging from the balcony.

'That's too far a drop!' exclaimed Beatrice.

'You wait!' grinned Nicobobinus. 'We've done this before.' He whipped his belt off, and before you could say 'Venice and chips!' Rosie was clinging to the end, and being lowered down into the street.

'Oo-er!' said Beatrice.

'Come on!' called Rosie.

'Are you sure this is fun?' whispered Beatrice.

'Well it beats enjoying yourself!' shouted Nicobobinus, as several guards suddenly appeared at the far end of the balcony.

'Hurry!' he said, and thrust the end of the belt into her hand.

'There they are!' shouted one of the guards. And without giving another thought, Beatrice followed Rosie down into the street.

'Nicobobinus!' yelled Rosie. 'How are *you* going to get down?'

'I'll be OK!' yelled Nicobobinus, although his main thought, as he ducked through a window, was actually 'Cripes!'

'I thought you'd done this before?' said Beatrice as she and Rosie legged it down the street.

'Well . . . maybe not from quite such a high balcony,' admitted Rosie, and they disappeared round the corner.

Nicobobinus meanwhile had made a discovery. He had discovered that the window that looked out onto the long balcony that looked over the Calle de San Marco was the window of the office of the Prime Minister. He also made a second discovery: it was office hours. The Prime Minister was sitting on a sort of throne, holding an audience with several rather scruffy individuals who looked scared out of their wits.

'. . . and then take their heads off,' the Prime Minister was saying, as Nicobobinus backed in through the window and landed in front of him.

'Ah!' smiled the Prime Minister, signalling to his guards, 'another customer.'

Some time later, Nicobobinus found himself chained and shackled and being dragged into the Grand Audience Chamber of the

Doge of Venice himself. It was a particularly magnificent room, and nowadays people come from all over the world to gaze up at the ornate ceiling and stare at the fine furnishings, while a guide talks too quickly in a language they can't understand and tells them about all the boring and pompous men and women with famous names that have come and gone through the doors of that famous place. But one story they never tell (and I don't know why) is the story I'm telling you now.

At that particular moment, however, the one thing Nicobobinus was *not* interested in was the magnificent decor of the Grand Audience Chamber. His one and only concern was how to get out again as quickly as possible (which, come to think of it, is probably what most of today's tourists are thinking too!).

'Bring the boy here,' yawned the Doge (who was actually wishing he was back in bed).

'We could start by simply cutting his feet off, and then move on up to his knees . . .' the Prime Minister was whispering in the Doge's ear as Nicobobinus was thrown onto the floor in front of them.

All eyes were upon him, and an excited buzz went around the Audience Chamber. The Doge looked at him for several moments and then said: 'What are your demands?'

Nicobobinus thought he hadn't heard right, so he said: 'I beg your pardon, Your Highness?'

'Where is she?' shrieked the Prime Minister, and suddenly everyone in the room was muttering and shouting the same thing.

'Silence!' commanded the Doge. Then he turned to Nicobobinus once more and said: 'You have kidnapped my daughter. I will give you what you want, providing you return her at once – unharmed.'

Nicobobinus was just about to say: 'No! I *haven't* kidnapped your daughter', but he didn't. Instead, he looked around at all the heavy, brooding faces, the wine-soaked noses and the sunken eyes of all the important, pompous folk of Venice, and he said: 'I want one thing.'

'Yes?' said the Doge.

'And it isn't for me,' went on Nicobobinus.

'It's for your master,' assumed the Doge.

'No,' replied Nicobobinus, 'it's for your daughter.' A gasp went up around the room. 'It's something you must give Beatrice.'

The Doge couldn't speak for a moment, but eventually he managed to say:

'And what is it?'

'Fun,' said Nicobobinus.

'Fun?' said the Doge.

'Fun?' said all the pompous and important people of Venice.

'Fun!' said another voice, and there was Beatrice, the Doge's daughter, standing at the entrance to the Grand Audience Chamber, holding Rosie's hand. 'We've been having fun!'

Well, to cut a long story short, the Prime Minister still wanted to chop off Nicobobinus's and Rosie's heads and drown them in the Grand Canal at midnight, until the Lord Chief Advocate pointed out (after consulting various medical authorities) that you can't drown someone once you've cut their head off.

'Then just drown them like the rats they are!' exclaimed the Prime Minister.

'But they're only children,' said the Doge's mother.

'That's beside the point!' screamed the Prime Minister. 'It's the *principle* that matters! If you don't drown them, soon you'll have all the riff-raff of Venice climbing into the palace and making demands!'

But the Doge had fallen asleep, and his mother ordered that Beatrice should decide what was to become of Nicobobinus and Rosie. Beatrice said they had to come and play with her every Monday. And so that was that.

Later that evening, as the Doge was getting into bed, and all the assistants were gone, he said to his wife: 'You know, my dear, a most extraordinary thing . . . Just now . . . Do you know what I found in my trousers?'

At about the same time, Nicobobinus and Rosie were sitting on Nicobobinus's doorstep laughing and laughing as Nicobobinus described how he had managed to slip the wriggling fish past the Doge's belt and into his trousers while the Doge's mother was kissing him goodnight.

'But one thing puzzles me,' said Rosie. 'When did you stick your tongue out at the Prime Minister?'

'I didn't,' replied Nicobobinus. 'That happened in a totally different adventure.'

'Was it the one where we set off to find the Land of Dragons?' asked Rosie.

'Ah!' said Nicobobinus. '*That* would be telling . . .'